Unforgettable
An Alessi Brother Novel

Sonia Stanizzo

Unforgettable Copyright © 2023 by Sonia Stanizzo

Publisher JRL Publishing

ISBN: ebook 9780645466621

ISBN: paperback 9780645466638

eBooks are not transferable. No part of this book may be used or reproduced without written permission, except in the case of brief quotations in articles and reviews.

This book is a work of fiction and any resemblance to persons, living or dead is purely coincidental. The characters are productions of the author's imagination and used fictitiously.

For my family

Chapter One

HARPER

Some people call this house a mansion, envy the life of luxury within these sandstone walls. I call this ten-bedroom monstrosity a prison, praying every day for the chance to leave. After nine grueling years, my prayers are answered. The chains that shackled me here are broken. All I have to do is get through today, and then I'll have my life back.

My fingers curl around the cold, crystal champagne flute as I stare at the guests gathered in the 'ballroom' as Derek liked to call the pretentious room, acting like it's a social event, not a wake. To me it's a celebration. My husband is dead and the reason I'll soon be free. This wasn't how I pictured my freedom, but I'll take it however I can get it.

For now, I must put my loathing for the man aside and play the grief-stricken widow. Judith, Derek's sister, has been giving me warning glares all afternoon if I so much as crack a smile. After today, she won't have to see me again. With Derek gone, we have no ties. There's no reason to be in each other's lives.

I want to hide in my room to avoid the 'mourners'. Instead, I shake their hands, accept air-kisses, and dab the corners of my eyes with a tissue at non-existing tears I couldn't push out if I tried. If one more person says they're sorry for my loss, I think I'll scream! No, it wasn't tragic. No, he won't be missed. No, there will never be another man like him—thank God! I know their condolences are meaningless. I see their knowing smirks when they think I'm not looking. It is no secret Derek died from a cardiac arrest while fucking another woman. How fitting for him. These people hated him. Only tolerated him because of what he held over their heads. He could destroy their reputation and businesses with a snap of his fingers. They're not here to share their grief. They want to gossip.

The afternoon drags on. My feet throb in my black Prada heels, and the pins holding my long hair in a bun are digging into my scalp. The aromatic scent of lilies and roses in ornate vases placed around the room is cloying, making my head pound. I'm so relieved when I say goodbye to the last of the guests and leave Judith to organize the clean-up crew and race to my room.

Kicking off my shoes, I pluck the pins from my hair and peel off my widow clothes, tossing them into a corner of the room. Not neatly put away in the walk-in closet like Derek would demand. *I hope in your special place in hell you can see the crumpled heap on the floor.* In my bra and panties, I fling myself onto the bed. A huge grin spreads across my face.

"I'm free," I whisper, looking up at the ceiling. "I'm free!" This time I yell it as I kick my arms and legs and toss my head from side to side. Derek is out of my life for good. Oh God, it feels amazing. I take a deep, fortifying breath. It feels wonderful to breathe again.

In the morning, I have a meeting with Derek's lawyer for the reading of his will, and after that, I'm getting my life back.

I can't wait!

The next morning in Mr. McCarthy's office, a mixed feeling of excitement stirs in the pit of my stomach. While waiting for the will to be read, I fidget in my chair as the lawyer shuffles papers on his desk. For a second, I wonder where Judith is. The thought disappears when the lawyer clears his throat. In a moment, he'll be handing me my freedom.

He props his glasses on the tip of his nose and reads. When he finishes, I sit stunned for a moment, my eyes blinking slowly. When the words sink in, I sit up straight. "What did you say?" Surely I misunderstood.

Mr. McCarthy's gaze flicks from the papers in his hand, then back at me. A trace of sympathy crosses his eyes. "Derek's estate, which includes all property, money, and personal items, are going to his sister Judith Richardson. He is leaving his chain of casinos to his business partner, Warren Goldman. You are to receive five thousand dollars and the suitcase of belongings you moved into his house with."

Like the lawyer's secretary knew when to enter, she rolls my gray luggage into the room, placing it next to me, and hands me an envelope I assume has money inside.

"I can't pack my own stuff? I have a few more things at the house that wouldn't fit in that suitcase I'd like to get." Who the hell had Derek arranged to do this? Probably Judith. Good riddance to them both. I'm surprised she's not here to witness this.

"I'm afraid not. You're not allowed back on the property."

I grip the arms of my chair, my chest heaving. "I've been married to that bastard for nine years. I've put up with the string of women he paraded in front of me—" Not that it bothered me; it kept him away from me. "—and…and…" I can't verbalize the mental torture of being married to such a toxic person. "And the shit he put me through. You know what? I want nothing from him or anything his money bought me. He can shove his money and possessions up his cold, dead ass. All I want is my parents' properties back. Tell me how I go about doing that please."

Mr. McCarthy runs a finger under the collar of his shirt. "About that. Derek owned your parents' estate. Therefore, it's all going to Judith."

An icy shiver rakes over my body. My mouth drops open. "No." The word comes out in a cracked whisper. "That's not possible. Their house in South Hampton and cabin on Mirror Lake belong to me." I knew the properties were still in Derek's name after the reading of my parents' will a year ago. All because of a gambling debt my father owed Derek that was supposed to be wiped clean when I married him. But because my father continued gambling after the marriage and continued to owe Derek, he signed the properties over to Derek to keep his gambling addiction quiet. The governor of New York did not want his dirty laundry aired. I sold my soul to keep them in the family and to protect my father's reputation. The cabin is what I want the most. It's the one place I was the happiest.

The lawyer uses a handkerchief to rub beads of sweat off his forehead. "The properties are in Derek's name, therefore they will now go to Judith."

I rub my palms on my thighs. "I've been married to him for years. Surely I have some rights?"

Clasping his hands together, he places his forearms on the timber desk. "Before you married Derek, you signed a prenup. It explained what you were entitled to in case of his death. Didn't you read it?"

The morning of my wedding was the worst day of my life. I remember signing something. Papers were thrown under my nose. My heart had been too broken, my eyes too swollen with tears to read a word of it.

"So, I have no house to live in and only five thousand dollars?" I can't control my voice from shaking.

Mr. McCarthy looks at me with sympathy. "I'm afraid so. He originally wasn't leaving you anything. I had to fight with him to give you any money. I wanted more, but..." He shrugs his shoulders. "I wish there was more I could've done."

For a moment, I stare at the marble floor. Surely I can contest this? But with what money? Derek took everything from me. "Even from the grave, Derek keeps proving he's nothing but an asshole." I won't let him get the better of me. I straighten my shoulders. "Thank you for trying."

Rising from my chair, I tuck the envelope in my purse and grab the handle of the luggage bag. With my head held high, I march out of the office.

As I walk through the reception area, the secretary who'd given me my luggage earlier, scurries from behind the desk. "I'm so sorry about Mr. Richardson's will."

"Thanks." I go to move on.

"If you need somewhere to stay, my niece's roommate just moved out of the townhouse she's renting in Brooklyn. She's looking for a replacement." She hands me a yellow post-it note. "Her name's Alyssa. I'm Susana. Tell her I gave you her number." The phone rings and she rushes back to the desk. Before she picks up the receiver, she smiles and says, "Good luck."

I try to smile back, but I think it was more of a grimace.

Outside, I stand on the sidewalk of the busy New York City street, pressed up against the cold, brick building, watching pedestrians rush past. Closing my eyes, I take a deep breath. Freedom was supposed to smell a lot sweeter. At the moment, my life smelled much like the street—a hint of landfill mixed with hotdogs. My stomach churns at the thought.

For the first time in my life, I'm on my own. Responsible for my own decisions, and with only five thousand dollars to my name, I don't know how to reclaim my life. Fear presses heavy on my shoulders, but I quickly shake it off. I will not let these circumstances ruin the moment. It will be difficult to live on the limited funds I have until I find a job, but I'll make it work. I must. There is no other choice.

Two weeks after the reading of the will, I'm still looking for work. Today's job interview at a nearby café was another one I was underqualified for. From office administration jobs to flipping burgers, no one will give me a chance. If I don't get a job soon, my money won't last much longer. Finding a job is harder than I imagined.

I pull the elastic band from my ponytail and let my hair fall down my back. Rubbing my temples, I trudge to my bedroom. I had called the number on the post-it note the secretary at Derek's law firm gave me. Thank God I did, or I'd be homeless by now. Walking into the tiny space, I kick off my heels and change into gray sweats.

My stomach rumbles, reminding me I haven't eaten since the buttered toast I had for breakfast. It's now five-thirty PM. In the fridge in the kitchenette there's leftover mac and cheese.

Nuking the meal in the microwave, I take it into the living room and sit cross-legged on the scratchy, threadbare rug and place the bowl on the chipped timber coffee table. Opening the ancient laptop someone had packed into my luggage with the other things I'd moved into Derek's house with, I wait for it to bootup. With sketchy wi-fi, it takes a few minutes.

I do another search for job listings. Every position I look at wants qualifications and experience. Something I'd have if it weren't for Derek. The moment I married him ended any studies or career path I had planned. The wife of a wealthy businessman trying to make his way into politics was supposed to support and serve her husband. You'd think he was born in the 1950s. Well, he was twenty years older than me, that might explain his old-fashioned behavior.

Thinking of him makes the mouthful of pasta I swallow churn in my stomach, and I push the bowl aside. *Get him out of your head. He doesn't control your life anymore.*

The jangle of keys at the door breaks me out of my depressive thoughts. A few seconds later, my roommate, Alyssa, walks in. "Hey, Harper."

I will be forever grateful to Alyssa's aunt for hooking me up with Alyssa. At twenty-three, six years younger than me, we've become fast friends. Alyssa has shown me more care and consideration in the two weeks I've known her than my high-society friends have in nine years. 'Friends' who dropped all communication after Derek's funeral. And the friends I had before my marriage; Derek kept me away from. By now, they've all drifted away. I'd be too embarrassed about my life to reconnect anyway.

Dressed in baggy, black cargo pants and an oversized sweater, the clothing hides Alyssa's slender dancer's body. She drops her bag by the door and flops on the sofa. With her hair in a tight, high bun, I'm guessing she's come back from dance class. For the last two years, Alyssa has been auditioning for a part on Broadway. She's shown me videos of her dancing and singing. She's amazing. It shocks me that she hasn't landed a principal role yet.

"Mac and cheese again?" She points to the bowl. "You going to finish that?"

"It's all yours." I lost my appetite.

Alyssa takes the bowl and leans forward in the seat. She looks over my shoulder at the computer screen. "How did the admin interview go?"

I blow out a frustrated breath. "No one wants to hire someone with no qualifications or experience." Resting my elbow on the table, I drop my chin on my fist. "I don't know what I'm going to do." Time and money are running out fast!

Around a mouthful of food, Alyssa mumbles, "Then we'll give you some."

"What do you mean?" I sit up straight and shuffle around to look at her.

"We'll adjust your resume a little and give you the qualifications and experience you need." Relaxing back into the sofa, Alyssa forks more food into her mouth.

"I can't do that. It's lying," I say with disapproval.

She makes a scoffing sound. "Everyone fibs a little on their resume."

"Yes, fibs. They don't give themselves qualifications they don't have."

Alyssa points the fork at me. "Think of it like an actor. They'll put 'can ride horses' on their resume, but they really can't. They'll learn on the job."

I shake my head. "I can't do that."

"Sure you can. But I won't do anything unless you want me to," Alyssa says, placing the empty bowl on the coffee table.

"I also don't have any references."

She taps her chest. "Meet Alyssa Martinez, executive assistant."

I giggle. "You're an entertainer, not an executive assistant."

Shrugging a shoulder, she grins. "I'm always assisting someone with something. I'm only throwing in the 'executive' part."

Nibbling my bottom lip for a second, I wonder whether I can lie on my resume. If I don't get a job fast, I'll be in a whole lot more trouble than fibbing. Before I change my mind, I pick the laptop up and hand it to Alyssa. "Don't go too crazy," I warn.

She throws me an excited grin, places the computer on her lap, and says, "Leave it with me. You'll be employed before you know it. I know you told me your husband didn't want you to work, but was there anything you did for him or any hobbies you took up?"

I told Alyssa briefly what my life was like. She was co-renting me her apartment. I felt like I needed to explain why I was unemployed.

"I painted." It was the only thing that gave me peace. I could shut out the rest of the world and the crap I was living in and get lost in the creativity.

"Really? Were you good?"

I chuckle. "No. Terrible." I'm glad the canvases stayed at the mansion.

Alyssa taps the side of her chin. "I'll spin that into something creative. What else?"

I take a moment to think. "Every day I organized the staff on their daily chores."

"Staff manager. Great organizational skills," she says as she types on the computer. "Anything else?"

"I arranged dinner parties and took care of the household admin."

"This is perfect. I can do a lot with this."

Oh God. What is she going to write? I might regret letting her do this.

Thirty minutes later, Alyssa turns the computer around to show me her work. After reading it, I gasp at my new resume. "I don't have a degree in business!" I point out. "Or have any of the office qualifications you've listed. I can't use this. I thought you'd add things like filing and answering phones. This is too much. I'll keep trying restaurants. Surely someone needs a dishwasher."

"You won't be washing dishes, because you've applied for three administrative management positions, and I've got a gut feeling you'll get one."

My mouth falls open. "What did you do?"

"Applied for three admini—"

"I heard you. Retract them!" I snatch the computer from Alyssa's lap and pound random keys on the keyboard like that will fix the problem.

"Relax. There'll be hundreds of applicants. You'll be lucky to get an interview."

I stop pressing keys and stare at her. "You said you had a gut feeling I'd get one."

Alyssa grins. "I like to be optimistic."

"You're so annoying." I drop the laptop back on Alyssa's lap.

"But you love me," Alyssa says with a sweet smile.

"The jury's out on that one," I huff, picking myself off the floor to sit next to Alyssa.

She puts an arm around my shoulders. "Don't worry, things will work out."

My stomach twists in a knot. "I wish I had your optimism."

Chapter Two

HARPER

After showering, I hang the towel neatly on the towel rail in a perfect line with the one next to it. I stare at them for a beat, my scalp prickling with unease. They're too perfectly aligned. I mess them up. Still not satisfied with how they look, I pull one off the towel rail and toss it over the shower curtain rail. "Derek would have a fit if he'd seen that."

I slap a hand to my forehead. *Why can't I stop thinking about him?* I was married for nine years and have only been free for three weeks. It's going to take some time to erase him from my mind. I wish I could reach inside my brain and rip all memories of him out!

In the kitchen, I make a cup of tea. God, I crave a caramel latte with extra caramel. But I don't have the money to waste on small luxuries. I need my money for more important things like food and a place to live. Taking the mug to the sofa, I place it on the coffee table, pick up the laptop and turn it on. Every morning I check job listings, and every day I get disheartened at not being employed by now.

Opening my emails, one makes me pause. I hold a hand to my mouth, my fingers trembling over my lips as I read the sender's name. *Alessi Fashion*. Why are they emailing me? The only connection I have—*had*—with them is Finn, and I broke all ties with him the day I told him I was marrying Derek.

I gasp as I read the subject line. *Position for Administrative Manager*. Alyssa had applied for a job at Alessi's! If I had known, I would never have allowed it. After a week of not hearing from any of the companies she sent my resume to, I assumed I was overlooked. Receiving this email feels like a bomb has exploded in my face. There's no way I can answer it.

Going back into the kitchen, I pour my tea down the sink and wash my cup, then I make my way to Alyssa's room and knock. When she opens the door, she takes one look at my face, grabs my arm, and drags me inside. "Why do you look like someone's died? What's happened?"

The shock at seeing an email from Alessi Fashion has shaken me. I haven't told Alyssa everything about my life before we met. She hasn't pried. What would she think about me if I told her I broke up with Finn Alessi to marry Derek Richardson for money? It looks bad—it *is* bad.

I sit on the edge of Alyssa's bed, and she takes a seat next to me. "I got a response from Alessi Fashion. You must have applied there."

My lips tremble. Why did an email affect me so much? It wasn't like I'd received a personal letter from Finn.

"What did they say? Wait...it was a rejection, wasn't it? That's why you look sad. Don't worry, we'll keep trying, and hopefully, more will get back to you with better news."

I fiddle with the hem of my t-shirt. "I didn't read it, but I'm assuming it's for an interview. I deleted it."

"Why? Don't tell me it's because you're not qualified. A monkey can do those kinds of jobs," she jokes.

I shake my head. "I can't work there even if I got the job. It's my ex-boyfriend's company. We didn't end on good terms."

"Oh wow. Your ex is an Alessi?" Alyssa's eyes widen. She obviously knows the company. Alessi Fashion is one of the biggest fashion houses in the world.

I nod.

"Well, it's a big company. Maybe you'll never see him." Alyssa leans over and picks up her cell from the nightstand and swipes at the screen. "What's his name?"

"Finn Alessi. Why?"

"I'm googling him." Alyssa must have found what she was looking for, because she sighs as she flicks through the photos. "He's a hottie. Looks like a bit of a player though. Look at how many women he's been involved with."

Alyssa turns the phone toward me, and I turn away. I've seen it before. It still hurts. Derek took great pleasure in showing me the beautiful women Finn dated knowing I was in love with him. Derek resented me for not throwing myself at him because of my loyalty to Finn.

"This still upsets you." Alyssa's smile drops, and she flips the phone face down on the bed. "I'm sorry for dragging it up."

I wave a hand like it doesn't bother me. But it's still like a knife twisting in my heart. "It was a long time ago."

"Did you break up because he's an asshole and cheated? Most men this good-looking and rich can't keep their dicks in their pants."

The anguish over our breakup squeezes my heart. He wasn't an asshole. Finn loved me, and I threw his love in his face. "Something like that," I lie. I didn't want to get into the details.

"If you're worried about bumping into him in the office, I read that he's living in the UK, running the London branch. So, if you get the job, you won't see him. You should go for it."

It had always been my dream to work in fashion. Finn had supported me and encouraged me to study. We'd fantasized about someday working together. I'd started my second year at fashion school when Derek put an end to my dreams. Who knows if I'll ever get the opportunity again? An administrative position might be a foot in the door in the fashion industry. If Finn stayed in London and I can keep away from his brothers, there shouldn't be a problem. Right? My heart flutters with anxiety. No. It's ridiculous to even think it could work.

"I'll consider it." But there's nothing to consider. There's no way I can go through with it.

I trudge into the apartment with a heavy heart after another failed attempt at finding a job. During the last five days, I've handed my resume to several restaurants and retail stores. I've had no response from the other positions Alyssa applied for, and I've given up hope they'll request an interview.

My phone rings in my bag and I dig it out. The number isn't one I recognize. Hope flutters in my belly. Maybe it's someone calling about my resume?

"Hello," I answer.

"Hello, this is Tamara Harris from Alessi Fashion. Am I speaking with Harper Madden?"

It was risky using my maiden name. I hope none of the Alessi brothers have anything to do with the human resource department and recognize it. But I can't stand calling myself Harper Richardson. That name died with Derek.

I sag onto the armrest of the sofa, my legs shaking at just the mention of the Alessi name. "Umm...yes...this is Harper." Why are they calling me? Did Alyssa reply to their email without telling me? I'll kill her if she did!

"Great. I'm just calling to ask if you received our email regarding an interview for the position you applied for. We've had problems with our email service, and some emails have been lost in cyberspace." She sighs. "It's been such a nuisance."

"Arrhh..." I don't know what to say. My brain seems to have turned into a jumbled mess.

"You did apply for an administrative management position?"

"Oh, arrhh...yes, I did," I manage to say.

"Great. Can you come into the office for an interview tomorrow at ten AM?"

"Umm...well..." Why is it so hard to form a coherent sentence?

"If it's not convenient for you, we can arrange another time," Tamara continues, unaware of the jumbled emotions rampaging through me.

"Yes, I can be there." The words fly from my mouth. What the hell? What I should have said was: *I'm not interested in the job anymore. Thank you for calling.*

"Excellent. I'll text you the address. I look forward to meeting you."

We say our goodbyes, and I disconnect the call and throw my phone on the sofa. "What have I done?"

Chapter Three

FINN

Lying in bed, I crack open my eyes. Bright, blinding light pierces through my brain, and I fling my arm over my face. Damn it. I must have forgotten to close the drapes last night. Rolling over onto my side, I'm met with a warm, soft, curvaceous body. The body shifts and shuffles closer to me.

I think back to the previous night. After landing in New York City from London, I headed straight to the nearest bar, had a few drinks, and brought a woman back to my hotel. *Crap!* They're always gone before morning. I never let a woman stay the night. Lack of sleep and one too many scotches and I must've passed out. Now I have to get rid of her.

I look at the woman. Her long, dark hair fans out over the pillow, and like she feels me watching her, her eyes flutter open, revealing chocolate-colored eyes framed with long, full eyelashes. Looking a lot like— God! Why do I do this to myself? Why when I'm back in the city do I sleep with women who resemble Harper? It's the reason I avoid coming home as much as possible. Whenever I step foot in the city, even after so many years, thoughts of her plague me. Living in London, I can pretend the time I spent with Harper never existed.

"Good morning." The brunette—I can't remember her name—smiles, caressing a hand across my bare chest and over my stomach.

I know what she wants, and it will not happen. Every time I do this, self-loathing at my weakness kicks in. "Morning." I slide out of bed and pull on my jeans that are lying on the floor.

The brunette props herself up on her elbow, letting the sheet drop to her waist, exposing impressive-sized breasts. A lot bigger than— *Fuck! Stop thinking about Harper.*

"I had fun last night. I'd love to do it again," she purrs.

Was it fun? I can't remember much. I throw on a t-shirt, collect her clothes discarded around the room and place them on the bed. "Sorry, I'm not here long, and I'll be busy with work."

The woman's eyes grow wide for a beat then narrow, no doubt realizing this was only a one-night stand. She huffs and rises from the bed, snatching at her clothes, then heads to the bathroom and slams the door behind her. Thank God she got the not-so-subtle hint.

A moment later, someone knocks on the door, and I answer it. Bianca, my assistant who flew from London with me, is standing at the threshold. Her gaze scans me from head to toe, her lips twisting to the side. Taking in my disheveled state, she says, "Are you not coming into the office this morning? Do I need to reschedule your appointments?"

I scrub a hand behind my neck. "Yeah, I'm coming in. Give me time to shower and change. I'll meet you in the lobby in fifteen minutes."

Just as I'm closing the door, the brunette pushes past me. Without saying a word, she storms down the hallway, and I watch her step into the elevator. Better to be pissed at me than upset because she was hoping for more.

Bianca also watches the woman. When she's gone, Bianca turns back to me with accusation glaring from her eyes. "Now I know why you're late." How many more women will I piss off today? Bianca had a strict work schedule and hated delays.

"I'll be down soon," I assure her and close the door.

After shaving, dressing, and downing two Tylenol, I meet Bianca in the lobby. She has a car waiting, and we slide into the backseat. Pulling out a phone from a bag, she informs me about my schedule for the day. "You have a meeting with Juliette Monet at ten. Then at one you have lunch at La Grenouille with Mr. Chavez. At three you have a meeting with Arnold Jameson to discuss fabrics."

"Are my brothers in the office today?" I ask as I prop an elbow on the doorframe and stare out the passenger side window, watching the busy streets and buildings fly by. My family are the only people I miss while living in London. Although not enough for me to move back permanently like they wish I would do.

Bianca taps on the screen of her phone for a few seconds. "Yes, they are. Would you like to arrange a meeting with them?"

"Yes, please."

More tapping. "Okay, they'll be waiting for you in the boardroom." Bianca puts her phone in her bag and smooths out her skirt. "So... Who was the woman in your hotel room?"

"A friend." I don't need to tell Bianca about my sick fascination of picking up random women who look like my ex and fucking them when I'm in New York.

Bianca scoffs. "She didn't look *friendly* when she left."

My brothers Hayden and Lucas have often told me that my assistant wants more than a working relationship with me. I always brush away their comments. Bianca is dedicated to her job and a stickler for details and punctuality. This isn't jealousy, she's just pissed because I made her wait for fifteen minutes.

When we arrive at Alessi Fashion, I make my way to the boardroom to meet Hayden and Lucas.

"Welcome back." Hayden slaps me on the back. Older than me by only a year, with the same wavy, dark hair and hazel eyes, when we were younger, we often got mistaken for twins.

"Good to see you. We miss you here," Lucas says, repeating the back-slapping gesture. At twenty-six, Lucas is the baby of the family and often has the maturity to prove it. With the strong Alessi gene pool, he too inherited the same coloring and build.

We take a seat at the table. "Don't get too used to me being here. You know it's only temporary." I've given Juliette Monet two months to finish the designs, then I'm on the first flight back to London.

"You're the head of the Alessi creative team, you need to be here more often. Will we ever see you here permanently?" Hayden asks not for the first time.

I cross my arms over my chest. My answer is always the same. "Not a chance." I conduct most of New York's business in London. "I'm only here because Juliette insisted I needed to see her designs in person."

Before Hayden can lecture me about moving back, Bianca walks into the room carrying a tray of coffee and places one in front of each of us. I'm grateful for the distraction. Turning to me, she asks, "Is there anything else I can do for you?"

"We're good for now. Thanks, Bianca."

She smiles and leaves the room.

"I know exactly what she'd like to *do* for you," Lucas says before blowing into his steaming mug.

I roll my eyes. They never stop.

I need to get this conversation directed to business and off me. "What do you think about Juliette's spring collection so far?"

"Once again, she's outdone herself. The budget is a little higher than we agreed on," Hayden says. In charge of finances, he can be strict with money.

I tap the side of my mug. "The collection is worth the extra dollars."

"I agree. You can't skimp on her designs. They are going to photograph well too. I already have ideas on what I want to do with them," Lucas adds. Lucas is a magician with the camera and our head photographer.

"Speaking of Juliette, I need to prepare a few things in my office before I see her." I knock back the rest of my coffee and say goodbye.

As I make my way to my office, a woman at the end of the corridor catches my eye. Drawn to her, I pause. She's tall, with long, dark hair that falls down her back in soft waves. Something in the way she gestures with her hands as she speaks with Tamara causes the hairs at the back of my neck to rise and sets my heart racing. Her head is slightly turned away, and I can't get a good look at her face. She's too far away to hear her voice.

No. It can't be who I think it is. It's just a strong resemblance. She wouldn't dare set foot in my building. This is why I avoid New York City as much as possible. Any woman with long, dark brown hair and similar features makes me think of Harper. I should leave and go to my office, but instead, like a magnet being pulled to her, I take a few steps forward.

"Finn," someone calls behind me. I ignore them and keep walking. "Finn," they repeat louder. Seconds later, a hand lands on my arm. "Juliette is waiting." I turn around. Bianca is staring at me with a quizzical expression on her face. "Are you okay?"

I rub my fingers over my eyes. "Yeah, I'm fine."

Glancing back, I discover that the woman is gone. Of course, it's not Harper. It was just another woman who looks like her. Being back in New York has the ghosts of my past playing tricks on my mind.

"Let's go." I guide Bianca to my office, but before I step into the room, I take a glimpse over my shoulder. I can't shake the feeling that the woman looked *too* much like Harper.

Chapter Four

HARPER

I twist my fingers together with nerves as I sit in a chair across from Tamara Harris, listening to her explain the position and what will be required from me. What am I doing? I shouldn't be here. This isn't a 'fake it 'til you make it' job. This position needs qualifications and experience. Tamara is speaking about budgets, financial reports, and using a computer system I've never heard of before. All I can do is nod my head and smile, hoping I don't look as confused as I feel.

Tamara pauses and pushes her bright pink, heart-shaped glasses onto the top of her emerald-colored hair and rests into the back of the chair. "You have no clue what I'm talking about, do you?"

"No...I mean yes... I—"

Tamara holds up a hand. "Stop. I can tell by the deer-in-the-headlights expression on your face that you haven't a clue as to what I'm talking about. Why did you apply for a job you're not qualified for?"

The pressure of the last three weeks reaches its limit and percolates from me. Before I can stop myself, I jump up from the chair. "Recently, my husband died, purposely leaving me with almost nothing to live on or a place to live. I've applied for a lot of jobs, all of them needing qualifications and experience. But guess what? That man never let me out of the house to study or work. Oh, unless it was to host his dinner parties. He said I was good at that, which it surprised me he actually gave me a compliment. Now I'm free to do whatever I want, but no one will hire me. Unless I wash freaking dishes, but that won't pay my rent." I gasp at my outburst and cover my mouth with my hand. "I didn't mean to say all of that. I don't normally spill out my life story to strangers." God, she must think I've lost my mind. I pick up my bag next to my chair. "I'm so sorry I've wasted your time." I rush toward the door.

"Wait," Tamara calls, and I turn back around. She rises from her chair, and her vintage 50s style black and white polka dotted dress swirls around her legs. The colors in her sleeve tattoo on her left arm pops against her caramel-colored skin tone. The dress is quirky and fun. Not like the serious black pencil skirt and blue blouse I bought from a thrift shop. "Your husband never allowed you to work?"

My shoulders sag. It's degrading and embarrassing. "It's true, unfortunately. Even when I begged him to let me continue studying. I love fashion. Being here has only reminded me how much I miss it."

"How long were you married?"

"Nine years." I wait for Tamara to ask why I'd stayed married so long, but she just stares at me, tapping a finger to her chin.

Tamara sits back down and gestures for me to do the same. "I can't give you the job you applied for. Unfortunately, we do need someone experienced. But we have a PA for one of our managers who needs help. It's only temporary—about two months. You'll be running around for her, making coffees, delivering files, that sort of thing. Are you interested?"

"I lied on my resume. Why would you offer me a job?" I'm shocked she'd even offer.

"Because I witnessed my mother in a similar situation. No one deserves to be treated that way. I get a good vibe from you. My gut is never wrong." Tamara smiles. "Will you take it?"

Will I take it? Tears prick the backs of my eyes. Finally, someone is giving me a chance. "Yes. Thank you so much. I'm so grateful for the job. When do I start?"

"You can start right now."

"Now?"

"Is that a problem? The temp agency I usually use has no one available until late next week. You'd be doing me a huge favor."

The sooner I start work, the sooner I'll make money. "Today is perfect."

Tamara claps her hands. "Great. Welcome to Alessi Fashion. I'll have a contract ready for you to sign shortly, until then, I'll introduce you to Bianca, the PA. She's already complaining about having to make coffee for the managers this morning." She rolls her eyes and walks behind her desk, opens a drawer, and pulls something out. She hands me a business card. "I don't want to stick my nose into your personal life—" I look at the card. It's for a therapist. My eyes flick up to Tamara. "If you need anyone to talk to about what you've been through, call the number on that card."

"I can't afford this." A therapist is *way* out of my budget. This job will hopefully pay next month's rent. I'll be lucky if there's any left over for food. I try to hand the card back.

Tamara doesn't take it. "She's my sister. Tell her I've sent you. She'll look after you. That's if you want to, of course. No pressure."

Now that Derek is gone, all is okay in my world, right? I can do what I want. Wear what I want. Go where I want. Eat what I want. I think back to the many times I've placed towels on the rail immaculately. Scrutinized what I'm wearing and how I styled my hair. When I colored my hair from blonde—the color Derek preferred—to brown, I broke out in a sweat. It was silly. Derek wasn't around, and yet going against his wishes made me sick to my stomach. I've had to purposely try and do the opposite of what Derek wanted to pull myself out of his toxic pattern. It was like flipping him the bird and also hard to break the cycle. Maybe I do need to talk to someone.

"Thank you. I'll think about it." I slip the card into my bag.

I follow Tamara from the office. We head down a long hallway. Hung on the walls are pictures of gorgeous gowns from the Alessi label worn by Hollywood superstars and even royalty.

Tamara stops in front of a frosted door, gives a quick tap on the glass, and enters the room. A woman with long, black, sleek hair and delicate features stands by the window. She glances up from the folder in her hands. Perfectly shaped brows crease above sky blue eyes. Tall and slender, this woman should be wearing an Alessi gown and walking on a catwalk, not be stuck in an office.

"Bianca, this is Harper. She's here to help you with all the run-around stuff you don't have time for while you're in town."

Bianca snaps the folder she's reading shut, struts to the desk and tosses it on the table in my direction. "Great. Take that to accounting then get me an almond milk latte." Her gaze travels from my blouse to the tips of my black heels. Her nose wrinkles. "You'll need to improve your wardrobe if you want to work here."

I glance at my feet and back up. I know my choice in clothing isn't the greatest, but it was the best I could do with the money I scraped together. My shoulders curl inwardly at having someone point it out.

"Harper looks fine." Tamara snatches the folder off the desk. "I'll show you where accounting is."

My face burns with embarrassment as I follow Tamara from the room.

"Ignore Bianca. She has the face of an angel and the sharp tongue of the devil. There's nothing wrong with your outfit," she says as I fiddle with the waistband of my skirt.

"Bianca's right. This is a fashion house. I can't show up to work wearing thrift store clothes." I sigh. "I can't afford anything designer. Maybe this job isn't for me after all." If only I could get access to the boutique-sized, walk-in closet at Derek's house to collect some of the pieces he bought me, but it's not possible.

Tamara waves her hand. "You won't need to buy anything. We have tons of clothing in storage that will never be worn."

"I can't take—"

Tamara interrupts me. "Hand it back when the job's over. No big deal. After work, I'll show you, and we can play dress-up." She smiles with excitement. "It will be fun."

How did I get so lucky finding Tamara? I'm so grateful for her help. Apart from Bianca's frosty encounter, I'm hopeful about this job. Sure, it's only temporary and I have to keep away from the Alessi brothers, but I'll now have some real experience to add to my resume.

After Tamara takes me to accounting, she gives me a tour of the building and the different departments. The sleek interior with bright colors and modern touches haven't changed much from what I remember when I'd briefly come here with Finn. Tamara also introduces me to staff along the way. There are so many people working here I'm hoping I can blend in and not be noticed by Hayden or Lucas. We pass a set of offices with their doors closed. I read the names: *Hayden Alessi*, *Lucas Alessi*, and *Finn Alessi* on shiny silver nameplates. My heart stops beating, and I suck in a quick breath. *Please don't stop here. Please don't stop here!*

"The managers are in a meeting now. I'll introduce you another time," Tamara says.

I breathe out a sigh of relief. I'd like to skip this introduction altogether and stay away from their offices. "I should probably make Bianca's coffee. She's waiting." I need to make a quick getaway before one of the Alessi brothers walk out of the office and find out I'm working here. I'm sure they would report it to Finn.

"I'll show you where the kitchen is." Inside the kitchen, Tamara says, "Bianca will let you know what she wants you to do, but if there are any problems or if you need anything, you know where my office is."

"Thank you. I really appreciate you doing this for me." She'll never know how grateful I am for the opportunity to work at Alessi Fashion.

She smiles and gently squeezes my arm. "Not a problem. Enjoy your day." With that, she sails from the kitchen.

After getting myself familiar with where things are, I make Bianca's coffee and head back to her office, glancing in every direction for any signs of the Alessi brothers. I breathe a sigh of relief when I don't see them.

My reprieve doesn't last long when I realize that Bianca's office is close to the manager's rooms. Is Bianca the PA to Hayden or Lucas? Tamara said she was here for a couple of months.

Wouldn't they have someone more permanent? Is she from another office?

For a second my blood runs cold. Oh my God! What if she's Finn's PA? No. I mentally shake my head. Alyssa said Finn is in London. There's probably another manager working here that I don't know of. I lost all contact with any Alessis, so I don't know who works here. Being here is already so stressful. If I didn't need the money so badly, I'd run out of here.

In Bianca's office, I place the coffee cup on the desk.

"How long does it take to make coffee?" Bianca taps a pen on the edge of the desk.

"I'm sorry it took so long. Tamara was showing me around."

Bianca rolls her eyes, picks up the cup, and takes a sip. Screwing up her nose, she puts it on the desk and shoves it aside. *Okay, I'll have to work on my coffee.* "Since you know your way around now, go to the fabric room and get me this bolt of material." She holds out a sample of light blue fabric. I take it, and it glides through my fingers. The color shimmers under the light. "Don't take all day." Bianca waves her hand in the door's direction.

Tamara wasn't wrong about Bianca having a sharp tongue. Is she always this bitchy? Oh well, it's only for two months. I'll put up with it if it means I get a paycheck.

Now, I have to remember where the fabric room is. Is it on the second or third floor? I don't want to go back and ask Bianca after I told her I had a tour of the building. Standing at the elevator, waiting for the doors to open, is a man carrying a bunch of folders. "Excuse me. Can you please tell me what floor the fabric room is on?"

He smiles. "Sure. It's on level three."

I smile back. "Thanks."

We step into the elevator. During my marriage to Derek, I was 'trained' to make small talk with strangers. Told to put on a smile and look interested in Derek's boring friends. So, my first instinct is to talk with this guy. Get to know a little about him. But I bite my tongue. Derek's not here now to tell me what to do.

So I stand in the corner, staring at the descending numbers, feeling awkward. I breathe a sigh of relief when the doors open on the man's floor and he steps out. What is wrong with me? Or I should say *damn you, Derek*. Just another thing to add to my ever-growing list of fucked up things you did to me.

On the third floor, I find the fabric room. When I step inside, my breath catches. Multiple colored and textured fabric line the walls. I slowly spin around to take it all in. It's like I've slipped inside a rainbow. It's glorious. I can imagine the beautiful gowns and clothing that could be made. I can picture the events celebrities and models would wear them to.

Unfortunately, I don't have time to daydream. I need to find the fabric and fast before Bianca has another reason to get pissed at me. The problem is there's dozens of bolts and swatches to search through, and none of them resemble the sample in my hand.

I scratch the side of my head, trying to decide where to start. This might take forever. "Looks like I'm going to piss Bianca off for the second time today after all."

What a great way to start a new job.

Chapter Five

FINN

In my office, I sit at my desk looking through Juliette's drawings. "I need your designs completed before I go back to London. Will that be a problem?" I ask as I flip through the pages. Once again, she's outdone herself with the sleek, elegant, whimsical designs.

"I have a few I'm still working on and a couple that need adjusting, but I'll have them finished by the deadline." She waves a hand covered in gold rings in the air. "Darling, have I ever let you down?" Not waiting for my response, because she knows the answer is no, she drags her chair next to me, flicks to a page, and taps her finger on the drawing. "The fabric for this has just come in. I want to see it before we work with it."

Pressing the button on the intercom, I connect to Bianca's office. "Bianca, I need you to bring the blue fabric in for Juliette, please."

"I've sent someone to get it." I hear a heavy sigh. "And she's taking her sweet time. I'll track her down."

"Don't worry, darling," Juliette says. "I'm leaving now anyway. I'll head down on my way out."

"I'll come with you," I say. "I'd like to see it too. If it's anything like the sample, it's amazing."

We take the elevator to the third floor. Just as we step out, Juliette's phone rings. "Excuse me, darling, I need to take this. I'll catch up with you in a minute."

Leaving her with her phone call, I walk into the fabric room. I'm greeted with a pert ass wrapped in a tight, black skirt bent over bolts of fabric that have been knocked onto the floor.

"Damn, I'm such a klutz," I hear her mumble.

"Do you need help?" I ask.

The woman pauses and doesn't turn around.

In a quiet voice, she says, "I'm fine, thanks."

With quick movements, she stacks the bolts haphazardly against the wall and clutches one to her chest. Hanging her head low, she turns around, her dark hair falling like a curtain, covering her face. She starts to step around me, but her foot hits a bolt left on the floor, and she stumbles. The material she's holding flies from her hands, and I catch her around the waist before she follows the blue fabric now lining the floor.

"Are you okay?" I ask.

She keeps her head down and shakes herself free from my grasp. "Yes. Thank you."

Is this the same woman I saw earlier in the hallway? The woman who reminded me of Harper. I'm desperate to see what she looks like. As she starts to leave, I wrap my hand around her wrist, stopping her, and pull her around to face me. Slowly, she lifts her face. Wide, dark brown eyes, framed with thick, black lashes stare back at me. For a second, I'm not understanding what I'm seeing. How can this woman look exactly like Harper? Then it hits me. Because it *is* Harper.

My heart jackhammers against my ribs. My first instinct is to pull her to me. At one point in my life, having her in my arms was as natural as breathing. As I stare in disbelief at her shocked face, it only takes a second for reality to punch me in the gut. I snatch my hand away.

"You need to tell me why the fuck you're in my building." Venom laces my words. Without answering, she spins on her heels and tries to rush from the room. Taking two long strides, I block the doorway. "Not so fast."

"Please move," she says, her voice shaking. Her chest is rising up and down like she's run a race.

I step away but pin her with a don't-fucking-move glare. "You need to explain what you're doing here." My body is vibrating with anger. I take a deep breath to keep my shit together.

"I…arrhh…" Her gaze darts toward the door.

Reading her intentions to flee, I say, "Tell me why you're here, then I'll personally kick your ass from the building." I clench my fists. The temptation to do it before an explanation is strong.

"What's happening here?" Juliette says from behind me before Harper can speak. "What's my fabric doing on the ground?"

"I'm sorry. I tripped and...and..." Harper drops to the floor and gathers up the material.

What in the twilight zone is happening? Does Harper work here? If so, why and for how long? Why hasn't Hayden and Lucas told me about this? Are they keeping secrets from me? Why would they do that? They know what she did to me. The questions tumble through my mind, making me dizzy.

"I'm sorry if I've dirtied it." Harper clutches the material to her chest.

Juliette pushes past me and kneels in front of Harper. "Darling, it's not a problem. It's for a sample. I'm sure it's fine." She puts a hand on Harper's shoulder. "You're shaking. Are you okay? It's really no big deal. There's no damage."

"I need to go." Harper gathers the bolt and rises, looking ready to sprint away.

"Come with me. I'll show you where to take it," Juliette says as she gets to her feet.

"Bianca wants it." Harper keeps her face turned away from me.

"Yes, darling. To give it to me. Let's take it to my office," Juliette says soothingly and guides Harper away.

I'm left standing alone in the room, watching the women leave, too dumbstruck to move or stop them. The familiar, sweet, fruity scent of Harper's perfume following them. I thought I'd never see Harper again. Never *wanted* to see her again. Now here she is carrying fucking fabric around the building with my head designer. What's been happening here while I'm working in London?

I scrub my hand through my hair and march to Tamara's office. Not bothering to knock, I storm into the room. "Why the hell is Harper Richardson here?" I demand to know.

Tamara's eyebrows rise over her glasses. "We have a Harper Madden, not Richardson, working here."

She's gone back to her maiden name. I thought she'd want to flaunt that asshole's name forever. "Why is Harper *Madden* here?"

Tamara rests back in the chair. "I gave her a job."

I slam my fists on my hips. "Why did you do that?"

"Because she applied for one. Bianca wanted an assistant, so I gave Harper a temporary position."

With all the money from her husband's massive inheritance, why would she need a temporary job? The hairs prickle at the back of my neck. Something doesn't feel right.

"Do my brothers know about this?"

"No. I just hired her today."

Today. It seems a little coincidental she starts working at Alessi's as soon as I'm back from London and not long after her husband's death. "I don't want her here. Fire her."

Tamara frowns. "Why? What did she do?"

"Fire her," I repeat without giving her a reason. I can't tell her that having Harper so near brings up the past. A past I've long ago buried. A past that almost killed me. One I don't want to revisit. Having her here will only dredge it up.

Tamara tosses the pen she's holding on the desk. "She's signed a contract for two months. So without a good reason, she stays."

I cross my arms over my chest. "I don't want her working here. That's the reason."

Tamara pushes herself from the chair and crosses her arms over her chest to mirror my stance. She never takes shit from anyone. Not even her bosses. "Not a good enough reason. If she's another one of your one-night stands you're trying to avoid, you'll need to put the company before your ego for a moment. I can't get any temps until late next week, and Harper is available now."

I clench my jaw. "Harper isn't a one-night stand."

"Then who is she? You don't usually fly off the handle like this." She pushes her glasses up her nose.

"No one. Just fire her."

Tamara's shoulders sag on a heavy sigh. "Not happening. I need her. No one else here will put up with Bianca."

"I can fire you both," I say in a warning tone.

Tamara shrugs a shoulder, wearing an I-don't-give-a-fuck expression. She knows I won't follow through with the threat. That's because for the past five years, she's been a valuable member of the company. And she knows it.

Placing my palms on the desk, I lean forward. "Fine. But you better keep her the hell away from me." Without waiting for a response, I push away from the desk and stomp from the room, slamming the door shut behind me.

There is a reason Harper took a job at Alessi Fashion the day I arrived. Before I leave for London, I'm going to figure it out.

Chapter Six

HARPER

In Juliette's office, my body is shaking, black dots float in front of my eyes, and I take deep breaths to stop myself from passing out. With trembling hands, I place the bolt of material on a white marble desk before I drop it again.

Did that just happen? Did I bump into Finn? Why isn't he in London? I mentally shake myself out of the shock. I always wondered how it would feel if I ever saw Finn again. Would I feel guilty…sad? Yes. Absolutely. What I didn't expect was to feel like a truck had hit me. Hearing his voice, seeing his face… All the love I had to bury deep to make it through a day—the pain and loss all came flooding back. He looked at me with so much anger and loathing. What did I expect? That he'd lovingly open his arms to me?

I have to pull myself together. I can't fall apart now. Not at work. Will I even have a job now? Probably not.

"I'm sorry again for dropping this." I skim a hand over the silk.

"Darling, there's no harm done. Take a seat. I'll get you like a glass of water." The petite designer with flaming, long, red hair is wearing an oversized pink coat with giant, yellow daisies embroidered into the fabric. Worn over skin-tight, orange pants, the outfit is bold. Not many women could pull it off. I may not have finished my fashion design course, but I loved to keep up with the fashion world online. Juliette Monet—a designer I've admired for years—looks amazing.

I drop into the nearest seat and take the glass of water Ms. Monet passes me. Glancing around the large room with floor-to-ceiling, arched windows, I take in the drawings and fabric samples pinned on boards on the walls. Mannequins dressed in unfinished garments stand in corners.

If I thought the fabric room was amazing, this room is heaven. This is where the magic happens. Where designs are drawn and given life. If I wasn't so shaken up by my run in with Finn, I'd love to explore the room. Well, that's if Juliette Monet let me.

After finishing the water, I put the glass on the desk, careful not to place it on any drawings scattered on the smooth surface.

"Are you okay?" Ms. Monet asks. "Back in the fabric room, it looked like something, or *someone* had frightened the life from you."

That *someone* was Finn Alessi. Why is he back from London? He shouldn't be here. I can't be near him. My heart won't take it. I have to tell Tamara I'm quitting. Unless I'm already fired.

"I'm fine," I reply. "I freaked out a little when I dropped the fabric. It's expensive, and I worried I might have damaged it."

Through narrowed eyes, Ms. Monet scrutinizes me like she's gauging whether or not I'm telling the truth. I shift in the chair.

Now that my hands have stopped shaking and my heartrate has slowed down, I'm feeling a little calmer. "Thank you for the water, Ms. Monet. I better tell Bianca you have the fabric before she wonders where I am."

Juliette rolls her eyes. Picking up a folding fan on the desk, she opens it with a flick of her wrist and fans it in front of her face. Who uses a folding fan these days? Juliette is fabulous. "Tell Bianca I needed help. That will shut her up. And please, call me Juliette. Ms. Monet makes me sound like an old woman."

Juliette could be anywhere from thirty to fifty. With her smooth features, it's hard to tell. I smile my thanks. "I'm Harper."

"Lovely to meet you, darling."

I rise from the chair and turn to leave. A drawing of a gown propped on an easel catches my eye. "This is gorgeous."

Juliette rounds the desk and sits on the corner. She screws her lips to the side. "Something's not quite right. I can't figure out what it is. It's for next year's spring collection. What do you think it could be?"

What? Juliette Monet, the famous designer, is asking for my opinion! "Oh, I don't know. I think it's stunning." Then I inspect it more closely. Can I really make a suggestion?

"I can see you've noticed something," Juliette says. "Darling, I'd love a fresh set of eyes."

Excitement bubbles inside me. Juliette Monet has asked me for my opinion. Can this day get any crazier? I trace a finger along the V neckline. "Maybe this needs to be lower?"

Juliette picks up a pencil with a long, pink feather attached from the desk and draws on the design. She glances back at me. "Like this?"

Oh God. Spending a year at design school had me dreaming of moments like this. "Yes, and maybe the skirt needs to be a little fuller here?" I point at the hips of the skirt.

Juliette makes quick strokes. When finished, she takes two steps back to look at the amendments. "That's it!" She places the back of her hand on her forehead and smiles at me. "I've stared at this for days and couldn't work it out. Such a simple modification and it's exactly how it should look. Thank you, darling."

I dip my head, a little embarrassed by Juliette's enthusiastic praise. "I'm glad I could help." Although, I'm sure Juliette would have eventually worked it out on her own.

"You have a good eye. Are you a designer?" Juliette asks.

"No. I went to school to study for a year but...arhhh...things didn't work out." Before she asks why I quit, I quickly continue, "I better find Bianca."

As I rush back to Bianca's office, I search for any signs of Finn. Thankfully, I make it to her office with no more run ins. I step into Bianca's office, and she's typing on her computer. Without looking up, she asks, "Where have you been?"

Twisting my fingers together, I say, "I gave the fabric straight to Ms. Monet. She also needed me to help her with something."

Bianca flicks her hair over her shoulder, not saying a word. Wow, Juliette Monet was right. It did shut Bianca up.

"Is Finn around?" I want to avoid him as much as possible. If I know where he is, it will be easier to stay away.

Bianca's eyes snap up from the screen, and she raises an eyebrow. "*Finn?*"

I shuffle my feet. God, Bianca makes me feel like I'm in trouble and have been sent to the principal's office. "I'm sorry. Is Mr. Alessi around?"

"I don't know why it's any of your business, but no. He left and won't be back until tomorrow."

My shoulders sag with relief. I can finish the day without fear of bumping into him again. Why haven't I been fired on the spot?

For the rest of the day, Bianca has me running around delivering documents, making copious amounts of coffee, and picking up dry-cleaning among many other things. I keep looking over my shoulder, half-dreading, half-hoping Finn comes back. My nerves are so wired from the stress, when I finish work, I'm a jittery mess. I make my way to Tamara's office and drop with exhaustion onto a chair in front of her.

"Busy day?" Tamara eyes me from over the rim of her glasses.

"I think Bianca took great pleasure in torturing me. She hates me," I say.

"Don't worry about her. She loathes anyone who rivals her beauty. Especially if they get near Finn. She's obsessed with him, but he doesn't look twice at her. Well, not in the way she'd like."

Bianca considers me a threat? If only she knew how much Finn hates me. The proof clear in his fierce gaze and harsh words. Besides, I won't be back tomorrow. "Tamara, I'm so grateful for the job. You didn't have to help me like this. But I have to quit. I'm sorry."

Tamara pushes the colored glasses on top of her head. Placing her elbows on the table, she leans forward. "Has this got anything to do with Finn? He came storming into my office demanding I fire you."

Even though I expected that, it still stung. "If I'm fired, why was I still working today?"

"Because I told him you signed a contract, and without a good reason, it can't be done."

I shake my head. "But I didn't sign a contract."

Tamara gives a cheeky smirk, pulls open a drawer, and places a sheet of paper on the desk, sliding it toward me.

"He didn't know that." Passing me a pen, she says, "Here, sign it."

"I can't. I'm not coming back."

"I don't know what's going on between you and Finn. It's easy to see there's history. You told me you needed this job. Are you going to let another man determine what you do with your life?"

I straighten in the chair and grip the pen in my hand. Oh my God. That's exactly what I'm doing. I spent nine years being commanded by Derek. Now I'm finally free from those restrictive chains. I'm not letting Finn scare me away from a job I need. It's not like I have options lined up.

Picking up the contract, I scan through it. It all looks good. My hand shakes as I sign my name on the bottom.

All I need to do is avoid Finn as much as possible. It's only for two months. How hard can it be?

After work, Tamara takes me to storage—which is more like a department store filled with beautiful clothes—to find suitable outfits for work. I choose skirts, trousers, and blouses I can mix and match. I have to ignore the gorgeous lace, silk, and satin gowns. They're not appropriate for work. It doesn't stop me from running my hands over the textured fabric and dreaming of wearing them one day.

"Thanks for helping me," I say when I have my selection.

"My pleasure. It was fun. I'll arrange an Uber and help you take them home." She picks up the garment bags.

"Oh no, that's not necessary. I don't want to bother you anymore."

"No bother. I have no plans tonight," Tamara insists and organizes an Uber.

Thirty minutes later, we arrive at my apartment. Tamara sits on a stool in the corner of my bedroom, watching me put the clothes into an old, scratched, faux timber closet.

"Let's go to a nightclub and celebrate your new job," she suggests.

"That's a great idea," Alyssa says from her propped-up position on the bed where she's snacking on an apple. She's dressed in her signature black cargo pants, black leather jacket, and black biker boots. Always dressed in black; the only way I can tell that she's come home from a dance class is the pink leotard peeking from under the jacket and her hair pulled on top of her head in a tight bun.

I pause with a blouse in my hand. "I don't think there's much to celebrate. It's only temporary."

"Of course there's a reason to celebrate! You have a job." Tamara holds up her hand, stopping me from repeating that it's 'only temporary'. "*And* you're young and single. I bet you haven't gone out since your husband died."

I bite my bottom lip in thought. She's right. I haven't been out. When I was married to Derek, we didn't go out either. His boring dinner parties he dragged me to don't count.

"Come on. I know this great club. Consider this another step to your new life."

It's like Tamara knows the buttons to press to fire me up. First it was about quitting my job because of a man. Now she's planted the seed of starting a new life. Wasn't that what I wanted to do the second I learned about Derek's death? To get my life back?

I toss the blouse I'm holding onto the bed. "You're right. Going out is another step in getting my life back. I want to dance, drink, and not give a damn about anything or *anyone*." That includes Finn and his reaction to seeing me. Although, he could be a little harder to push from my mind.

Tamara claps and cheers, "That's my girl! Now put on that little black dress I can see in the closet poking out from your clothes."

I pull it out and hold it in front of me by the hanger. It's one of the dresses I moved into Derek's house with. At the time, I didn't know what I was throwing into my luggage, and I didn't care. It was a dress I'd worn when I was about nineteen and never wore again. "This won't fit."

"Put it on and we'll see," Alyssa encourages.

I seriously have doubts about it, but I go into the bathroom. I slide into the dress and tug it up my body. Glancing in the mirror, I'm shocked to see only a small scrap of material clinging to my every curve. This is definitely smaller than when I last wore it. I can't wear this in public.

"Don't hide in the bathroom. Come out and show us," Tamara calls from the bedroom like she knows I'm having second thoughts about leaving the outfit on.

Walking timidly back to the bedroom, I tug the hem of the skirt lower with no success. Tamara's eyes bug from their sockets as they trail me from head to toe. "You look amazing. Do *not* think about taking it off."

"It's too skimpy." I skim my hands over my hips.

"The right amount of skimpy. Sexy skimpy, but not giving away all the goods," Alyssa says. "I love it."

God, it has been so long since I've dressed up in clothes other than something Derek deemed suitable for his wife. He liked me in conservative clothes. If I never wear another blazer again, it will be too soon.

"Can I really wear this in public?" I ask as I gaze with uncertainty at my reflection in the mirror.

"Of course you can. You look gorgeous." Tamara slaps the palms of her hands on her thighs and rises from the stool. "Put some heels on and let's go. I'm going to text my wife, Erica, to let her know where I am."

"Why don't you ask her to come too?" Alyssa says.

Shaking her head, Tamara says, "She can't tonight. She's a nurse, and she's working nightshift."

I look at Alyssa, needing her opinion. "What do you think? Should I wear it?"

"If you're not comfortable, then don't. It's up to you. But if I had tits like yours, I'd be proud to show them off." She giggles playfully.

This is my time now. No more restrictions. No one telling me what to wear and where to go. It's going to take some time to get used to being in control of my own life. Nerves flutter in my chest. I shouldn't feel this way about an innocent night out with friends. This anxious feeling is Derek's fault. I can't have fun without thinking it's wrong. It's not wrong. So why does it feel like it is? I think about the business card Tamara gave me. Maybe I should give her therapist sister a call. I want to live my life with no doubts and insecurities.

"Okay, I'll wear it," I say on an exhale of breath.

"Excellent," Tamara says at the same time Alyssa says, "Watch out, boys!"

I'm happy to just go out, have fun, and forget about my messed-up life and not complicate it with men. I want to forget the biggest complication—Finn Alessi.

Chapter Seven

FINN

Knocking back a shot of whiskey, I smack the glass on the table. In the busy club, Alto, colored lights ricochet off the mirrored walls and ceilings. The music pulsing through the speakers is pounding through my brain.

How did I let Hayden and Lucas convince me to go out? Being around people is the last thing I want to do tonight. Hayden's buddy, Theo Campbell, owns the trendy nightclub, and Lucas insisted I needed to check it out, telling me it's what I need to pull me out of my foul mood.

"Are you going to tell us why you ran out of the office like your ass was on fire?" Lucas asks. He'd called me multiple times today asking where I was only to be told to fuck off.

Not a *what* but a *who*. I have no intention of telling them what happened. Because I can hardly believe it myself. So I keep my mouth shut.

"Come on, man. Were Juliette's designs so bad? She's been experimenting with different ideas lately. Did she scare you?" Lucas jokes, not taking offense by my rejected phone calls.

I wish it was as simple as bad designs. I tap my left ear, implying I can't hear the conversation over the music. Hayden and Lucas make identical I-don't-believe-your-bullshit eye-rolling gestures.

"If you left to screw another Harper look-alike, I'm going to be pissed. You had meetings you missed," Hayden says disapprovingly.

A red haze fogs my vision. "You don't know what you're talking about."

Not caring that I'm aiming a death glare his way, he continues, "Do that shit in your own time and keep it in your pants during work hours."

My hands ball into fists on the table. "Maybe you should go home to your daughter." I see a flash of parental guilt across Hayden's face. A good way to get the subject off me and Hayden thinking of something else.

"She's at a friend's house tonight." He points a finger at me. "Don't think I don't know what you're doing. I'll drop it—for now."

I never want to talk about how Harper had me running from the office like a scared rabbit with a hunter chasing after me. I hate she has that effect on me. Instead of attending meetings and getting work done, to avoid her, I spent the afternoon wandering around the streets, freezing my ass off. I thought if I focused on the cold, I wouldn't think about Harper. It didn't work. She was front and center in my mind. For a moment, my hands had touched her. I'd breathed in her sweet scent. Fuck, my heart had jumped to my throat seeing her again. And that's what scared the hell out of me. Yet, while walking around the city, it didn't take long for the memories of our time apart and the knife she stabbed in my back to fill me with rage.

Through the dim lights of the club, my attention is drawn to the entrance. Like I've conjured her up, Harper walks in the club with Tamara and a woman I don't recognize. They head straight for the bar. Tamara must have said something funny because Harper tosses her head back and laughs, her dark brown hair falling down her back. Shifting restlessly in my seat, the urge to go to her is pulling me to her. Like she hadn't ripped my heart from my chest and broken every dream we ever made.

What is wrong with me? I thought I'd laid my feelings to rest. It must be the shock of seeing her again. Annoyed with my reaction, my jaw clenches and I stand up from the chair. I need to get out of the club. Get as far away from Harper as possible. I fucking hate that she keeps chasing me away.

"Hey, where are you going?" Hayden yells over the music.

I don't bother answering and walk away. Instead of leaving the club, my feet have a mind of their own, and I weave through the crowd and tables until I find a spot near the bar. Close enough but not too close to be seen by Harper. I tell myself I'm only here to gauge what she's up to—like, is she following me? Yet, my eyes drink her in like I'm dying of thirst.

Concealed by a granite column, I watch Harper as she sips a cocktail and chats with the women. She's wearing a figure-hugging, black dress that clings to her every curve. When we were together, she'd worn one just like it. Over the years, she'd filled it out nicely. I hate myself for noticing. Hate myself for spying on her. Yet I can't drag myself away.

For the next half hour, I watch her laugh, dance on the spot, and order another cocktail. She smiles politely at men who approach her, declining whatever they are offering. They should consider themselves lucky she rejected them. I know first-hand the pain she can inflict. But here I still am with my eyes glued to her every move. What kind of sick fuck does that make me?

Harper excuses herself from the women and heads toward the restrooms. Without thinking, I peel myself away from my hiding spot and follow. When I catch up to her, I wrap a hand around her wrist, stopping her from entering the restroom.

She lets out a squeal and spins around. When she sees me, her eyes widen. "What are you doing?" She glances at her arm and back at me.

Warmth spreads up my arm, and I quickly drop her wrist. "We need to talk. Come with me." She doesn't refuse, and I lead her to an alcove tucked away from the crowd.

"Finn, what are you doing?"

"You followed me to the club," I accuse, not bothering to answer her question.

She narrows her eyes. "No. I didn't know you were here."

I scoff. *Bullshit!* "Why are you here?"

"Tamara asked me to come out with her."

I shake my head. "Not at the club. Why are you at Alessi's?"

She fidgets with a delicate chain around her neck that dips behind the neckline of her dress. My gaze follows its descent between her breasts. Breasts that are practically spilling out from the dress. My cock tightens behind the zipper of my jeans. Fuck! She's supposed to repulse me, not turn me on.

"I needed a job. Alessi's had a position," she says, unaware of how my body is reacting at being so close to her. Why can't I seem to fight it?

"You don't expect me to believe that, do you?" I give a mirthless laugh.

"It's the truth. What other reason can there be?"

I pin her with a hard stare. "To get to me."

Leaning toward her, that damn fruity scent of her perfume surrounds me. For a second, I want to bury my nose in her neck. Breathe her in. To hell with how much I hate her. Thankfully, I snap myself back to my senses before I do something stupid. Like run my tongue over her smooth skin.

"Now that your husband's dead, do you think we can pick up where we left off?" I rake my eyes over her with disgust. "Well, I'm not interested." *Liar!* my body screams.

She presses her lips together, then says, "I told you, I'm here for the job."

"Quit."

"No." She crosses her arms over her chest. Which pushes her breasts up further. My mouth waters. I peel my gaze away.

"You don't need the money. If you want to work, find someplace else."

Sighing, she drops her arms to her sides. "You wouldn't understand." She starts to step around me.

"What wouldn't I understand?" I ask. She stops and turns back. "I really want to know why the hell you're back." *Back in my life and tormenting me all over again*, I want to say. But I keep that to myself.

Her eyes waver from mine. "Finn, It's true. I need a job. Things aren't what they... I don't have... I didn't want..." She shakes her head. "It's complicated." She's not making any sense. A deep frown creases her forehead. Her shoulders droop on a heavy sigh. "I never wanted to hurt you. There's so much you need to know. If I can just explain—"

I place a finger over her lips, stopping whatever lies were going to spew from her mouth. Because what else could there be? Our relationship was based on deceit. Whatever she has to say won't change that.

Her lips tremble under my finger. Her eyes hold a puzzled look. Now's the time to pull away. Tell her to get the hell out of my life because I never want to see her again. Any second now I will... For whatever sick reason, I just need a moment.

Instead of dropping my hand away and stepping back, I skim my finger along her full, bottom lip. Her mouth parts slightly, sucking in a startled breath. Standing with her in front of me, it's like I've traveled back in time, and we're two young lovers sneaking away from a family dinner to get some alone time. How many times did we do that? Too many to count.

My hand floats across her cheek and cups her jaw. Taking two steps closer, our heaving chests bump together. For a beat, our eyes lock. I lower my head, my lips ghosting over her mouth before I place a soft, feather-like kiss on her lips. She tastes of sweet alcohol and…Harper. A taste I could never forget and never find in other women.

Wrapping a hand around her waist, I draw her closer, the fingers of my other hand tunneling through her hair. This woman is a drug I thought I'd kicked out of my system a long time ago. But with one kiss, I'm desperate for another fix.

As I deepen the kiss, she hooks her arms around my neck, pressing her breasts against my chest. My hand travels up her waist to cup her left breast. She draws in a shuddery breath as my thumb glides over a peaked nipple. I shouldn't want this. Yet I can't step away.

The music and sounds of the club dim in the background, leaving Harper's sighs of pleasure filling my mind—spurring me on. Pressing her against the wall, the kiss turns more frantic. I need to taste more of her. Rip the clothes from her body. Bury myself deep inside her. Do everything I've dreamed of since the day she left.

The words *she left* shoots through my brain, and like a splash of icy water is poured over my head, I propel away from her. Shocked and disgusted by what I have done.

"Finn?" Her glassy eyes stare at me with confusion.

No…no…no… Why am I doing this? Reality rears up and punches me in the chest, knocking the oxygen from my lungs.

This can't be happening. I should be telling her I never want to see her face again. Instead, two minutes in my arms and I was ready to fuck her up against the wall in a busy nightclub.

Fuck! Even after what she put me through, I want her.

Chapter Eight

HARPER

God, I longed for the day I felt Finn's hands on my body again. Felt his lips pressing on mine. Felt our hearts beating against each other's chests. I've often dreamed of a moment like this—being wrapped in his arms with him loving me again. Dream Finn can't hold a candle to Real Finn. I miss him so much it hurts. If he's kissing me, does that mean he misses me too? A surge of hope bubbles in my chest.

When I take one look at the thunderous expression on his face, I know immediately it was too much to hope for. The bubble pops, leaving a heavy blanket of disappointment over me.

He points a finger at my face. "Stay away from me."

Gasping, I hold a hand to my chest. "Me?"

"Yes, you!" He shoves his fingers through his hair.

"I was on my way to the bathroom, minding my own business, when you stopped me. You're the one who approached me. You dragged me away into a dark corner to *talk*. Then *you* kissed me! This..." I flick a pointed finger between us. "...is on you. If you can't control yourself, maybe *you* need to stay away from me!"

God, if I'd ever spoken to Derek that way, he'd have a fit. He would have yelled at me for being insolent and then given me a lecture on how women are expected to always treat their husband with respect. If I ever refused, he'd pull out his trump card—threats to my family and Finn. I eventually learned to keep my mouth shut. It was easier that way. Now, it felt liberating to finally be able to speak my mind with no repercussions.

"Fine. That won't be a problem," Finn says through gritted teeth.

"Good. Excellent!" Our chests rise and fall as we stare at each other. No one taking the first move to leave. When I don't think he'll step aside, I say, "Move away so I can pass. I don't want to 'accidentally' touch you and have you get the wrong idea."

For a second, he doesn't move. He stares at me so intently while standing so close. When his gaze drops to my lips, I wonder if he's going to kiss me again. My heart trips with anticipation. Would I let him even though I know he hates me? Probably. That's how desperate I am to feel his touch again.

He finally steps aside, gesturing with his arm for me to leave. "Don't bother coming into work tomorrow."

My back stiffens at his command. "I will not let another man tell me what to do ever again. I *will* be at work tomorrow. But don't worry, I'll stay away from you as much as possible." With my head held high, I push past him and hurry into the restroom.

Inside, I place my hands on the vanity counter and drop my head, trying to catch my breath.

Oh God. What just happened? I drag in deep breaths through my nose, trying to steady the nausea churning in my stomach. Snatching paper towels from a dispenser on the tile wall, I run them under water and press them against my flaming cheeks, forehead, and neck. I take a long look at myself in the mirror. My cheeks are flushed. My eyes are wide and glassy. If this is what being so close, touching Finn, does to me on the outside—I press a hand over my heart and bow my head—what it's doing on the inside is tearing me apart.

The shock and surprise of the day is too much. I'm so overwhelmed with emotions, I can barely stand upright. I need to get out of the club. As far away from Finn as possible. Racing from the bathroom, I give a quick scan of my nearby surroundings. It's clear of Finn, so I make my way back to Alyssa and Tamara.

"What took you so long? I was about to come and search for you," Alyssa yells over the music.

Ignoring her question, I say in a rush, "I have to go."

Alyssa's glass pauses at her lips, and she puts it on the table. "Why? We haven't been here very long."

I tug at the ends of my hair and risk glancing around the club. Like magnets, my eyes zone in on Finn. He's slouched in a booth on an upper level with Hayden and Lucas. A glass of amber liquid at his lips. While his brothers chat among themselves, Finn pins me with a narrow gaze. Breaking away from his stare,

I say, "I can't stay here. I'm sorry." I pick up my purse from the chair.

"Hey, wait. Are you okay?" Alyssa asks.

"You're looking a little pale. Can I get you a glass of water?" Tamara signals to a waiter.

I shake my head. "I don't need water, thanks," I say to Tamara. To Alyssa I say, "I bumped into my ex."

"Your ex?" Alyssa frowns.

"The one I was telling you about the other day."

Tamara puts a hand on my arm. "Finn is your ex?"

My eyes widen. "How...who..."

"I saw Finn storming away from the direction of the restrooms. A few minutes later, you're running out as white as a ghost and saying you want to get away from your ex. After he wanted to fire you today and you wanting to quit...I knew you two had history."

"He wanted to fire you? What a jerk," Alyssa says with disgust. Then softening her tone, she says, "Are you okay seeing him again?"

I nod although my legs are still shaking. I flick a quick glance at Finn. He's still giving me a death glare. "I'm going to go. You two stay and have fun."

Tamara taps her hand on the table. "If you really want to go, then go. But we came here tonight to have fun. Are you going to let him run you out of the club? Don't let him dictate what you do."

Every time Tamara mentions not letting a man interfere in my decisions, it sparks a fire in my belly. My spine stiffens. Gone are the days I'll let that happen again. Decision made, I signal to a passing waiter. I say to the girls, "I think we need cocktails."

"That's the spirit!" Tamara cheers.

We give the waitress an order of espresso martinis.

While waiting for our drinks to arrive, Tamara says, "Do you want to talk about Finn?"

Do I? What can I tell them? That he was the love of my life, and I threw away that love and broke his heart to marry a man for money? I've only recently met Tamara and Alyssa, and although we've instantly clicked, I can't tell them the full story. The shame cuts too deep.

I run my finger along the seam of the table. "We dated a few years ago. It ended badly. Finn is still angry and hasn't forgiven me." How could he? I stomped all over his love.

"He may not have forgiven you, but he hasn't taken his eyes off you," Tamara says. "What happened while you were at the bathroom?"

I shift in my seat. Our cocktails arrive, and I wait for the waiter to leave. What happened? Finn kissed me like no time had passed. Like love still beat between us. No, that isn't completely true. The kiss was different. Deeper. Harder. Punishing.

I clear my throat. "Nothing much," I lie. "He wanted to know why I was working at Alessi's, and he wants me to quit."

"In my office today, Finn called you Harper Richardson. Is your late husband Derek Richardson, the owner of Black Casino?"

I hate the word husband. We coexisted in the same house. That's all. I was called to stand by his side occasionally. But he was never a husband. "Yes."

"Finn looked like he'd swallowed razor blades when he mentioned your married name. I'm guessing he wasn't a fan of the marriage."

I twist the stem of the cocktail glass between my fingers. "Finn wasn't happy when I got married." That was an understatement if ever I heard one.

"Finn is one of the nicest guys I know. Hopefully, he'll cool down and stop telling you to quit your job."

"I'm not sure he'll ever 'cool down', but I'm not going to quit. I need this job. Even if it means I have to put up with Finn's bad mood." I shrug my shoulders.

Alyssa drops her elbows on the table and props her chin in her hands. "We're supposed to be out having fun, not talking about depressing shit. We need another cocktail!"

Two cocktails, three vodka cranberry shots, and a dance marathon later, we stumble off the dance floor. My feet are throbbing and my head's spinning slightly. The last time I had this much to drink was at my wedding. I tried drowning out the day and what my future looked like with alcohol. It didn't change anything, just left me with a bitch of a headache.

"I should go home. I have to work in the morning." I glance with blurry vision at my watch, bringing it closer to my face. "Actually, it is morning. I need sleep."

"I don't have class until tomorrow afternoon. Do you mind if I stay?" Alyssa asks.

"Sure. No problem."

"Will you be okay getting home on your own?"

I roll my eyes. "I'm a big girl. I can take care of myself. Thanks though."

"Okay, great, because there's a cute guy over there checking me out. I'm going to go say hi. Don't wait up for me." Alyssa smiles with mischief, then her graceful dancer's body threads through the crowd.

Tamara and I make our way outside to wait for the Ubers that we ordered. I should save my money and walk to the subway, but my feet ache, my head's a little fuzzy, it's drizzling, and I'm freezing. Thank God I have a job now, because tonight has done damage to the pathetic amount of money I have left. Looks like I'll be eating cheap ramen noodles until I get paid.

Tamara's Uber pulls up first. She pauses at the passenger door. "See you at work tomorrow?" After what happened tonight, I'm not surprised that she'd be wondering if I'll show up.

My heart says 'no'. How am I supposed to see Finn again? My pockets says 'get your ass to work or you'll be out on the streets'. "Yes, see you in the morning. Thanks for a fun night."

Tamara waves and smiles as she slides into the backseat of the car.

The temperature has dropped since leaving my apartment, and my coat isn't doing much to keep out the icy chill. Waiting for the Uber, I huddle closer to the building, rub my hands up and down my arms, and bounce on my toes to get warm. "God, it's cold."

As soon as the words leave my mouth, something warm drapes over me. Tilting my head to the side, I see a thick, black coat hanging from my shoulders. For a moment, I squeeze my eyes shut and breathe in the familiar scent of sandalwood and citrus, knowing exactly who's standing behind me.

Slowly turning around, I come face to face with Finn for the second time tonight. Now his expression is unreadable. Much better than the hard glares he'd been giving me all night. I tried pretending he wasn't in the room, but I couldn't help giving him sneaky looks.

"What are you doing?" I start to shrug off the coat.

Finn stops me by holding onto the lapels. "Keep it on. You'll freeze."

"Why do you care if I freeze?" In the dim light of the streetlamp, I search Finn's face for any signs of the man I once knew. For that fun, full-of-life man I'd fallen head over heels for. The man who held me, loved me. The man who wanted to spend the rest of his life with me. A tight fist squeezes my heart. Someone harder, fiercer, stood in his place. The man I once loved is gone, and it breaks my heart.

He shrugs, lets go of the jacket, and steps back. A look of confusion slides across his face, like he isn't sure what he's doing here. "I don't." He turns to leave.

The alcohol in my system gives me the courage to hold onto his arm—an arm more muscular than I remembered—and pull him around. "What is your problem?"

His gaze zeros in on my hand and he shrugs it off. He can't stand an innocent touch, yet he had his hands all over me a few hours ago.

"You're my problem. There's a reason you're working at Alessi's, and I'm going to find out why."

Pent-up frustration pours from me, and I jab a finger at his chest. "There's no sinister reason. I'm working at Alessi's whether or not you like it!" I try to jab my finger at his chest again, but Finn grasps my finger before I hit the mark. He tugs me forward, and I stumble toward him, my hands landing on his chest. His muscles bunch under my palms, feeling bigger and firmer than nine years ago.

For a moment, Finn stares down at me. Anger blazes from his eyes. Even though the love is long gone from his eyes, I can't pull away. "Fine. Keep working at Alessi's. It will only make it easier for me to figure out what your game is. And I will figure it out." With that, he spins on his heels and marches back into the club. Even with his coat still on my shoulders, I feel colder than ever before.

Chapter Nine

FINN

Inside Alto, with my hands on my hips, I drag in deep breaths. What the fuck am I doing? It's bad enough that I kissed Harper...touched her. When I saw her leave the club, I propelled my ass from the chair and followed her for the second time tonight!

I had no reason to talk to her again. I'd already made it clear I wanted her to keep away from Alessi's...keep away from me. Yet, *I'm* doing the chasing. It's like I have no control over where my feet lead me. Like a sleepwalker walking through the night unaware of what they're doing. Being led by a dream. Maybe I'm clinging onto the dream I once shared with Harper. No, that was a nightmare I violently woke up from.

There's no point sticking around the club. Hayden and Lucas have already gone home. Normally, I'd find a woman to take back to my hotel. I'd spend a couple of hours pretending I wasn't thinking of Harper while fucking a nameless woman. It's sick. I know. Every morning I wake up with the shame of what I've done. Yet, I keep doing it again and again and again.

I give a quick scan around the room. With all the beautiful women in the club, not an ounce of interest stirs in me. These women are a poor imitation to the real thing. There's no denying I'm still drawn to Harper. She's beautiful. Even more so than before. It's what's inside I have to remember—cold and unfeeling. She'd rip a person's heart out in the blink of an eye.

I leave the club, and a blast of icy wind blows through my shirt. I shiver in the night air as I wait for the valet to bring my car around. I could do with my coat. Why did I have to put it on Harper?

Shit! My coat. I pinch the bridge of my nose. What have I done? If Harper happens to check the inside pocket, she'll discover the memento I've kept all these years. Something to remind me to never fall in another trap again.

The engagement ring I bought her.

Chapter Ten

HARPER

THE NEXT DAY, I step out of the elevator and into the brightly lit reception area of Alessi Fashion and make my way to the cubicle Tamara assigned to me. I put my bag under the desk and hook my jacket over the back of the chair.

I place Finn's coat in the crook of my arm. A blast of jittery nerves rakes over my body. I need to give it back to him. That means I have to see him again. Maybe I should give it to Bianca to give to him, that way I don't have to have any contact. Bianca will probably question why I have it. Do I want to deal with that? No. Can I sneak it into his office when he's not in there? God, I'm such a coward. If I want to change my life, I need to face the hard parts too.

Before finding Finn—courage takes time to build—I duck into Tamara's office. "Good morning."

Tamara is cradling her head in her hands. She tilts her face up to look at me. "What's so good about it?" she groans. "And why don't you look like death warmed over like I do?"

I should. I'm functioning on only a couple of hours of sleep. Thoughts of Finn had kept me awake. "Coffee and plunging my face into an ice bath has helped."

"I'm never drinking again." Tamara rests her head on the back of the chair.

I giggle. "I hope you feel better soon."

Tamara rubs her temples. "Thanks."

"Do you know if Finn is in the office yet?" I ask. As much as I'd like to, I can't avoid him forever.

"Yes, I saw him come in a few minutes ago. His mood looks as dark as I feel. Today's going to be peachy," she says sarcastically while giving two thumbs-up.

Great. Time to face Finn and his bad mood. Well, what difference will it make? He's always in a bad mood when he sees me. Except for when he kissed me, pressed me up against the wall, and put his hands on my body. If he hated me so much, why do it? Was it some kind of punishment? I'd spent hours tossing and turning in bed, trying to figure it out. I need to talk to him. He can't kiss me like that without an explanation.

"Drink coffee. I'll see you later," I say.

Tamara presses her lips together like she's trying not to throw up and waves.

When I reach Finn's office door, I draw in a deep breath. I raise my hand to knock then hesitate for a moment. Maybe I should just give him his coat back and forget about asking about the kiss. No point dragging it up. I'll chalk it up to nostalgia. A moment of weakness. Surely that was it.

"What are you doing?" A sharp voice comes from behind me.

I jerk like I've been caught with my hand in the cookie jar. Turning around, I see Bianca staring at me with a raised eyebrow. This woman who looks like a goddess scares me like the freaking devil.

"I need to see Finn—I mean, Mr. Alessi."

Bianca's gaze drops to the coat draped over my arm and shoots back up. "Is that Finn's coat?"

Crap! So much for keeping this from Bianca. "Yes, I need to give it back."

"Why do you have Finn's coat?"

I shuffle my feet. "I saw him last night and—"

"Are you sleeping with him?" Bianca's voice rises, and her eyes narrow with accusation.

"What? No!" My cheeks grow warm, and I glance around to see if anyone can overhear our conversation.

Bianca must have mistaken my flaming red cheeks as guilt, because hate shoots from her eyes. She gives a mirthless laugh. "Oh, you work fast, don't you?"

"Excuse me?" Who the hell does Bianca think she is? It's none of her business who I'm sleeping with or not sleeping with, but before I can say anything, the door swings open. I breathe a sigh of relief even though the interruption is Finn.

Finn looks at us standing in front of his door with a slight crease between his brows. "Is there something wrong?"

"Just going over what's happening today with Hayley." She smiles sweetly. Like a flick of a switch, Bianca's gone from devil woman to angel face.

Finn frowns. "Her name's Harper."

I inwardly smile at Finn's correction. Would he care she'd gotten my name wrong if he truly hated me? I'm clinging onto the smallest things. Anything that shows he might care even in the tiniest of ways.

Not glancing at me, her lips thin as she says, "Oops, my mistake. Finn, I have a few last-minute details I'd like to go over with you before tomorrow's photoshoot."

With Bianca's attention focused on Finn, her eyelashes batting like a lovesick puppy, I understand her hostility toward me. She assumes I've slept with Finn. Bianca's in love with him, or she wants to jump his bones. Either way, she sees me as a threat. Didn't Tamara say something to me like that? I'd brushed it off as nonsense. If only she knew she had nothing to worry about. Finn hates me. From the look on his face and the tone of his voice last night, nothing will happen again.

"Not now," Finn says to Bianca. He turns to me. "Is there something you need to see me about?"

What the... He's brushing off Bianca for me! His face is expressionless. His tone neutral. No anger from last night is visible. Should I worry? Is it simmering underneath his cool exterior, waiting to explode the moment we're alone?

I see Bianca's back stiffen. I'm assuming she doesn't enjoy being dismissed. Or hates Finn choosing me over her. Again, she has *nothing* to worry about.

"I want to talk to you about something, but if you're busy with Bianca, I can come back later."

"I'm not busy. Come in." Finn gestures for me to enter his office. My jaw wants to hit the floor in shock. Why is he being so polite?

Bianca's expression hardens. "Finn, this is important."

"It can wait a few minutes. I'll call you when I'm free." With that, he closes the door on Bianca. But not before I see that her jaw *did* fall open. Bianca looks as surprised as I feel.

Finn walks around his desk, putting his hands on the top of the leather chair. His gaze fixes on the coat in my hands.

"I came to return this." I lift my arm that's holding the coat. Instead of passing it to him or placing it on the desk, I hold onto it. Like this piece of soft, woolen fabric is going to be the closest I'm ever going to get to Finn. Taking a deep breath, I pluck up the courage to say, "Can we talk about last night?"

"What about it?" His tone is nonchalant, but I notice the way he squeezes the top of the chair. He's not as detached as he's trying to make out.

"You approached me at Alto's, you kissed me—touched me. I can see you hate me, so why would you do that?"

He shrugs a shoulder. "It was a moment of insanity."

I shake my head. "You had plenty of time to stop yourself." I know it's too good to be true that he did it because he still has feelings for me. So why? "Were you punishing me for…for…" The words stick in my throat.

"Marrying another man after you told me you loved me? Said you wanted to spend the rest of your life with me? Even naming the babies we were going to have?" The neutral expression from moments ago hardens as he clenches his jaw.

I hang my head with shame. "I *wanted* all those things." With Finn. No one else.

"You wanted an old man with deep pockets and a social circle," Finn accuses.

I gasp as his words hit me hard. Of course that's what he saw. If he only knew the truth. Is now the time to tell him the real reason I left him? Well…most of the reason. There's a part about his father's infidelity I'm not sure how to deal with yet. Would he even believe me?

"That's not what I wanted," I say.

Finn pushes away from the chair and scrubs a hand down his face. "I don't care anymore. Whatever you say will only be a lie. Now, is that all?" He nods his head toward the door. Now is not the time to tell him. By the way he's throwing me death daggers, he definitely won't believe me.

Annoyance ripples through me at being dismissed. I'm not done. So I take the conversation back to last night. "Why did you approach me in the club? And why did you kiss me?" I don't believe his 'moment of insanity' comment.

Instead of answering my question, he sneers. "I didn't see you complaining."

He's being nasty to avoid answering the question. What was I expecting? For him to tell me his love for me has never died? That he wants to start over? Yeah, right. Talking to him is going nowhere. If he doesn't want to discuss it, I will not push.

I huff, "Here, take your coat." I toss it on the desk. As the coat lands on the wooden surface, something falls from the pocket, rolls on the desk, and drops to the floor, landing by my feet. I bend to pick it up.

"Leave it!" Finn snaps a moment too late. In my hand is a white gold ring with a sizeable solitaire diamond sitting on a delicate band of tiny diamonds. We would often look at rings together; I even picked out one just like this one. My gaze flicks to Finn. His expression darkens as he walks around the desk. "Give me that." He snatches the ring from my hand and shoves it into the pocket of his trousers.

"Is this an engagement ring? Why do you have it in your coat?" I ask.

Finn tugs at the cuffs of his shirt. "None of your business."

The air knocks from my lungs. There's only one reason I can think of why Finn has an engagement ring. "While you were kissing me, you have a girlfriend you're going to propose to?"

He clenches his jaw as his gaze flicks away. I take that as a yes.

Nausea rises to my throat. "How could you do that?" The Finn I used to know had respect for women. He'd never act like such a dirty dog. Have the years changed him so much? "How can you do that to someone you love?"

My heart aches. Once upon a time, I was the woman he loved. The woman he said he couldn't live without. What did I expect? That he'd stay single for the rest of his life? Live a miserable life like I had? No, he'd moved on.

Finn digs his hands into his pockets. "You're one to talk about love. All your sweet words and promises meant nothing. You were waiting until you got a better offer. You have no right to judge."

I throw my hands in the air. "I never cheated on you."

Tossing his head back, Finn gives a mocking laugh. "You don't expect me to believe that, do you? So, Derek was love at first sight and you couldn't wait to marry him?"

"No," I say, my voice trembling.

His mouth twists. "You're such a liar."

Again, I want to tell him the truth. But with the way he's looking at me, accusing me of being a liar, I know he'll never believe me.

"Next time you have the urge to cheat on your girlfriend, *do not* use me to do it! I have had enough of men using me for their benefit." My chest heaves with each word I speak.

He leans down and stares at me with a fierce expression, our noses almost touching. "I don't have a girlfriend. The engagement ring was for you."

Chapter Eleven

―◆―

FINN

What the fuck! The words flew out of my mouth before I could stop them. Wanting to propose to Harper was something I'd buried in a deep hole, pouring concrete over the top. Chain me to a chair, rip my fingernails out, pull my teeth, and I was still sure I'd never tell a soul. I was embarrassed to let anyone know that I'd fallen in love with a woman I thought would one day be my wife, who, with a snap of her fingers, easily chose another man.

Harper stands as still as stone. "The ring was for me?" she whispers. "You were going to propose?"

"Yes." I scrub the back of my neck. The day I bought the ring was one of the happiest days of my life. I had the proposal planned out in my mind. A trip to Positano, Italy—a place Harper always wanted to visit—with a fancy dinner on a private yacht. I couldn't wait to spend the rest of my life with her. Yes, we were young, but I knew she was it for me. Nothing or no one could change that. But things did change. She tore my fucking heart out of my chest. Since then, a black, cold stone sits behind my ribs, never to beat with love again.

The color in Harper's face turns white. Unshed tears shine in her eyes. "I'm sorry. I never meant to hurt you. I want to explain why…" She bites her bottom lip to stop it from trembling.

I take two steps toward her. My hands clasping her shoulders. We stand so close she has to tilt her head back to look at me. Something sweet, like the scent of strawberries, floats around me. I have to stop myself from burying my nose in her neck and breathing her in.

Frustrated with myself for again not being able to keep my distance, I push away and step back. "There's nothing you can say that will justify what you did."

"Finn, please."

The heartfelt way she says the word *please* stabs me in the chest. Softening me against her a little. She's come back into my life. With a word, a look, a touch, she's chipping at my walls. I steel my spine. I won't let that happen.

"I don't want to hear it," I say through gritted teeth.

Her shoulders sag with a sigh. "Fine. Then tell me why you kept the ring."

My hand slides into my pocket, and I clench the band in my palm. The stone digs into my skin. "I keep it as a reminder."

"A reminder of what?" She frowns.

I look her straight in the eye. "A reminder to never fall in love again. To never let another woman close enough to wreck me the way you did."

Harper covers her face and sobs. Instinct has me wanting to pull her into my arms to comfort her. Instead, I stay rooted where I stand, remembering to lock down any emotion that might resurface.

I refocus the conversation on Harper, because I don't want to talk about the ring anymore. "Tell me why you're working here. Your *husband*—" The word tastes like acid in my mouth. "—gave you a life of luxury and wealth. Why are you working as an assistant at Alessi's?"

Harper wipes her eyes. "Things aren't always what they seem."

"The man owned a chain of casinos. Are you telling me he had no money?" I lift an eyebrow. "I'd heard rumors about the money he threw around—was it all for show?"

"No, he had money. He just didn't leave me any. Well, that's not entirely true. He left me with five thousand dollars and the belongings I owned when I marr—moved in with him."

Just say the word. Married! You fucking married a man twice your age! I want to scream at her.

Harper hangs her head. "I'm working here because I need money. This was the only place I could get an interview. My friend Alyssa tweaked my resume and applied for a job here without me knowing. Believe me, this was the last place I wanted to be."

"You're joking, right?"

She shakes her head and stares at her hands. "I'm not joking."

"What about your parents' estate? The cabin?" I ask. Her gaze flicks up to mine. The lake where we spent so much of our time. A place where we planned our future together. I clear my throat. "I was sorry to hear about their accident." I truly was. They'd welcomed me into their home and treated me like a son.

Except for the day of Harper's wedding. I'd arrived at their house, desperate to see Harper. Desperate to believe it was a bad joke. The truth was written on their faces. With sad expressions, they turned me away. I'd left my pride at their doorstep and yelled for Harper. Hoping she'd hear me call her name. I tried barging inside the house. It took three security guards to drag me away. I don't remember much after that. I woke up in a hospital bed, connected to tubes with machines beeping around me.

I'd loved her so much. Over time, that love turned to hate. A much better emotion to deal with.

"Derek took it all. After he died, everything went to his sister."

Before I get to ask why Derek would have possession of her parents' inheritance, the intercom buzzes on my desk. "Mr. Lavigne is on the line for you," Bianca snaps.

"I need to take this," I say to Harper. I pick up the phone. "Fabien, thank you for calling me back."

Behind me, I hear the click of the door closing. I turn back around. The room's empty.

Chapter Twelve

HARPER

I close the door behind me and lean against it. Squeezing my eyes shut, I take deep breaths to settle my racing heart. When Finn said he was going to propose, I had to lock my knees, because they were shaking so hard I thought I'd fall to the floor. All I ever wanted was to be Finn's wife. To have his babies. Then Derek came along and crushed my fantasies under the sole of his Prada shoe.

Finn had kept the engagement ring all these years. A ring I would have proudly worn. But he didn't keep it because it evoked beautiful memories for him. No, he needed the reminder of what I'd done.

God, I hate what I did to him—to us. The damage cut so deep. Unrepairable. Unless... I tell him the truth. I wanted to in his office, but he didn't want to listen. He looks at me with so much hate, will he ever want to hear what I have to say? And if he did, how much can I tell him without it destroying his relationship with his father? Can I cause him more pain? I need time to think. Sort things out in my mind, and hopefully figure out what's the right thing to do.

At my desk, I pick up my mug. Before I can get any work done, I need to settle my nerves with a cup of tea. Making my way to the kitchen, I find Bianca and Tamara sitting at a table with coffee mugs and a plate of cookies sitting in front of them.

"Hey, Harper. Just in time for chocolate chip cookies. Flora at reception baked them, and they are divine!" Tamara takes a bite, and her eyes roll back. "So good."

Switching the kettle on, I search the cupboard for tea. As I wait for the water to boil, I grab a cookie and take a bite. I moan as the chocolate goodness melts in my mouth.

"Told you they're good," Tamara says as she takes another one off the plate.

I can't help noticing the scathing look Bianca is throwing my way. I know she's curious as to why I had Finn's jacket and probably livid that he chose to speak to me over her. I inwardly sigh. I don't think there's anything I can do to get her to like me.

Once the water has boiled, I make tea, ignoring the evil glare Bianca's sending my way.

"I see you've given Finn back his coat."

Tamara looks between Bianca and me and frowns, obviously unaware of what's going on. She'd left the club before Finn had given me the coat.

"I bumped into Fi—Mr. Alessi last night as I was leaving a club. It was cold, and he was kind enough to lend me his coat." *Not that it's any of your business Bianca*, I want to say. I keep my face as neutral as possible so she can't read too much into things. If she knew Finn kissed me, she might explode.

Bianca narrows her eyes.

Keep eye contact. Don't show fear.

"Oh, I have something absolutely adorbs to show you both." Like Tamara could sense the tension in the room, she pulls out her phone from the pocket of her flared skirt. I was never more relieved for the distraction. "Look at this photo of the King Charles Cavalier I'm adopting from a shelter. I'm so in love. Erica and I can't wait to pick her up." Tamara holds the phone out for me to see.

A moment ago, I was thankful for the subject change. Now, I'd rather give Bianca a blow-by-blow enactment of last night and deal with whatever she had to say about it.

"Isn't she gorgeous?" Tamara asks, unaware of the fear rippling through my body.

I assume people would see an adorable dog in the photo with its big, brown eyes, floppy ears, and fluffy coat. What I see is a monster. A killer. Something that causes cold sweat to bead on my forehead and suck the air from my lungs.

"Hey, are you okay? You've turned green." Tamara stands and places a hand on my shoulder and guides me to the chair she vacated. Thankfully, Tamara put the phone back in her pocket and the threat of fainting passes.

I give an embarrassed chuckle. "I'm fine. Just not a fan of dogs."

Tamara takes the seat next to me. "It was only a photo."

"I know it's silly." I clench my shaking hands in my lap.

"It's not silly. You obviously have a fear. Did something happen to you?" Tamara asks with concern.

"When I was a kid, I was attacked by a dog." I twist my hair and place it over my shoulder to expose my neck. I trace a finger over the faint, slightly raised scar. "While at the park, a dog knocked me down from behind and bit into my neck."

Tamara leans forward to get a closer look. "Geez, that's so close to the jugular."

"The doctors said I was lucky. Any closer and then, well…" I shrug, letting Tamara work the rest out for herself.

"I don't blame you for fearing dogs." Tamara shivers. "That must have been traumatizing."

Bianca chuckles. "After getting bitten by a dog, you're scared of them all now? Even a small ball of fluff in a photo?"

I pick up my forgotten mug of tea and take a sip. I wish I had something stronger than tea. Today my body has been one jittery mess after another. "I know it seems silly to others. I can't help it."

With an eyeroll, Bianca rises. "Yeah, it is stupid." With that she heads toward the door, pauses, and turns around. "Go see Juliette and pack garments. We have an on-location photoshoot tomorrow. You need to be there by seven AM. I'll email you the details," she says with a smirk on her face, like she knows something I don't, before she prances out of the room.

"What was that look about?" I ask Tamara. "Are photoshoots bad? Is this some kind of punishment?"

Tamara picks up another cookie and takes a bite. "Oh God. I can't stop eating these!" She licks the crumbs off her fingers. "I've never been to a photoshoot before. I've been told it's a lot of work, although no one has complained about it. You never know what's going on inside Bianca's head. Thank God she's not here permanently."

With Bianca gone in two months, that means Finn will be gone too. Gone again from my life. My chest tightens. I wish things could be different. There's nothing I can do to change the past. Is this my opportunity to change the future? Can I even attempt to when Finn can barely look at me?

My tea is now long cold, so I pour what's remaining in the sink. I say goodbye to Tamara and make my way to Juliette's office.

"Darling, I'm so glad you're here," Juliette mumbles around pins between her teeth, kneeling in front of a mannequin. For a second it surprises me. How many world-famous designers would be crawling along the floor hemming a gown? Don't they have people to do that for them?

Then my eyes are drawn to the gown. An ice-blue, fluffy cloud of tulle surrounds the mannequin. Soft, light, and flowy. The plunging V neckline, which mirrors the back, is beaded delicately with crystals and pearls. The sheer, lacy skirt flares from the waist, reaching gently to the floor. It's the most stunning creation I've ever seen.

"Where's Bianca?" Juliette tilts her head to the side to look past me.

"With Finn I guess."

Juliette plucks the pins from her mouth and pricks them into a cushion strapped to her wrist. Pushing herself from the floor, she dusts her hands. "She's supposed to bring me the list of the itemized gowns for the shoot tomorrow."

"I can run back and grab it for you."

Juliette shakes her head. Her flaming red locks bounce around her shoulders. "No, I'll sort it out. After all, they are my designs. I can add whatever I want." She gives a jaunty wave of her hand.

I giggle. I love the confidence and flamboyance of this woman. "Bianca said you need someone to pack the gowns?"

I have to admit, I'm feeling a little nervous touching such beautiful garments. What if I dirty them, or worse, rip something by accident? I have dropped a bolt of expensive-looking fabric before. I give my hands a quick glance. They look clean.

"Before you pack, darling, I need a favor." Juliette taps her chin with her finger as she trails her gaze up and down my body. Then she flicks her eyes to the mannequin and back at me.

"What do you need?" I ask.

"I need to see this dress move."

"Move?"

"Yes, I've made some adjustments to the hemline, and I want to see the way it flows. Put it on for me, darling."

My eyes widen and I point to the mannequin. "You want me to wear that dress? What if I damage it?" This is so much worse than packing gowns into a garment bag.

Juliette waves her hand. "You won't damage it." She lifts the gown from the mannequin and hands it to me. "There's a changing screen over in the corner."

How can I refuse to wear a gown from such a talented designer? Gently, I drape the dress over my arm, careful to not drag the fabric on the ground, and duck behind the privacy screen. I undress and gently shimmy into it. Stepping from behind the screen, I can't help but hold onto the sides of the skirt and swish it around my legs like I'm Cinderella after her fairy godmother magically whisked her up a gown for the ball.

"Let me fluff it out." Juliette fiddles with the skirt then gives my shoulder a tap. "Slowly walk toward the door, then turn around and walk back."

I do as I'm told. "This dress is gorgeous. I feel like a supermodel on a catwalk." I'm surprised it actually fits. Another reason I love Juliette's gowns so much is they are made for real women.

Juliette has a hand on her hip and a finger on her chin, examining the dress. "You look like one too. The gown fits like a glove. Like it was made for you."

Warmth spreads across my face at the compliment. "You're so talented. It's a privilege to wear one of your designs. Even for a few moments. Thank you."

"My pleasure, darling. The hem is perfect. It moves beautifully. You may take if off now."

"Not yet. I want a closer look," a deep voice says behind me. The sound of Finn's voice sends goosebumps exploding over my skin.

I turn my head to see Finn leaning a shoulder against the doorjamb, an appreciative gaze raking over my body. I know he's only looking at the dress. He usually looks at me with hate or mistrust.

"What do you think? Doesn't Harper look fabulous?" Juliette says.

Finn steps into the room and stares straight into my eyes. "Stunning."

My heartbeat quickens. Is he talking about the dress or *me* in the dress? I'm so caught up in Finn's gaze, and with the sound of my heart pounding in my ears, I hardly hear Juliette saying something about a dress emergency as she dashes from the room.

Slowly, Finn circles around me, stopping behind my back. His hot breath fans over the curve of my neck. I swallow hard. He's so close, if I lean back a fraction, we'll be touching. Does he want me to? Should I do it? What will he do? I take a deep breath to stop my panicky thoughts. Before I decide, Finn trails a finger down my spine. The exposed back of the dress gives him access to my skin, which I'm sure has scorched his fingertip.

"Finn," I say on a heavy breath. My body wanting... Wanting more of his touch. Wanting him to pull me in his arms and tell me all is forgiven. Wanting him to help me forget about how I screwed up our lives. I turn my head to the side. His gaze drops to my lips. I want to lean in...in fact, my body is already moving. My lips hover over his mouth.

Loud laughter and chatter from outside the office shatters the moment, and Finn jerks back. His expression changes from desire to confusion and then anger. Spinning on his heel, he blows from the room like he can't get away from me fast enough. A lance of pain spears my chest. All those things I wanted...I can forget about. There is no forgiveness in his eyes.

Chapter Thirteen

FINN

What the fuck is happening? I pound the steps leading to my office. I take the stairs to my floor instead of the elevator, because I need to work off some frustration. God, it's more than frustration. I'm disappointed at myself. I fucking loathe how I feel whenever I'm near Harper. I can't be in a room with her without wanting—no, *needing* to touch her! My body is drawn to her. Like she's the air I need to breathe.

Damn it. What is wrong with me? The sight of her should make me sick. Instead, I want to pretend that the last nine years of my life never happened. My stomach twists in a knot. I can't let that happen.

Before I can hide away in my office, Bianca intercepts me. "Finn, I need to speak with you."

I give a heavy sigh. "Not now."

"But we need to discuss—"

"I fucking said not now!" My hands are shaking with rage as I open the door to my office and slam it shut behind me.

A few seconds later, a sharp knock hits my door. I spin around to tell whoever it is to get the fuck out when Hayden and Lucas saunter in.

"Get out," I order. "I'm not in the mood for whatever shit you're here for."

My brothers raise their eyebrows as they look at each other then back at me. "Why are you biting Bianca's head off? The ice queen looks like she's about to cry," Lucas says, dropping into a chair, not giving a shit that I want to be alone.

I pull out a chair and deflate into it. As soon as I've calmed down, I'll apologize to her. It's not her fault Harper makes me crazy.

Dropping my elbows on the table, I cup my head into my hands. "Harper's here." I dig my fingers over my eyes to try and remove the image of Harper in Juliette's gown from my mind. How stunning she looked. She's still the most beautiful woman I've ever seen.

"Harper Richardson?" Hayden asks, taking a seat opposite me. "Why?"

"She's back to calling herself Harper Madden. She's Bianca's assistant while we're here."

They both stare at me with eyes wide with surprise. "Why the hell is she working here?" Hayden asks. His face turns cold and tight. He stands like he's ready to find Harper and personally escort her from the building. My brothers—my best friends—saw the mess she'd left me in. So broken I'd wrapped my car around a pole. Barely surviving the accident. It's no surprise they're not happy to hear she's working at Alessi's.

"I don't know. She said she needed a job. After Derek died, she said he left her with nothing. She needs money."

"Tell her to leave. It's not your problem she's broke," Lucas says. "I don't want her anywhere near you." My brothers are always on my side. Hell, they'd cut off their right arm if I needed it. I'd do the same thing for them in a heartbeat.

I plow my fingers through my hair. "She stays."

Hayden is pacing in front of the desk, and he abruptly stops. "What? Why? Out of all the places in New York City she can work, there must be a reason she's here. And it can't be good."

"Exactly. I want to know what game she's playing."

Hayden frowns. "She's up to no good. That's the game. Don't do this to yourself. Get rid of her. Now!"

Hayden is right. I don't need to do this to myself. I should make her leave. Today. What's stopping me? Is it this sick desire I have to torture myself? Is the engagement ring in my pocket no longer enough to remind me of the past? Do I need the woman who caused the chaos to be the reminder?

To appease my brothers, I say, "I'll think about it."

They both stare at me like I've grown two heads. Hayden says, "What's there to think about? Nothing good can come out of why she's here."

"I need time. Please. Let me do this my way."

Hayden stares long and hard at me. He nods and sits back down.

To change the subject, because talking about Harper is making me sick to my stomach, I say, "Have you spoken to Dad lately?" Even though our father retired two years ago, he still likes to pop into the office from time to time—keep an eye on things.

"Not for a few days. He's been out of town with his golf buddies," Lucas says, hooking his ankle over his knee.

"Anyone know if he'll be at the photoshoot tomorrow?"

Hayden shrugs, looking uninterested in the conversation, yet I see a slight clenching of his jaw. For years I've felt friction between Hayden and Dad. I've asked my brother about it several times, but he says it's nothing, they're just different and sometimes clash. He's not wrong about the differences. Our father has a larger-than-life personality. When he enters a room, he commands attention. And loves it. Hayden is quieter. More serious. A thinker more than a talker. Although, he wasn't always like that. I remember a time when he was loud and fun. Things changed for him when his daughter was born six years ago. Being left with sole custody of a newborn wasn't easy on him.

"Dad loves a shoot. I'm sure he'll turn up." Lucas is right. Dad loves the busy activity.

Hayden and Lucas stay for a few minutes, discussing some details for the shoot, then leave. Once I'm alone, I blow out a long breath, letting my head drop on the back of the chair. I stare at the ceiling. Pictures of Harper in that damn dress play in my mind. Not only in that dress; I'm seeing her every time I close my eyes.

Nine years ago, after I recovered from my accident, I made myself a promise. I promised I wouldn't let myself get close or have feelings for another woman again. I'd gone through too much pain. My legs may have visible scars from the accident, yet it was my heart which had the most damage. It never recovered. So, I made my life simple. Work, hangout with my brothers and friends, and fuck whoever I wanted with no strings. Except, most of the women I've slept with have a striking resemblance to Harper.

I really am a sick bastard.

I meant what I said when I told Hayden and Lucas I want to figure out what Harper's game is. Is the story about her being broke true? Derek was an asshole; would he do that to his wife? Was their marriage an unhappy one? Were there problems? Did he fuck her every night until she screamed his name? Christ! I blow out a breath and toss the pen in my hand on the desk. Rubbing my palms over my eyes, I try to scrub the image away. Why am I thinking about that shit? Because I haven't stopped since we broke up. I thought I'd lose my mind.

Well, I will not let her fuck me over again. I'm going to keep an eye on her. Starting now. On my way to Bianca's office, I pass by Harper's desk. I stop and watch her. She's reading something on the computer, tapping a finger to her lips. A little crease forms between her eyebrows. She looks adorable concentrating so hard. My heart gives off a flicker of electricity. Like something or *someone* is trying to jumpstart it.

As she shakes her head with what looks like annoyance, her eyes lift, and she catches me watching her. I jerk back, clear my throat, and point to a file on the desk. "I need to take that to Bianca." What the hell am I saying? I have no clue what's in the file.

Harper looks at the file and back up at me. "This one?" She taps the top of it. "Are you sure? It's only—"

"Yes. That file." I snatch it from her hands. I know I sound like a prick. Getting busted staring at her as flustered me.

"Ooo-kkkay." Amusement glimmers in her eyes.

I spin on my heel and march to Bianca's office. Before I go inside, I open the file. Inside is a list of instructions. How to make Bianca's coffee. What sandwich to order her for each day of the week. When to drop off and pick up her dry-cleaning. I flick the page over. The list continues. No wonder Harper looked at me strangely. This file has nothing to do with work and everything to do with Bianca and her list of demands. Embarrassed at my mistake and annoyed at Bianca, I knock and enter her office.

Bianca smiles at me as she swivels on her chair away from the computer. "Finn, I'm glad you're here. I've been wanting to go over—"

"What's this?" I drop the file on the desk.

Her eyes narrow as she flips it open.

Without giving her time to answer, I say, "Harper is here to work, not be your personal servant."

Why am I defending Harper? Maybe because I don't like people being mistreated in my workplace. *Yeah right, that's what it is.* There's something about her I can't shake. No matter how hard I try.

"Harper is new. She has no experience in the fashion industry. There's only so much work I can give her."

"In the future, keep what she needs to do for you to a minimum. She doesn't work for you." Bianca's lips thin with annoyance. "What work for the company do you give her to do?" I take a seat. Bianca tilts her head to the side as if she doesn't understand the question. "How much of my business does she know about?"

"She files, delivers things to other departments, just general running around for staff who needs things done."

"That's it? Does she have access to any accounts, projects we're working on, things like that?"

A quizzical eyebrow rises above her right eye. "Nothing like that. Why, is there a problem with Harper?"

I scratch my chin. "No, just checking. You wanted to see me about the photoshoot?"

After I finish with Bianca, I make my way to my office. Again, I'm drawn to where Harper is sitting. I stop by her desk. "What are you working on?"

Harper's eyes lift to meet mine. She smiles slightly. Damn, I'm a sucker for those deep brown doe eyes. I give myself a mental shake.

"Just making sure I get Bianca's order for lunch right. Yesterday I forgot the extra pickles on her sub. She wasn't happy." She chuckles.

"I've told Bianca that you're not her servant."

She lifts a shoulder. "I don't mind."

"Hey, Harper. Mr. Alessi. We're having cake in the breakroom for Riccardo's birthday," Theresa from sales informs us. "Come join us."

"I have work to do. Maybe you can save me some?" Harper says.

Theresa laughs like Harper has said something funny. "As if there is going to be any left to save. Better get in now or you'll miss out. Oh, did I mention it's a chocolate and Oreo cake?"

I see the spark of interest in Harper's eyes when Theresa mentions chocolate. Harper can never say no to a chocolate cake.

"I really shouldn't—"

"Go have cake. The work can wait," I say.

Harper looks at me with surprise. Like why am I being nice to her since every interaction has been hostile.

She gets up off her chair. "Only if you have some too."

I'm supposed to be meeting someone for lunch in twenty minutes. Filling up with cake is the last thing I should be doing.

"Who can pass up chocolate cake?" This will give me an opportunity to keep my eye on Harper.

In the breakroom, the cake gets cut and Harper hands it out to the staff with paper plates, chatting and laughing as she goes along. It's only her second day here and she's already friendly with everyone. Is this a ploy? A way of sliding her way in for whatever the reason she's here? But she seems genuinely happy. There doesn't seem to be any conniving or scheming going on. Just general interest in everyone. That's something that hasn't changed about her. She loved being around people, and people loved having her around.

She comes to me and hands me a plate. I notice she doesn't go back for one for herself. "Where's your slice?"

"Nothing's left. Theresa was right. You need to get in quick for cake around here." She laughs.

"Here, have this." I push mine toward her.

Harper waves it away. "No, that's okay. I probably shouldn't eat it anyway." She taps her hips as if that's where the cake would be heading.

Another thing about Harper that hasn't changed—putting others before herself. Even if it meant giving someone her last piece of cake when she really wanted it herself. Is that the person she still is? Or is it all an act? Was it always an act? Because she didn't put me first when she ran off with Derek. My spine stiffens at the thought.

"Take it. You'll enjoy it more than I will." I shove the plate into her hands. "I have to go." Trying to figure out who the real

Harper is, is making my head spin. This is all too much. I'll have to figure out what she's up to another day.

Chapter Fourteen

HARPER

Wrapped tight in my coat, I step out of the subway and into the icy morning air. I blow warm air into my hands before slipping them into my gloves. To stop any chilly air wafting down my neck, I twist my scarf around my neck one more time. I give a quick glance around at the street signs so I can navigate myself to the botanical gardens.

I make my way to the entrance I was told to go to, and once at the gate, I flash my work ID card at the security guard. Up ahead I see trailers, tents, lights, heat lamps, and other paraphernalia needed to take photos. People are bustling around getting everything set up. I must admit, I'm excited about seeing what a photoshoot is all about.

Walking through the botanical gardens, I take in my surroundings. With manicured hedges and lawns, beautiful, colored flowers, and pristine gardens, it makes me want to roam around and explore. That will have to wait until another day. I'm here to work.

When I find Bianca, her mouth twists to the side like she's not happy to see me. Will she ever look happy to see me? "Good morning," I say with a smile. I'm not letting her ruin my excitement for the day.

Bianca acknowledges my greeting by handing me a file. "These are the photos of the dresses and the models who need to wear them. There are five models. Make sure they are dressed and ready. When they're called, take them to the tent over there." She points to a spot near the camera crew.

I look over, and the first thing I see is Finn. He's talking to Lucas, who is adjusting a light stand. Finn's hair is hidden underneath a black beanie, and he's wearing a thick, woolen coat. It looks like the one he draped over me at Alto's. Is my ring still in the pocket? Now that I know about it, has he tossed it away like it's trash? Like he can feel my gaze on him, Finn turns his head in my direction. Our eyes lock, and my breath catches.

"What are you waiting for?" Bianca snaps. I break eye contact with Finn and give her my attention. "We haven't got all day. The models are in the first trailer."

The morning is a busy hive of people scurrying around. Lighting is being set up. Equipment is getting checked. Models are in hair and makeup and getting dressed in their gowns. When the first model, a black-haired beauty with chocolate-colored skin and deep brown eyes is ready, I guide her with a warm robe over her shoulders to the heated tent. I glance around at the setup. With a cherry blossom canopy, and smoke machine, it looks like something from a fairy tale. It's so pretty and ethereal.

On my way back to the trailer, someone calls my name. Stopping, I turn around. Finn's father, Marco Alessi, is standing by the catering tent looking at me. I haven't seen him since Finn and I broke up. Nerves clutch at my stomach. He's the last person I want to see.

Mr. Alessi saunters toward me. He's dressed in a navy coat and scarf, and gray hair is sticking out from under his beanie. He's not as tall as Finn, nor had he ever had the same strong, solid build. The only resemblance Finn shares with his father is their hazel eyes.

"Hello, Harper," Mr. Alessi says with a smile. A smile that looks tight around the mouth and doesn't reach his eyes. "It's been a few years."

"Hello, Mr. Alessi." I want to get away from him as fast as I can. I shuffle away slightly, hoping he won't engage in any chitchat.

"What a surprise it is seeing you working at Alessi's." His face hardens.

This man is well-loved by his family, friends, and work colleagues. Once upon a time, I was one of those people. I grieved with his family when Mrs. Alessi's cancer triggered a stroke and she was only given hours to live. I believed Marco when he said he tried moving heaven and earth to get to her. I never suspected he was with a mistress. Why would I? Finn never once told me he thought his dad was cheating on his mom. I only found out about the affair after I married Derek, and he took great joy in showing me photos of Marco and his mistress together. Loved hanging it over my head. Tormenting me with how easy it would be for him to give the evidence to Finn and his brothers and destroy their relationship with their father. It was his way of showing me that with a snap of a finger he could ruin people. Including me and the people I loved.

"I'm grateful for the opportunity. I better get back to work." I go to walk away, but his hand shoots out and grabs onto my forearm, stopping me. When I glance down at his hand and back up to his face, he drops his arm to his side. "You're not welcome here."

I tilt my chin and glare at him. "Why? Because I might expose your dirty, little secret?" I can't believe I said that. I should've kept my mouth closed and walked away.

Mr. Alessi's eyes widen with surprise. Leaning forward, bringing his face inches away from mine, he says through tight lips, "So, Derek told you. I'm not surprised. The man had a big mouth. Well, he may have taken the secret to his grave, but I see you know a little too much. If you've come here to spill secrets to Finn, think again. I will ruin you."

Would my life ever be free of threats? First Derek and now Marco Alessi. I step away from him. "I don't know how you can look at yourself in the mirror. Your wife was on her deathbed. She loved you. Trusted you and you...you—"

Mr. Alessi points a finger in my face. He grits his teeth. "I'm warning you. Keep your mouth shut or else." With that, he retreats to wherever the hell he crawled from, leaving me rooted on the spot.

I'm shaking so hard from the confrontation, I don't notice Bianca until she's standing in front of me. Throwing something into my hands, she says, "Take these to the set. They're waiting for them." And she scurries off.

Glancing down at my hands, I see I'm holding white leashes with pink diamantes stuck to the leather. Leashes? There's only one thing I can think of that can be attached to them. With trepidation, I look at the ground. My heart stops, my head spins, and I sway on my feet. Four white, fluffy dogs are scampering around my ankles. Then they lift themselves on their haunches to scratch at my legs like they're trying to win my attention.

Fear grips at my throat, stopping me from screaming. I can't move my feet to run away. It's not long before black spots flitter at the edges of my vision. Just as my legs are about to give way, someone rips the leashes from my hands, and strong, warm arms wrap around me.

Finn.

"Someone get these dogs out of here! Who the fuck gave the dogs to Harper?" Finn's voice roars through the garden. Like the air has deflated from my body, or I've found my safe place, I collapse against Finn's chest. "It's okay, it's okay. I've got you," he soothes, kissing my temple.

My body is shaking as I bury my face in Finn's neck. I know I'll be okay because I'm in his arms. Finn understands my fear. Understood how real my reactions are and had always protected me. Just like now. "I-I feel like an i-idiot." My teeth chatter from the shock.

"Shhh. You're not an idiot." He gives me another kiss on the temple and runs his hands from the top of my head down to my shoulders. "Let's get you away from here so you can calm down." He places an arm around my shoulders and guides me to the nearest trailer. Once inside, he barks orders, "Everyone out. No one is to disturb us." The crew scurries out, no one questioning why they've been asked to leave. Sitting me down on a bench seat, he crouches in front of me. He cups my face and kisses my cheek. "Are you okay?"

Just having him near me—holding me—has made things better. "Yes, thank you."

He rubs his hands up and down my arms. "You've stopped shaking. That's good."

Finn's hands rest on my shoulders. It's like we've stepped back in time when Finn once looked at me with love and concern, ready to slay dragons, or in my case, fluffy, white dogs, to take away my fear. God, I miss those days. Miss *him*. I want to curl up in his arms and never let him go again. Tears of regret trickle down my cheeks.

"Hey, don't cry. The dogs can't get you now," Finn says, mistaking the reason for my tears. He brushes them away with his thumbs. "I won't let anything happen to you."

I give a ghost of a smile. "I can't understand why such small dogs make me react like that. They could barely reach past my ankles." With his hands still on my face, his thumbs float over my jaw, making my head spin. Having Finn touch me again with compassion is overwhelming. More tears fall.

"I can." Finn sweeps the hair from my shoulder and twists the scarf off around my neck, tossing it on the bench. With his finger, he traces the pale scar. "Doesn't matter the size of the dog. What you went through was horrific."

At the memory of the attack, I shudder. Finn rises from his crouched position and sits by my side. Lifting an arm, he places it over my shoulders, pulling me closer. The warmth of his body comforts me like a warm blanket. His first instinct is to always protect me. Whether or not he likes me. That's one thing that hasn't changed.

There was a time when I had to protect him too. Protect him from his father's secrets and Derek's vindictiveness.

Finn's hand caresses my hair. If I close my eyes and don't say a word, I can imagine all the animosity he's felt for me during the past couple of days is gone. Laying my head on his shoulder, I sigh long and deep, wanting to soak up the moment before it ends.

"Things really got fucked up." His chin rests on the top of my head. Another onslaught of tears threatens to spill.

I don't even try to pretend I don't know what he's talking about. "I know saying sorry can never undo the damage I caused. The pain..."

His fingers pause at my neck. "What's done is done." I feel his body stiffen against me, and I wonder if he really means what he's saying.

Pulling away, I twist in my seat. If I told him the full story, it would cause major problems with his father. Probably tear their relationship apart. As much as I loathe Mr. Alessi, Finn has had enough loss in his life. I sat with him after his mother died while he cried in my arms. I can't watch him lose another parent. But if I tell him some of it, maybe he'll eventually stop hating me.

"Finn, I want to tell you—"

"I don't want to hear it," he says flatly, cutting me off.

"But—"

"Look, I don't want to talk. All I've wanted to do from the moment you dropped that bolt of fabric on the floor is to fucking touch you. Kiss you. Dive so far into you I forget where I am, who I am, and what you've done. I hate that I want you so much. But I do. Every minute of the fucking day I want you. I don't know what to do about it." He screws up his face as if it's causing him pain to admit it.

His words are far from romantic. Painful even. I shouldn't want this—not this way. Whenever Finn came to me in my dreams, it was with love and longing. Not anguish. Not this tug of war between desire and hate. Yet, I want him to do all those things to me. I'm *desperate* for those things. "Kiss me." This should feel wrong—him wanting me like this, but my yearning for him beats logic. Maybe I'll regret it. Maybe I won't. I'm willing to take the risk.

With hooded eyes, he asks, "Are you sure?"

I'm unbuttoning my coat and shrugging out of it. The room suddenly feeling like a balmy summer day. "Yes, I'm sure."

Finn pulls off his beanie, tossing it on the floor, revealing his brown, flat hair. Next, he removes his coat. It too gets thrown on the floor. Left in a dark green pullover that brings out the color of his eyes and faded denim jeans, he makes my mouth water.

Clutching my face in his hands, he presses his mouth to my lips. He angles his head, swipes his tongue into my mouth, and deepens the kiss. This kiss doesn't feel punishing like the one he gave me in the club. This one seems more desperate. Wanting. Urgent. Yet, still not the tender, passionate kisses from the past.

Our tongues twirl in each other's mouths with our lips sealed together, and I can barely breathe. My chest is heaving as I press closer to Finn. He slides a hand between our bodies and massages my breast through my top. At the sheer pleasure of his hand on me, my head falls back, and I let out a low moan. An explosion of sensations is traveling through me like the speed of light from my head to my toes.

Finn replaces his hand with his mouth. Mumbling, he says, "Your tits are bigger than I remember. They're beautiful." I suck in a gasp as he lifts my sweater up and licks over the lace of my bra from one peaked nipple to the other. "I could never get enough." He pays tribute to each breast, licking, sucking, and caressing until my body trembles with need. I grab my sweater and pull it over my head, giving him the hint that I need to take this further.

Thankfully, he knows what I want and stands up to remove his top as I kick off my boots and socks and shuffle out of my jeans, leaving me in only my bra and panties. The heating in the trailer isn't exactly piping hot, but with the way Finn is looking at me, my body is burning up. He slowly unbuttons the fly of his jeans and leaves it hanging open low from his hips. He tosses a foil packet on the bench next to me. I know where this is going. And I need it.

Shuffling along the bench, I give him room to join me. He pushes me onto my back and kneels between my legs. Nudging my knees to open wider, he nestles himself over me. He gives me open-mouth kisses at my neck, my pulse kicking up with speed. Soon he's venturing down to my breasts; they feel so trapped in my bra. He moves lower, skimming over my stomach and taking soft bites of my hip. I wiggle under him, so desperate for something! Anything!

When he gets to the V between my legs, he tilts his head up, looks me in the eye, and smiles—a smile so hot and sinful it practically melts off my panties. I barely have time to catch my breath when he pushes my panties aside and covers me with his mouth. As he flicks his tongue over my sensitive bud, my hips buck off the bench. "Oh God. Finn," I cry. My legs fall further apart like they've lost all muscle. "Feels...so...good," I pant, tunneling my hands in his hair.

The sweet torture of his mouth is making me want to hold his head there for hours while he fucks me with his tongue. But my body is trembling, ready to come. It's been years since I've been touched like this, and I don't know how much more I can take.

Finn hooks my leg over his shoulder to delve in deeper. My head tosses from side to side, no longer able to take the beautiful torture anymore. "Finn, I'm going to...to..." When he continues lapping me up like I'm his favorite ice cream, I tug at his hair. He stares up at me with glassy eyes. "I can't take much more." My voice sounds low and husky.

Sliding himself up my body, he kisses me long and deep, and I taste myself on his tongue. Our bodies twining together, I melt against him, feeling at home in his arms. Like this is where I'm meant to be. Where I've *always* meant to be. This is too good to be true. Am I dreaming? If so, I never want to wake up.

I don't dwell on that thought for long because his erection is pressing against my inner thigh. My hands skim over his broad shoulders, down his toned back, and slide between our bodies until I feel the bulge pressing against the fabric of his underwear. Slipping my hand under the waistband, I clutch his hard length, my thumb ghosting over the tip.

"Oh fuck. You're going to kill me." He squeezes his eyes shut and groans as I stroke him. He slowly pumps in my fist, then faster. I want him inside of me. Now!

"I'm not going to last much longer." I whimper as my hips, like they have a mind of their own, are thrust toward his penis.

Finn pulls back and stares at me. "God, I want you, Harper. So much." My heart ripples with happiness at his confession.

"I want you too." Every day of my life I've wanted this man.

"This is so messed up," he says, his voice sounding strained.

The words spear through my heart. I should remove myself from under him, get dressed, and walk out, forgetting all the feelings and desires I have fighting their way to the surface. But my good sense lays dormant, my conscience suddenly keeping quiet.

If this is all I can get from Finn, I'll take it. I've spent years not getting what I want. This moment right now is what I want. I'll deal with the consequences later. I'll never get Finn back. Never have the life we planned. I've lived too long without this connection. This moment is mine, and I'm taking it.

"Let's not overthink it and just have this moment." I want to add *for the love we lost, for the lives that were meant to be*. For *us*. But I keep the words to myself.

If his mind and body are battling over what to do, it doesn't take long for him to make up his mind. His lips slams against mine. Not for the first time today knocking the breath from my lungs. Finn then pulls back, fumbling for something on the bench. A condom. Something we've never used before. We'd only ever slept with each other, and I'd been on the pill. Things are so different now. The knife keeps twisting deeper in my heart.

Not bothering to pull his underwear or jeans off, he shuffles them down enough past his hips to roll on the condom. I'm fascinated by the act. Fascinated at the size of him. Fascinated at seeing his desire for me again. Wet heat pools between my legs, and I squirm.

Pulling my panties down my legs and tossing them on the floor, Finn kneels between my legs. Our eyes lock, his gaze piercing through me. Something is missing. There's something about the way he looks at me that doesn't seem right. I don't have time to dwell on it, because Finn drops his hands on my knees and spreads my legs further apart. With a quick, hard thrust, he enters me. I cry out with a mixture of pleasure and pain. It's been so long, and with his size, I need a moment to adjust.

Finn stills, sensing my discomfort. "Are you okay?"

I bite my bottom lip and nod. After a few seconds, my muscles relax, and pleasure takes over from the pain.

"Fuck, you're so tight," he groans into my neck, licking over my racing pulse.

Wrapping my legs around his waist, I hook my ankles together like I don't want to let him go, urging him to pump into me. My hands run over the hard planes of his back. His muscles quiver underneath my palms.

As he thrusts harder and deeper inside me, I clench around his cock. The pressure rising, I'm ready to explode. My body trembles, and I tilt up my pelvis and bite back a moan. "Finn…I'm almost there."

"Let me give you a hand," Finn says between deep, wet kisses. He slips his hand between our bodies and finds my clit, giving it a rub and a flick with his fingers.

"Finn!" I moan long and low as my body spasms and falls apart.

He pumps once, twice, three times, and cries out his release. Dropping on top of me, he holds his weight on his forearms. His warm breath fanning over my neck. My body is quivering. Feeling alive again. Reminding me how great sex with Finn is.

When our bodies stop shaking, Finn shifts onto his elbows. I can't hold back the grin that spreads across my face. I feel amazing! When I chance a look at Finn, it soon drops when he stares back expressionless at me.

It finally hits me what's missing from Finn's eyes. It's love and affection. Of course, it couldn't be more obvious if I'd been hit over the head with a hammer. From the moment our paths crossed again, any affection was long gone. Getting so caught up in the moment, I ignored how he really feels about me. I turn my face away. I can't bear to see any loathing he fires my way.

Chapter Fifteen

FINN

I pull away from Harper and turn my back on her. I remove tissues from a box sitting on the counter and use them to wrap up the condom, and I dispose of it in the trash under the counter. While I lift my pants and put my sweater back on, the sound of clothes rustling behind me tells me Harper's getting dressed too.

What the hell am I doing? Things weren't supposed to go this far. The dog incident had freaked her out so much, I was only supposed to calm her down. Instead, wanting to touch her, taste her, became more important than breathing. Nostalgia had blinded me to reality. Clouded my judgment. No matter how much Harper had fucked up my life, my body still wants her. But she did fuck up my life. I can't pretend it never happened, nor do I want to forget, or I could end up falling back into the dark hole she left me in.

Scrubbing my hands through my hair, I turn back around. Harper is sitting on the edge of the bench seat, twisting her fingers together. God, she's beautiful. My chest aches as I stare at her. I have to remind myself Harper is vindictive and uses people for her own benefit. Her sweet, gentle demeanor will not fool me again. I'm not a pushover anymore, and yet, the moment she's in trouble, I'm at her side. What an idiot! I have to forget how natural she feels in my arms. Or how am I supposed to keep the rage that burns in my soul from fizzling out the second I get near her?

"We should get back to work," I say, not quite meeting her eyes. *Coward!*

Harper rises, placing a hand on my arm. "Finn, we need to talk. Please."

Before I can reply, Bianca thunders into the trailer, stopping short at the threshold. Her gaze flicks between me and Harper as she takes in our disheveled state. Her eyes narrow in on Harper's hand on my arm, and she frowns with menace.

Harper's hand quickly drops to her side.

"I said no one was to interrupt us," I snap. Again, the urge to protect Harper flaring to the surface. Whether from dogs or judgment from others, it's like a built-in mechanism I can't control.

Bianca's eyes grow wide at my tone. "You've been in here for a long time. Everyone's waiting for you."

"We'll be out in a minute." I soften my tone. It won't do me any good if I keep pissing off my assistant.

She nods. "I'll let the crew know you're on your way." With one last, scathing glance over her shoulder at Harper, she leaves the trailer.

"She hates me," Harper sighs.

"Don't take it too personally, she doesn't like anyone." I gesture toward the door. "We better go."

Harper places her hand on my arm again. "Please, can we talk? I need to tell you something. Especially now after what we've done."

"You think because we had sex I want to talk? There's nothing to talk about. You played me—"

"No." Tears fill her eyes as she shakes her head.

The sight of her tears is twisting in my gut, but I have to ignore them. "You left me to marry another man, for what? Money? Your parents had money. I had money. Or was it for his social status? You wanted to be a trophy wife? I never thought you were like that. I guess I didn't really know you at all, did I?"

"It wasn't like that. If you'd listen..." She clutches my arm, but I shake her hand off.

"I have no reason to listen to you. You made your choice, live with it." Fuck, I feel like the biggest asshole for speaking to her this way after having sex with her. I know it's to cover the God damn pain slicing through my heart.

I can't bear to speak or look at her a moment longer. I'm ashamed of what I've done. So, I race from the trailer, leaving Harper behind.

In the distance, dogs are yapping. To no one in particular, I yell, "Get those fucking dogs off set. Now!"

Chapter Sixteen

HARPER

Trudging home from a long and mentally draining day, I arrive at the apartment at the same time as Alyssa with her dance bag slung over her shoulder. She looks as dejected as I feel.

I unlock the door, and we head inside. "You look like you've had a great day too," Alyssa says with sarcasm. I must look worse than I thought. "Wanna debrief over wine and pizza?"

The offer sounds good, but I haven't been paid yet, and I'm running out of money.

Like Alyssa could read my mind, she says, "My treat. My tips were great last night."

When Alyssa isn't auditioning or taking dance and singing classes, she dances at a strip club called The Temple. She makes decent money and could afford some place better to live. Apparently, she believes living like a poor, down-on-her-luck dancer waiting for her dream role gives her more depth and life experience.

She dumps her bag on the floor, drops with exhaustion on the sofa, and kicks her feet up onto the coffee table. Pulling out her phone from her pocket, she asks, "Pepperoni good for you?"

"Yes. Thank you. Next time it's my treat."

"No problem. Pizza is on its way." She tosses her phone on the sofa. "God, I'm hungry. I should really eat a salad. The pizza is going to go straight to my ass. Just another reason to be rejected at another audition."

I take a seat next to Alyssa. "I gather the audition didn't go well today."

Alyssa blows out a long breath. Her head falls back on the sofa. "I'm ready to give up. I don't know what they are after. I can dance. I can sing. I take acting classes. What more do they want? I have no clue."

Although I've never seen Alyssa dance in the flesh, she's shown me videos of her performing. The elegance and style in her movements took my breath away. She also sings like an angel. Talent pours from her. "Don't give up. You're going to make it. They don't know what they're missing out on."

Alyssa smiles. "Thanks. I'll give it another year. If nothing happens…" She shrugs. "…I'll reassess. Anyway, tell me why your day looks as shitty as mine."

Mirroring the way Alyssa is sitting on the sofa—head back, feet on the coffee table—I stare up at the cracked, yellowing ceiling. Where do I start? There is too much to unpack, and I'm not even sure the day's events happened or if I'm in some kind of crazy dream. "We had an on-location photoshoot. I'm just tired."

Alyssa taps her biker boot against my foot. "I know we haven't known each other for long, but my bullshit radar is pointing at you. Did something happen with Finn?" She straightens and turns to look at me. "Sorry, you don't have to answer that. You can tell me to mind my own business."

I can see Alyssa is genuinely concerned and that she really means to stay out of my business if I want her to. Yes, we haven't known each other long, and yet, I feel like I can trust her. "No, that's okay. I tried talking to Finn. I wanted him to know the reason I left him. Try to get him to understand." I can't tell her about having sex with him. That's something I'm still trying to process. "He's so mad at me, he won't listen."

"This conversation needs wine." Alyssa rises, goes to the small kitchen, and grabs a bottle and two glasses. Filling them up to a generous level, she passes me a glass. "Why did you leave him?"

Taking a large sip, I place the glass on the coffee table. For years I couldn't speak a word about this to anyone. Not that I had anyone to tell. All my 'friends' were Derek's people. Socialites and fakes. "Derek blackmailed me into marrying him." It still makes my skin crawl thinking about the day he propositioned me.

Alyssa chokes on her wine. Wiping her mouth with the back of her hand, she exclaims, "He what? Why?"

I rub my palms over my thighs. "My father got into massive debt at Derek's casino. Derek offered to wipe out the debt only if I married him. If I didn't, he'd leak my father's addiction to the press. Being the governor of New York, it would've ruined his reputation, maybe his career."

Alyssa's glass pauses at her lips. "You're Charles Madden's daughter? Why didn't I figure that out?" It was more a rhetorical question. "Sorry." She waves her hand for me to continue with the story.

"Derek wanted to get into politics and had big ambitions of one day taking over my father's position. He didn't care how, who, or what he had to do to get there. Being the son-in-law of Charles Madden, he believed was his ticket. He died before he got the chance to test that theory."

Alyssa places her glass on the coffee table and sits cross-legged on the sofa. "Wow! To save your father, you married Derek." She shook her head with disbelief. "Did your parents know about the blackmail?"

This is the part that hurt the most—well, not as much as leaving Finn, but it was close. "They knew, although it was never spoken about. After the wedding, they couldn't look me in the eye."

"I'm so sorry. That must have been awful. Your parents passed away last year. Why did you stay?" Alyssa reaches for my hand and clasps it. I'm grateful for the comforting gesture. I don't see any judgment in her eyes.

"Because of Finn."

Alyssa frowns. "Finn? What do you mean?"

I reply without going into too much detail; if I can't tell Finn the whole truth, I can't breathe a word about it to anyone else. "Derek believed being the son-in-law of the late Charles Madden would still help him obtain his goal. Because he knew I still loved Finn and I wanted desperately to see him again, Derek threatened to destroy Finn's family business if I attempted to leave him. The risk was too high."

Alyssa cups her cheeks in shock. "This is like a Hollywood movie. Who really lives like that?"

For years it felt like a nightmare. One I never thought I'd wake up from. Now, without Derek's threats hanging over my head, the grogginess is lifting like morning fog.

"Now you can tell Finn the truth. Derek can't hurt anyone."

Plucking a lose thread on the sofa, I say, "I wanted to tell him today. He wouldn't listen. He doesn't want to hear what I have to say. And I'm not sure he'd believe me."

"Do you still have feelings for him?" Alyssa asks.

I pick up a cushion and hug it to my chest. My feelings for Finn have never died. To survive without him, I had to bury them deep. Now with him back in my life, the box has broken open, spilling everything I've ever felt into my heart.

"By the look on your face, I'd say yes. What are you going to do about it?"

Tears clog in my throat. I cough to clear away the lump. "He doesn't want to talk to me. What more can I do?"

Alyssa gives a dramatic shrug. "Don't take no for an answer and *make* him listen! Tie him down if you must—that actually sounds fun." She winks. I know she's trying to lighten the mood. "If he knows the truth, maybe you can pick up where you left off."

"Too much time and heartache has happened. It will never be the same," I say with regret.

Someone knocks on the door. "That will be the pizza." Alyssa rises, opens the door, and pays the delivery man. Setting the box on the coffee table, she says, "If things can't be the same, make them better."

Can I make things better? The only way I'll know for sure is if I tell Finn the truth. Well, as much of it as I can. A spark of hope flares in my chest. Are we back in each other's lives for a reason? Is the universe giving us a second chance?

I'll never know unless I try speaking to him. This time, I *have* to make him listen.

Chapter Seventeen

FINN

Jab-jab-jab. My fierce punches echo through the gym as I bounce around on the balls of my feet in a boxing ring, slamming into the pads covering Hayden's hands. I swing a right hook, and Hayden takes a quick step back, shielding his face. "What the hell, man? Are you trying to knock me out? What did I do to you?"

"Sorry, it's been a long day." My chest heaves, and I drag in deep breaths. Swiping the sweat off my brow with my forearm, I rip the Velcro off my gloves and shake my hands free. Leaning on the ropes, Lucas, from outside of the ring, throws me a water bottle.

"Well, next time you feel like punching the shit out of someone, ask Lucas. He could use someone messing up his pretty-boy face."

Lucas flips Hayden the bird. "You're just jealous."

Sidling up next to me, Hayden says, "You wanna tell us what's eating at you?"

"No." Tilting the bottle in the air, I squirt water into my mouth. I see Hayden and Lucas exchanging a strange look.

Hayden pulls the pads off his hands and tosses them on the floor next to my gloves. "A little birdie told us something happened at the shoot."

Lucas snickers. "More like an angry bird."

Snatching a towel off the rope, I wipe at the back of my neck and flick the towel over my shoulder. I pick up my gloves and duck under the rope, making my way into the changing room. Unfortunately, my brothers follow close behind. I have a solid idea what they've heard. It doesn't mean I want to talk about it. Sitting on a bench, I unwrap the strapping from my hands. Hayden and Lucas lean on the lockers opposite me.

"Are you going to tell us what happened?" Hayden asks.

"Why don't you tell me what you know?" Sometimes I wish they left me the hell alone. They nag more than our mother ever did.

"We'd rather hear it from you. Bianca's take on it was kinda nasty. That woman's claws were out and were ready to slice Harper to shreds," Lucas says.

I need to have a talk with Bianca. Treating Harper the way she has is unacceptable. God, I can't talk. I'm just as big an asshole as Bianca is—only worse. I fucked Harper! I wonder if there's a special place in hell for people like me. "Harper had an incident with the dogs on the shoot. She's scared of them, remember? I took her into a trailer to calm her down."

Hayden crosses his arms over his chest. "Yeah, I remember. It's what happened *in* the trailer we want to know about."

Getting to my feet, I open a locker and pull out my bag, stuffing my boxing gear inside. I will not tell my brothers what I did with Harper. It isn't any of their damn business. Plus, I'm still pissed at myself for my lack of self-control.

"She wanted to talk. I didn't want to listen. That's all." I slam the locker door shut.

Hayden steps in front of me, blocking my way out of the changing room. He ignores the annoyed glare I throw at him. "Why didn't you want to talk?"

With a heavy sigh, I set my bag on the bench. "I don't care about whatever she has to say."

"Why don't you care what she has to say?" Hayden insists.

Man, Hayden is a tenacious bastard. I huff with frustration. "It's been years since I've seen her. It's old news. I don't care anymore."

Hayden leans back on the locker. "I don't think that's true. You never truly got over her."

I jerk back like he's slapped me. Why would he say that? "I've been over her for years."

"That's why almost every woman you sleep with has a striking resemblance to Harper," Hayden points out with a raised eyebrow.

"They can be Harper's doppelganger," Lucas pipes in.

I throw Lucas a shut-the-hell-up look.

"Am I wrong?" Lucas smirks, not giving a shit. I want to smack that grin off his pretty face.

I take a step toward him, ready to follow through with it.

Hayden puts a hand on my shoulder. "*Anyway*, would it hurt to hear what she has to say?"

"Why is this so important to you? A few days ago, you were ready to kick her out of the building. Have you forgotten what she did to me?"

Lucas' smile drops, and Hayden squeezes my shoulder. "No, we haven't forgotten. We almost lost you. I hate what she did to you. Maybe if you talk to her, you can finally get some closure and move on." I open my mouth to reject his words, but Hayden cuts me off. "You *need* to move on. What you're doing—sleeping with these women who look like Harper—is not helping. Think about it."

Picking up my bag, I sling it over my shoulder. "I'll think about it."

This time Hayden lets me pass. Maybe if I talk to Harper, it will get her out of my system. God knows I've tried everything else to no avail. Even having sex with her didn't help; only made it worse.

If talking to her doesn't work, what will?

Chapter Eighteen

HARPER

Monday morning, I step from the elevator into reception. My heart is racing. My hands are sweaty. All weekend, I kept going over in my mind what had happened between Finn and me. The moment he left the trailer, he avoided me. So, for the rest of the day, he never once gave me eye contact. I went from being happy being back in his arms to feeling rejected. I had to drag myself to work today. Even contemplating sending Tamara my letter of resignation. Then what? If I quit, I'd be back to being broke and struggling to find another job. All because I found it difficult to face Finn. So, instead of cowering at home, I'm going to pull back my shoulders, lift my chin high, and pretend being with Finn again hasn't affected me at all. I can do that, right?

As I head to my desk, Finn steps out from his office, reading something on his phone. My steps falter as I catch sight of him. My breath hitches in my chest. When he lifts his head, our eyes lock. My heart gallops behind my ribs. How can I pretend this man doesn't affect me? It's not possible.

"Harper!" Jumping at the abrupt way my name is called, I spin around. Bianca has her arms crossed over her chest, glowering at me. "I need you in my office, now."

"I'll just put my bag and coat away and I'll be straight there." When I turn back around, Finn is gone. It's probably for the best. My legs are already a little shaky. Having him close by would only make it worse. Hopefully, whatever work Bianca has scheduled for me keeps me away from Finn.

After tucking my bag in the drawer and hanging my coat over the chair, I make my way to Bianca's office. I wonder if—hope—Finn's there. Taking a deep breath, I step inside. The air gushes from my lungs with relief and disappointment. My emotions are in such a jumbled mess. It's only Bianca sitting at her desk.

Without taking her eyes from the computer, she points to a stack of files on the edge of the table. "Take these down to the creative department. When you get back—"

"Knock, knock," Juliette sings as she enters the room, interrupting Bianca's instructions. "I was told I'd find you here, Harper."

"Oh?" Why is Juliette looking for me? The hairs at the back of my neck prickle. "Is something wrong? Please don't tell me I ruined your gown. I promise I took care taking it off." It would be just my luck if I damaged a Juliette Monet gown. I'll be paying it off for the rest of my life.

Bianca's eyebrows shoot into her hairline. "You wore a gown? Raiding the sample department for work clothes is one thing, but under no circumstances are you to wear any gowns!" Bianca's face screws up with irritation.

Juliette taps a long, red fingernail on the desk. "Darling, I asked her to. The gown fit her like a glove. She looked stunning."

"It... She..." Bianca splutters.

Twirling around to me, Juliette smiles. "Can you come to my office later today? I have a couple of designs I'd love your opinion on."

Juliette Monet wants my opinion! Again! Doesn't she have a million qualified people to ask before me? What is happening? "Sure. Yes. No problem," I say, not doing a good job at hiding my excitement.

"I have work for her to do," Bianca snaps, finding her voice.

Juliette turns her head over her shoulder to look at Bianca. Not saying a word to her, Juliette just raises a manicured eyebrow. Returning her gaze to me, Juliette says, "Come see me at four."

I guess no one tells Juliette Monet what she can and can't do. I nod. "See you then."

When Juliette flounces from the room in a swirl of whimsical skirts, Bianca rises from the chair, plants her palms on the desk, and leans toward me. "What's your game?"

I take a step back. Away from Bianca's menacing expression. "Excuse me?"

"You're chummy with our head designer, and you're fucking the boss. What are you after?"

I suck in a gasp. She knows about what happened in the trailer? Did Finn tell her? "I'm not after anything."

"Oh, please." She gives a mirthless chuckle. "Your sweet-and-innocent act isn't working on me. I'm onto you, and I'll figure it out. Just give me time. In the meantime, stay away from Finn. We wouldn't want the office gossiping about how you fucked him in a trailer at the photoshoot."

The blood in my veins turns cold. After I left the trailer that day, I put all the sideway glances at me down to my reaction over the dogs. Oh God, had Bianca told them what we did? I want to crawl in a hole and see no one again.

"Bianca!" Finn's deep voice booms from the doorway. Stepping inside, he gives Bianca a hard look. "If I hear you speak like that to Harper again, you can pack your things and get the hell out of here."

"But...Finn...she—"

"Understood?" The warning tone leaves no room for argument.

Bianca slams her lips tight, nostrils flaring. "Understood."

"Good. I have a meeting in ten minutes. Please get coffee and bring it into the boardroom."

Bianca's mouth drops open. "That's Harper's job."

Finn slides his hands in his pocket, giving him a casual stance. But I can see the tension pinching his expression. "I'm asking *you* to do it."

"Fine," Bianca says, not arguing. Although, before leaving the room, she glares at me.

My eyes follow Bianca from the room. "I wish you hadn't done that." I sigh, collecting the files from the desk.

"Why? She was being a bitch. She shouldn't speak to you or anyone like that."

Clutching the files to my chest, I spin around. "Oh, but it's okay for you to talk to me like crap?"

Finn pinches the bridge of his nose. "Harper, that's different."

"Right. So, you can speak to me like I'm the most hated person in the world, refuse to listen to me, but I'm okay to fuck."

On a long breath, he drops his head and stares at the floor. "We—*I* should never have let things go so far." He lifts his head back up. "I'm sorry."

"Will you listen to what I have to say?"

"I'm not sure."

My heart trips at the sadness shining from his eyes. He wants to hate me so much for what I did, but underneath that anger, lies a man who is still hurt. "When you're ready to talk, let me know." On trembling legs, I leave the room. Hoping and praying he'll come to me soon.

During the rest of the day, Bianca has me running around the office. She either communicated with me through two-word grunts or email. I prefer the latter. The less time I have to spend with her, the better. Finn has been in meetings for most of the day, and our paths haven't crossed. Or maybe Bianca planned it that way. It doesn't stop me from trying to catch a glimpse of him though.

When four o'clock hits, I excitedly head down to Juliette's room. I have no idea how I can help the designer, but I can't wait to see what she wants me to do. Juliette is in the office, pacing in front of multiple easels with drawings of stunning gowns on them. Colored and textured fabric are draped over the corners.

When she spots me, she whisks open her folding fan and waves it in front of her face. Today's fan is gold with a black sequence pattern. "Darling, thank you for coming."

Like I would say no to Juliette Monet! "I'm not sure what I can help you with?"

Juliette opens her arms out wide like she's a model on a gameshow. "My collections are almost complete. Only a few adjustments and confirming fabric choices and they're set to go."

"Again, I'm not sure what I can help you with? I'm not a fashion designer. Don't you have people who are qualified for this?"

Juliette gives a dismissive wave of her hand. "You don't need to be qualified to have a good eye. I have a feeling you do. Besides, they tell me what they think I want to hear. They don't have the guts to speak the truth. Fresh eyes and an honest opinion are what I need."

"Yes...but—"

"It's not rocket science. You'll be fine. Ahh, finally you show up," Juliette says to someone behind me.

"Sorry, I got caught up in a meeting. What did I miss?" Finn's voice, so smooth and deep, washes over me.

"I was telling Harper she doesn't need to be a qualified designer to appreciate great designs."

"What happened to the fashion degree you started?" Finn asks me.

"I never continued after..." I was going to say *after I got married*, but I don't want to keep bringing that up. The reminder only drove a bigger wedge between us. Instead, I say, "...after the first year."

"Why? You loved it. Oh," he says, giving a curt nod. "Too busy being the wife of a billionaire."

My back stiffens. So much for keeping Derek out of this. "No, that's not why. Derek never allowed it." *Derek took everything away from me. Including you.*

Finn pulls a dubious expression.

Like Juliette could sense the tension in the room, she ambles herself between us and says, "Darlings, let's go over everything." Turning her attention to me, she points to the designs. "Once Finn decides everything is perfect, we can start production. Then he can head back to London."

So, this is why Finn is in New York. Will he stay the full two months or go back early if the designs are finished? Of course, he'll leave when the job is done. There's no reason for him to stay.

Juliette taps the fan closed in her hand, breaking my depressing musings. "We have a lot to do while Finn is in town. We better get started."

Finn and I put aside the tension between us and focus our attention on the designs. I stay quiet and listen to Juliette explain fabric choices to Finn. Soaking up this moment because when will I ever get the opportunity again? Juliette drapes the material over her arm and shoulder to get the feel of the texture, pulling me into the conversation, genuinely interested in my opinion.

"I'm torn between two fabulous samples." Juliette picks off the fabric hanging over an easel. A soft midnight material falls smoothly over one arm, the light picking up shimmers of silver threaded into it. On her other arm is something very similar except with no silver threads, making it less dramatic. She hands the silver threaded one to Finn. "Drape this over Harper so I can get a better look. This is gorgeous. I'm leaning toward it. I'd love to make every gown in it if I could." She chuckles.

Finn cocks an eyebrow. "You want me to put it on Harper?"

Juliette shrugs a shoulder. "Unless you want to wear it?"

Does Juliette know about my history with Finn? Would Finn discuss our past with her? If they're close, maybe he would have. Or...my cheeks flame hot; she heard about what happened in the trailer at the photoshoot?

"Not my style," Finn says.

"I think you'd look spectacular in one of my gowns," Juliette jokes.

Maybe I'm just being paranoid.

Finn steps behind me with the fabric and drapes it over my shoulders, his fingers brushing over my skin. Did his hands stay a moment longer than necessary? I lock my knees, trying not to fall back and sink into him.

Propping one hand on her hip, Juliette pulls her lips to the side as she studies the material. "Drape it around the front. I can't see the full effect if it's on her back."

Finn steps in front of me, adjusting the fabric. He's standing so close I breathe in the faint woodsy scent of his cologne. I tilt my face. The air gets trapped in my lungs. He watches me with such an intense gaze. When his eyes drop to my mouth, I bite my lip. So desperate for him to kiss me again. Finn squeezes his eyes shut like it's taking all his effort to resist.

"I can't see the sample with you standing in front of Harper." Juliette's laughing tone snaps me back to attention. For a moment, I'd forgotten the designer was in the room.

Finn clears his throat and steps away, the heat leaving his eyes.

"Which one do you like best, Harper?" Juliette asks.

It's blowing my mind the way Juliette really wants my opinion. I look down at the sample I'm wearing and then to the one hanging over Juliette's arm. I pull mine off and drape it over a mannequin. I take the one Juliette is holding and place it over another mannequin. I take a few moments to examine them both.

Juliette seems to love the one with the silver threads, but as I look at the fabric and then the design on the easel, I know which one I'd choose. Can I really tell Juliette what I think, knowing how much she loves the silver thread? It's not like my opinion really matters. Juliette is the professional. She knows best.

"The ruffled tiered skirt on the design is so dramatic and eye-catching I think if you use the silver thread it might take away from the structure of the dress. Do you want people more focused on the design or the color? If I made something as spectacular as that sketch, I'd want everyone to be aware of every detail and not get distracted by silver threads." My heart is racing as Juliette narrows her eyes. Oh crap. Have I offended her? She did say she wanted people to be honest.

After a moment that felt like hours but was probably only seconds, Juliette's face splits into a wide grin. "Exactly, darling. I knew you'd tell me the truth. I was never torn between the two. I knew what I wanted."

I frown with confusion.

"Like I said, I want honest opinions. You passed the test with flying colors." She taps her fan on my shoulder.

"Oh..." I give a relieved chuckle. "I'm glad."

"You would have crushed her spirit if you'd told her she'd failed. Harper never could cope with bad grades. She'd sulk for days."

My mouth drops open. "I did not!"

Finn rolls his eyes. "After getting a B-minus on your English report, you wrote Mr. Rodriguez a two-page letter on why you thought he'd graded your paper poorly."

"Oh my God. I forgot about that." I hold my fingers to my mouth and giggle.

"What about when you got a C in math—"

"Okay. Okay." I laugh. "I'm a high achiever."

"That's an understatement." Finn chuckles, and we share a smile. Warmth spreads through my chest at having him smile at me again.

The afternoon turns into early evening, and I'm having so much fun looking at designs and fabrics. What makes it better is that Finn is no longer glaring and snapping at me. For a moment, it's like we're friends again. I want to hold on to this moment so tight and never let go.

"Well, that will do for now. It's getting late." Juliette places her hands on my shoulders and air-kisses both my cheeks. "Thank you for your help."

I blush. "Anytime. I had fun."

Leaving Juliette's room, Finn and I make our way back to our floor, not saying a word, but giving each other the occasional glance and smile. My heart wants to explode with happiness.

Bianca walks out from her office, popping my moment of bliss.

"You're still here?" Finn flicks out his wrist and glances at his watch. "It's seven-thirty." Wow, time really does fly when you're having fun. The office is quiet. Everyone has gone home. "You should have left two hours ago."

"I stayed to make sure there isn't anything you need before I go home." She's one loyal assistant. Although, I'm not sure if 'anything you need' is work related.

"I'll leave you two to it. I'll grab my stuff and head home. Goodnight." I turn to leave.

"Harper, wait. I need you to stay back a little longer if that's okay," Finn says, stopping me.

Bianca steps in front of Finn. "I'll stay and help you with whatever you need."

Finn looks over Bianca's head at me. "Go home, Bianca. There's nothing I need from you tonight."

Glancing over her shoulder, Bianca pins me with a sharp look filled with hatred. To Finn, she says, "Are you sure?"

"I'm sure. Goodnight, Bianca. See you in the morning."

Bianca's jaw is clamped tight as she goes into her office. She comes back out moments later with her coat and bag. Without saying a word, she marches to the elevator.

We watch her enter the cart, and when the doors close, Finn turns to me. "Can you come into my office, please?"

I follow him, and he stands with his back to me, hands in his pockets, looking out the window into the night sky. "I'm ready to listen." His voice is so low, I'm not sure I've heard him correctly.

I step further into the room. "What?"

He turns, and my breath catches at the look of anguish etched on his face. Like years of pain has come flooding to the surface.

"I'm ready to listen to what you have to say." Uncertainty flicks over his features.

My heartrate kicks up in speed. Now that I can finally tell him why I left him, nerves are bouncing around inside me. "Are you sure?"

He nods and gestures to a black, leather sofa along the wall. I take a seat. Finn sits next to me, keeping space between us. Waiting expectantly. God, now that I have the chance, where do I start? If I'd known he wanted to talk tonight, I would've been better prepared.

Taking a moment to gather my thoughts, I take a deep breath and rub my palms down my thighs. "Telling you I was marrying Derek was the worst day of my life."

Finn tosses his head back and scoffs.

Frowning, I say, "I thought you said you were ready to listen?"

"Then don't tell me crap like that."

"It's not crap. It's the truth!" I jump up from the sofa and pace the floor in front of him. "Derek was blackmailing me." There, I've finally said it. The words that have pressed me down so much I could barely breathe, release from me.

Finn's eyes widen. "What do you mean he was blackmailing you?"

I stop pacing and sit back down, my legs too shaky to support my weight. "My father got himself in a lot of trouble." The man I loved. The man I thought would always protect me like he did when I was a little girl and believed a monster lived under my bed. In the end, it was me protecting him. "He had a gambling addiction. Spent millions in Derek's casinos. Got himself into debt he couldn't pay off. When Derek approached me about it, I was shocked. I didn't know he had a problem. How kind of Derek to tell me about my father's addiction so I could get him help. I even *thanked* him." I shake my head at the memory. "That made him laugh. He said he had a reason for telling me. That he didn't give away information for nothing." The further I got into the story, the more Finn's jaw clenches. I'm not sure if he's believing me and is pissed at Derek or angry at me because he thinks I'm lying to him. Either way, I continue. "That's when he hit me with his 'proposal'. To clear my father's debts and stopping his addiction from hitting the media, he wanted to marry me. My father was his ticket into the world of politics, and he wanted to use me to get there."

"If that's what he wanted, why not blackmail your father to keep his addiction from the media? Why did he need to include you?" Finn's tone is deep and harsh. I'm still not sure where his anger is pointing at—me or Derek. Maybe both.

"He believed a wife made him look more respectable. Especially the daughter of the New York governor."

"So, you accepted just like that?" Finn snaps his fingers in front of my face.

I pull back my shoulders. "No, not 'just like that'. I refused. Told him there was no way in hell I'd marry him. He said if I didn't agree with his terms, he'd make my family's life a living hell. And I believed him. I'd heard about how he'd been involved in ruining people's lives. It wasn't just a threat—it was a warning."

Finn propels off the sofa, throwing his arms up. "Why didn't you come to me? I had money."

"It was millions of dollars!"

"I would have gotten the money any way I had to. You know I would." He slaps a hand to his chest.

I hang my head. "I know you would."

"Then why didn't you come to me?"

Rising from the sofa, I step closer to him. Careful not to come too close that it might make him skittish and back away. "He threatened you too."

Finn shrugs. "I wouldn't have given a fuck what he did to me. He could have taken everything I owned. Left me penniless. Slandered my name. All I wanted...*needed* was you. Everything else meant nothing without you."

Oh God. I hold back the tears burning the backs of my eyes. The anguish etched on his face, the pain I caused him, is killing me. I hold it together so I can get through the rest of the story. When I get home, in the privacy of my bedroom, that's when I can fall apart.

"Do you remember a few days before we broke up, designs from one of the collections you were working on were stolen? Alessi Fashion lost hundreds of thousands of dollars."

Finn nods.

"That was Derek. He did that because I refused to marry him. He laughed at how easy it was to destroy you." I wrap my arms around my waist and curl my shoulders inward. "I'll never forget the mocking look of triumph on his face." He knew I would never let anyone hurt Finn.

Taking two steps toward me, Finn cups my face in his hands and growls, "If you had told me, I could've taken care of it myself. You ruined us!" He flings his hands away, his chest heaving.

"I was protecting you," I say, my voice cracking.

"I. Didn't. Need. Your. Protection." He grounds out each word through gritted teeth. "I needed *you*!"

The tears burning in my eyes break free. "Finn—"

He cuts me off. "What about after your parents passed away and you didn't have that threat hanging over your head? Why didn't you come to me then?"

My bottom lip trembles. "I tried. When I told him I was leaving him, he organized the fire at Alessi's in Paris. You're lucky he didn't have the entire building burned down."

"You still should've told me. Derek could have burned it to the fucking ground for all I'd care." He shoves his hands in the pockets of his pants.

"Put yourself in my shoes, I felt like I had no choice," I plead, hoping he'd understand.

"People always have a choice. If it were me, I would have chosen you. *Always*. I wanted to marry you!" He removes one hand from his pocket and shakes his fist in the air close to my face.

I flinch, taking quick steps back.

"What the hell?" Finn's expression changes from anger to concern. "Did you think I was going to hit you?" He opens up the palm of his hand; the engagement ring he was going to give me once sat in his palm.

"No...sorry...it's just..." My body trembles.

Finn's face turns dark and murderous. "Did that fucker hit you?"

The strength in my legs gives way, and I sink onto the sofa. Putting my elbows on my knees, I drop my head into my hands. I drag in deep breaths to help stop the churning in my stomach. I feel the seat next to me dip, and Finn's arm slides across my shoulders.

A sob escapes from my mouth. Hot tears stream down my face, splashing on my skirt—so much for waiting to breakdown at home. During the years I was married to Derek, I never cried. I never wanted him to have the satisfaction of breaking me. No matter what he did to me, what he said, I held back the tears. Oh, it pissed him off. Toward the end, when he couldn't get a rise from me, things changed. The insults and degrading comments weren't enough.

Finn pulls me to his chest. I bury my face in his neck. Letting all the tears I never let Derek see, fall. Finn brushes a hand from my head down my hair, mumbling at my temple, "Ssshh. It's okay. Ssshhh. I've got you." The words only made me sob harder. He might have me now, but as soon as this is over, he'll let me go. Cocooned in Finn's arms is my safe place. I never want to let go.

A few minutes pass and my crying subsides. I pull away and dry my face on the back of my sleeve. I'm sure I look like a mess.

Feeling a little silly over my outburst, I give a sheepish smile and point to his damp shirt. "I'm sorry about that. I'll get it dry-cleaned."

"I don't give a fuck about the shirt." He swallows hard, pushes his fingers over his eyes, and with a strained voice asks, "Harper, did that bastard hurt you?"

I hang my head and tug at the bottom of my shirt. Yes, he hurt me. Taking me away from everything I loved. From the one person I loved the most. But I know that's not what Finn's asking.

When I don't answer—can't because my throat is tight—he says, "Earlier, did you think I was going to hit you?"

Looking him straight in the eye, he stares back at me like my answer is the only thing that matters. Like I could break him if I say yes. "No. I know you'd never do anything like that. It was just a reflex reaction."

His shoulders slump on an exhale of breath. "No. Never in a million years would I lay a finger on you. I'd rather cut off my hands."

"I'm sorry I made you think that." I place a hand on his shoulder.

With a surprised look on his face, he says, "What do you have to be sorry for? Derek did this. *He* hurt you. If he wasn't already dead, I'd kill him!" A muscle twitches in his jaw.

Even with all the hate Finn has thrown my way, deep down there's a part of him that still cares. My heart swells. "Derek never hit me," I say to soothe him.

Finn narrows his eyes with disbelief. "So, why did you flinch when I raised my hand?" He must have tucked the engagement ring back in his pocket, because he's no longer holding it. I wish he didn't keep it as a reminder of the bad times.

I pull my legs up onto the sofa and tuck them under me. "Derek was very controlling. He told me what to wear and how to behave. I had to eat what he told me to, and he made me exercise every day. He was heavily into health and fitness and looking after himself. Which is ironic since his heart gave out." I don't feel a twinge of sorrow. Does that make me a bad person? "The only thing he couldn't control were my feelings. He knew I loved you when we got married, yet he found it unbelievable that I didn't fall madly in love with him. All women loved him, he said. They'd give up anything to be in my position. When he realized I didn't worship the ground he walked on, he threw his affairs in my face. It frustrated him that I didn't care. So, he started showing me all the women you were involved with. He'd smile with malicious glee as he gave me details." I avert my eyes. "Trying to stay expressionless was a lot harder when I saw photos of you with other women. But I did it. Although it cut so deep to the point where I felt like I couldn't breathe. After years of this and not getting the reaction he wanted from me, the derogative insults and verbal abuse got more intense. I knew if I gave in, and showed any emotion, he won. So, he…arhh…started…"

Finn holds onto my fidgeting hands; his are strong and warm. Linking our fingers together, he brings them to his mouth and kisses my knuckles. "You don't have to talk about it if you don't want to."

The comforting, loving gesture almost brings me to tears again. Not because of Derek's horrible memories, but because I could see the old Finn again. The one who loved me. Cared for me. Would slay dragons for me. I never want this moment to end.

"It's okay. I need to talk about it." Gathering my thoughts for a moment, I continue. "Like I said, nothing he did got a rise from me. It frustrated him. He called me an emotionless bitch and a bunch of other names. He'd get right up in my face and yell at me. One night, he raised his fist. I was sure he was going to hit me. I think he wanted to, but at the last second, he punched a hole in the wall next to my head."

"Fucking bastard!" Finn growls, not letting go of my hands. "What did you do?"

"I ran and locked myself in my room."

"You still stayed after that? Protecting your family and me was more important than your safety?"

"After a couple more similar episodes, I knew I had to get out of there. It was only a matter of time before he'd replace the wall with my face. I was preparing to leave. My parents were dead. You were in London. I was going to warn you that something might happen. Then Derek died. You were safe. I was free."

Gathering me to his chest, Finn wraps his arms around me. Rubbing his hands over my back, my body shudders. He presses his lips to my ear and whispers, "It's over. It's over." The vibration of his deep voice and the caress has a calming effect on me.

Derek is out of my life forever. That part of my life is over.

I'm back in Finn's arms but not back in his heart.

Chapter Nineteen

FINN

Harper's body trembles against mine. I pull back slightly and cup her face in my hands, brushing my thumbs over her damp cheeks. What the hell did she put herself through? All because she wanted to protect her father—protect *me*. Fuck, I didn't need protection. All I needed was Harper. We could have worked out everything else.

"You're still mad at me." She lowers her eyes, probably mistaking my tense body for anger.

Yes, I am angry. But not with Harper. Angry with the fucked-up situation. So angry with Derek it burns in my gut. "Not with you. Now that I know everything, I can understand why you left me. I don't like it. Wish you would've come to me. But I understand. I'm glad I know the truth now."

Harper's gaze flicks away, and she rolls her lips inward. Is there something else she's not telling me?

"*Have* you told the truth?" I ask.

She hesitates slightly before saying, "Yes."

I search deep in her eyes for the truth, and she blinks rapidly, causing a spike of suspicion to coil in my gut. "Is there more?" There is something in her eyes, something that pokes a thread of doubt through me.

Again, she pauses. "I...well...I... It's difficult talking about my time with Derek. He took a lot away from me. For years I'd lost myself. I'm trying to find my way back. Tamara gave me her sister's number. She's a therapist. I've made an appointment to talk to her."

Of course there'd be scars. "I think that's a great idea. Let me know if there's anything I can do to help."

"There is something you can do," she says.

"Name it."

"I want to forget about Derek." She slides her hands up my torso and links her fingers behind my neck. "Make me forget. Please."

The intent on how she wants me to help her forget is clear on her face. I grab onto her wrists. "This isn't the way. I don't want to have sex with you if you're still healing from Derek. If I'd known any of this before, I would never have let things go as far as they did in the club and especially in the trailer. It kills me knowing you had to sleep with a man you hated. But I'm not sure this is the right way to help you forget."

"I never slept with Derek."

I jerk back. "What?"

"I never had sex with him or shared a bed. The thought made me sick to my stomach. To his utter horror and disbelief—remember, he had women throwing themselves at him—I told him no every time he came to my room. I made it clear to him that the only man I wanted touching me was you. That has never changed."

The words shoot through me. "What about other men?" Just because she didn't want her husband touching her, didn't mean there weren't others. Surely she hadn't been celibate for the last nine years.

"No. You were all I wanted. *Still* want." Her hands stay linked behind my neck, and she shuffles closer. "Please make me forget about those years. It was the worst time of my life." Her lips quiver above mine.

They were the worst years of my life too. A time I want to forget. In this moment, we both need to slay our demons. Get lost in each other. Try to heal the damage caused.

Clamping my hands on her waist, I lift her onto my lap, straddling her legs on either side of me. I hiss as she lowers and rubs herself against my erection straining behind the fly of my trousers. I cup her face in my hands and press my lips against her mouth. With gentle prodding, she opens to me.

She clings to my shoulders as she rocks against me to the tempo of our kiss. Slow at first. It doesn't take long for the speed to pick up. The pressure is building. I fucking want this woman. It's taking all my willpower to hold back and not end things fast. With her skirt bunched to her waist, I slide my hands up her thighs and grasp her hips, easing her rocking motion. I love the way she's letting go. I just don't want to come yet. I have more I want to do with her.

When our pace is under control, I skim my hands along her torso, brush my fingers across her heaving ribcage, and cup her breasts. As I pinch and pluck at her nipples, she moans with pleasure. Breaking the kiss, she tilts her face up to the ceiling and arches her back, pressing herself harder into my hands.

"Oh God." Her voice is laced with pleasure. She tunnels her fingers through my hair, encouraging me closer to her chest. I don't need to be told twice. I want my mouth on her tits as much as she wants me there.

I lave at her nipples peeking through the thin fabric of her blouse. With each lick and suck, her tempo kicks up. Her breathing is deep and choppy. The damp material is plastered against the lacy fabric of her bra. A bra I madly need to see. Tits I desperately need to taste.

With jerky fingers, I unbutton the top, surprised I don't tear off any buttons in my haste. Within seconds, her full breasts covered in pink lace are on display. Man, they've only gotten better with age. I dive into her chest, sliding the straps of her bra down her arms. She reaches behind her back to unhook it and tosses it on the floor. I kiss and massage as she squirms on my lap.

"I...want...your...shirt...off...too," she pants.

Hearing her so turned on gets me harder than I ever thought possible. We both work on the buttons. Once released, I shrug out of it and toss it toward her bra.

She splays her hands over my pecs and nibbles her bottom lip. Her eyes brimming with appreciation as she stares at my chest. "You've been working out. You used to be scrawny."

"Scrawny! I've never been scrawny." I squeeze her hips.

Her lips twitch with a smile, and she giggles at my disgruntled expression. "Okay, maybe not scrawny, but you were never this big. I like it."

"I can show you something else that's *big*." Clasping her hand, I push it down my body and place it over my cock. "How about that?" Our easy joking banter we once shared is as natural as having Harper back in my arms.

She twists her lips to the side as if she's thinking. "Is it bigger?"

"Of course it is!" I say with feigned offense.

Stroking her hand along my length, she gives it a squeeze. My eyes practically roll to the back of my head. Slowly, I thrust my hips in her clenched fist. "Hmmm, I'm not sure. I'll have to see for myself."

I open my arms out wide and slide them onto the back of the sofa. "Be my guest." She wants to look, who am I to stop her?

She strokes me again from root to tip, pumping me into her hand. I drop my head on the back of the seat and squeeze my eyes shut. I feel her shuffle off me. When I open my eyes again, Harper is leaning over my crotch with her hair falling like curtains. Her tits inches above my fly. It's the hottest thing I've seen in a long time.

Harper is kneeling on the floor in front of me. Flicking open the button of my pants, she slowly drags the zipper down.

Pulling my pants and underwear down my legs, she pauses at the mean-looking, jagged scar running down my thigh.

"What happened?" She glances at me with a frown.

"Nothing." I don't want to talk about this now. I want to fuck. If I talk about the accident, it will ruin the mood.

She runs a finger along the puckered skin. "It doesn't look like nothing."

"I had an accident a few years ago."

"What happened?" she asks again.

"Long story. Do you want to talk about it now or do you want to fu—*fuck me!*" I groan as she lifts me to her mouth. My body jerks from the sofa as her warm, wet mouth envelopes me.

She sucks me in deep. On her way back up, her tongue swirls over the tip before sliding back down. Her enthusiasm builds, her head bobbing up and down. I tunnel my fingers in her hair and pump into her mouth. If she keeps this up, I'll come in her mouth within seconds. That's not how I want this to end. I want my turn to play.

I set my hands on her shoulders and pull her up to me, laying her on my chest. "You're going to fucking kill me," I growl before slamming my lips on her mouth. Grasping her waist, I flip her onto her back. I hover above her on my hands, my gaze traveling the length of her body. I can't wait to taste every inch of her. She squirms under my perusal like she's impatient for me to start. "You're more beautiful than I remember."

Her hands ghost over my shoulders, down my back, and grips my ass. "You're not so bad yourself." She smiles, giving my behind a squeeze.

We kiss again. I could kiss her sweet mouth all day, but I have more pressing matters to attend to, and it's pressing against her panty-covered pussy, desperate to break through the barrier and bury myself deep inside her. She must be reading my mind, because she tilts her hips and rubs herself against my cock. She's going to have to wait. I'm not done with her yet.

I get lost in her drug-inducing kisses for a few moments longer before breaking away and taking soft bites along her jaw and neck. As I flick my tongue over her beating pulse and swipe it over her collarbone, Harper's hands clutch my ass. With me nestled between her legs, she pulls me closer and rocks against me. I know what she needs. It's what I need too. Yet there is so much more I want to explore. I want more than the quickie we had in the trailer.

For a second, I drop my head onto her shoulder, pulling in deep breaths to settle my raging arousal. Harper groans with frustration. "Patience, honey. We'll get there." I'll die if we don't.

I suck her nipple into my mouth. "Oh yes...Finn," she moans. Her back arches off the sofa, and her fingers dig deep into my shoulders. I dot kisses across her breasts, swirling my tongue over her nipples. I can feel her body jerking with every suck.

My exploration of her body continues south with open-mouth kisses over her flat stomach. I take bites of her hips as I position myself further down the sofa. I tug her panties down her legs, toss them aside, and prop Harper's legs toward her chest and spread her thighs apart. I tilt my head to watch her as my mouth closes over her sex. Her heavy-lidded eyes flutter closed, and she bites her bottom lip. My tongue strokes through her folds from top to bottom and back up to circle around her clit.

"Finn," she gasps my name. "Finn, I need...want..."

"Yeah, honey. I know." I know exactly what she wants. To be fucked. I'm just not ready to give it to her yet.

Sliding a finger inside her, I thrust in and out at a fast pace as my thumb puts pressure on her swollen clit. Her head swings from side to side as she bucks under my hand. While I'm finger-fucking her with one hand, my other one slides over her belly to her breasts, squeezing them and twirling her nipples between my fingers. Her body trembles. I'm not sure how much more she can take. Removing my finger, I give her sex one last lick and suck and position myself above her.

"You were always so good at that." Her husky voice is the stuff from fantasies. She caresses her hand between our bodies, clasping my erection in a tight grip, and strokes. My cock throbs like hell, ready to explode.

"And you were always good at handling my cock," I say. With a hard thrust, I pump into her hand. "I can't hold back much longer. I need to be inside of you. Now!" My low, gravelly voice is almost unrecognizable.

"Please...don't hold back," she begs.

As I position myself between her thighs, a sudden thought shoots through my mind. I can't believe I nearly forgot a condom. I *never* forget protection. Only with Harper could I forget something so important. "We need a condom. I have one in my wallet." Which is in the pocket of my pants, which I tossed along with the rest of our clothing. I can't stand the thought of breaking away from Harper right now.

"I'm on the pill. It helps keep my cycle regular," she says.

I've never not used a condom since we broke up. Damn, I want to feel her without restrictions. "I'm clean. I get tested regularly, and I've always used a condom. Are you okay with that?" I need to be certain.

Nodding her permission, she guides me to her entrance. I pause over her, our gazes locking for a beat. Dipping my head, I claim her lips as I thrust inside her, catching her gasp in my mouth.

Harper is tight and wet. It takes all my willpower to not pump like a sixteen-year-old boy and finish the job in two point three seconds. Buried to the hilt, I need a moment to catch my breath. "You feel so fucking good," I groan against her lips.

Wrapping her legs around my waist, she anchors me to her. She whispers in my ear, "Fuck me, Finn. I can't wait any longer." Her hips push up, encouraging me to move.

I start off slow, watching as Harper's eyes roll to the back of her head before she closes them. I give a satisfied smirk for putting that expression on her face. Moving onto my elbows, I pull in and out, picking up speed. Then I grind my pelvis against her in slow, circular motions before thrusting in and out again at a brisker pace.

"Yes...Finn." She mumbles words I can't understand against my neck. I'm guessing it's something good, because she's bucking against me like she's riding a bronco.

Resting my forehead on Harper's brow, I say through gritted teeth, "I'm almost there. Please fucking tell me you're almost there too. I don't know how much longer I can hold on."

"I'm almost there," she pants.

Thank God!

I pound into her harder and faster. She digs her fingers into my ass, meeting me with every thrust. I grasp a breast, giving it a squeeze as my tongue flicks over her nipple. Then I travel between our joined bodies, pressing my thumb over her clit.

"Oh God!" she cries. Her hands skim over her breasts, along her stomach to meet my hands, joining in helping me with what she needs.

Holy fuck! That's sexy. Her eyes squeeze shut. Her body trembles. The pressure is building. I press firmer on her clit. Crying out, her hips lift under me as an orgasm rips through her. I plunge faster, deeper, without finesse. Just wanting to reach the end goal. I don't have to wait long. Tossing my head back, my mouth drops open as an orgasm explodes through me as I spill myself into Harper.

I fall onto my elbows and drop my head onto her shoulder. Once the trembling and twitching subsides, I roll onto my side, pulling Harper along with me. It feels so natural having her in my arms. Like we've never spent time apart. Except, we have. For a moment I'd forgotten why. By the satisfied smile on Harper's face, I'd say she'd forgotten too.

Isn't that exactly what we wanted?

Chapter Twenty

HARPER

Finn's body stiffens next to me. I feel the last tendril of desire and warmth slither away. Sex in the trailer had been more urgent, like our bodies were starved for each other. This time, it felt more like healing. Our joining something deeper and more personal. Maybe I was the only one who felt that way. With Finn lying as stiff as a log next to me, it's obvious that's not the case for him. He pulls away from me and swings his legs over the side of the sofa. I wiggle my skirt down, pick up my shirt from the floor, not worrying about the bra and panties, and hastily button it up. Finn sits with his elbows on his knees, staring at the floor.

"Are you regretting what we did?" I ask with dread. It will slice through me if things between us haven't changed. If he once again looks at me with hatred in his eyes.

Rising from the sofa, he plucks his boxer briefs from the floor and tugs them on. Next, he slides his legs into his pants. With a long, hard stare, he says, "No. I don't regret what we did." He links his fingers and puts his hands behind his head. "What I am is fucking confused. I've spent the last nine years hating what you did to me. I know now there was more to it, but..." His arms fall to his sides. "It's going to take time to get my head around it. If you want something more..." He waves a hand between us. "...to pick up where we left off—"

"No," I say, stopping him. I drop my head and stare at my hands sitting in my lap. Even though I want to be with him, never stopped loving him, too much has happened. We've made a breakthrough in our relationship tonight, yet I can't ask for more. "I don't expect us to continue like nothing has happened. That things will be the same." I lift my head and stare at him with pleading eyes. "I do hope that we can be friends." As hard as that will be to have him so close and yet not have him in all the ways I want...well, it's better than not having him in my life at all. "*Can* we be friends?"

Finn blows out a long breath. "Yeah, we can be friends." He reaches out his hand for me to take. I rise and grab hold, thinking he wants to shake on it, but he pulls me into a hug. The strength of his arms around me almost has me in tears. For what we lost. For what I'll never have again. For a future that isn't how I imagined.

The hug goes a little longer than a friendship hug should probably last, and his hands slide close to my ass. I clear my throat and say, "Arrh... Do friends hug like this?"

Finn pulls back but doesn't let me go. "I don't know. I've never had a friend who's a woman before."

"Never?" I chuckle with surprise.

He grins. Oh, that smile melts my bones. "You're my first."

"I seem to remember I was your first for a lot of things."

"Oh yeah? Like what?" I know he's pretending to not remember. He knows damn well what our firsts were.

I pull an arm free to tap a finger to my chin. "Hmmm. Let's see. I was the first girl you sat next to in kindergarten. The first girl you let play dodge ball with you."

When I pause and don't continue, he quirks an eyebrow. "Is that all?"

I shake my head. Of course, he's going to make me spell it all out. "The first girl and *only* girl you picked up to show off your new car to."

"The car was a guaranteed way to get into your pants." He grins.

I choke on a laugh. "Well, that brings us to the first girl you kissed." I tap a finger on my chest. "Me. And I was the first girl you had sex with." But I won't be the last. A tight, fist-sized knot forms in my chest.

"Ahh, sex in my new Porsche was outstanding." He chuckles.

"Not exactly how I remember it. The backseat was cramped. I had a seatbelt buckle digging into my butt, and we nearly got caught by the police. Not how I planned *my* first time." I try frowning my displeasure at remembering the past, but I can't hold back a smile.

"If I remember correctly, I offered to take you to a hotel. You were so scared that someone would spot us and call your parents."

God, I miss this—being in his arms, exchanging playful banter. "We did have some fun."

"Yeah, we did." We stand holding each other, not rushing to let go. I'd give anything to have that time back.

Finally, Finn pulls away, breaking the moment. Picking up his shirt from the floor, he shrugs into it. As he puts himself together, I find my panties and shimmy them on. I don't bother about the bra; I tuck it into the pocket of my skirt.

"I better get you home," he says with his back toward me. I don't know what he's thinking, feeling.

I slide my feet into my shoes. "That's okay. I'll take the subway."

"It's too late."

"My apartment isn't far from the station. I'll be fine."

"Grab your things and I'll meet you at the elevator." There's no point in arguing. He'll only keep on insisting. Catching the subway this late isn't appealing anyway.

"I'll get my bag." I dash from the room.

We make our way to the parking garage and into Finn's car. "Still into Porsches I see?"

He shrugs with a grin. "I had a lot of great memories in one." Then a frown flickers over his face like he remembered that they weren't all good. Will that look ever go away? "Derek really took your parents' estate and left you nowhere to live?" he asks.

"Yes. He took everything. Even the cabin." It hurts my heart to know I'll never see that house by the lake again. All because my father couldn't stop his gambling addiction, which led to Derek getting the properties.

Finn's fingers grip around the steering wheel. "I'm sorry. We—*you* loved that cabin." He clears his throat. "Where am I taking you?"

I tell him and he punches the address into his GPS. I know *we* both loved that place. Like everything else, our times at the cabin are now just memories.

He pulls out of the garage and navigates through the busy streets. Finn puts the radio onto a rock station, and heavy guitar sounds fill the car. I guess he's done talking. There's a lot to process.

When we pull up to my red brick townhouse, Finn says nothing about the run-down building. To me, living in this apartment without Derek is better than thousands of mansions.

"Would you like to come in for a coffee?" I fiddle with the strap of my bag. When he hesitates, I add, "Just coffee. Nothing more. We're friends." I'm not ready for the night to end. Not when the hate from his eyes has gone.

"Sure." I'm so happy he seems to not want the night to end either.

We make our way inside the apartment and find Alyssa sitting on the sofa with her leg propped on the coffee table, a bag of ice covering her ankle. "Hey, Harper—oh..." She forms an O with her mouth when Finn steps out from behind me.

I try to communicate to her with my eyes and fierce expressions. Warning her not to say anything that might embarrass me. "Alyssa, this is Finn Alessi. Finn, this is my roommate and friend, Alyssa Martinez."

"Nice to meet you," Finn says.

"Likewise." She smiles brightly.

Before she can say anything else, I point to her leg. "What happened?"

"I rolled my ankle in class tonight. Nothing too serious. The ice should help."

"If you need anything, let me know." I turn to Finn. "Alyssa is an amazing dancer. She's been auditioning for Broadway."

"Impressive. Have you been in anything I might have seen?" he asks with genuine interest.

Alyssa pulls a face. "Nothing yet. The rejections suck."

"Hopefully, that will change for you."

Alyssa smiles. "Thanks." She turns her attention to me. "I'll leave and go to my room." She shuffles to the edge of the sofa, preparing to rise.

I hold out my hand to stop her. "No, don't move. You need to keep icing your ankle and stay off it as long as possible."

"That's okay, I can do this in my room." She gets to her feet and winces as she puts pressure on her ankle.

"Here, let me help you." Finn rushes to her, placing a supporting arm around her waist. "Where to?"

She points to her bedroom door. As they head that way, Alyssa turns her head over her shoulder, away from Finn. *He's hot!* she mouths.

I know! I mouth back with a grin.

While Finn is helping Alyssa to her room, I quickly get the coffee ready. When he steps back into the living room, I set the mugs on the coffee table, and we take a seat on the sofa.

"Alyssa seems nice," he says with a funny smirk.

"Oh God. What did she say to you?" I palm my forehead and groan. "Her brain-to-mouth filter doesn't work sometimes."

Finn chuckles. "Let's just say she has your best interest at heart."

I'll have to talk with Alyssa when Finn leaves. "I haven't known her long, but it's like we've been friends for years. I got lucky finding her. I'm glad she applied for the job at Alessi's for me."

"Me too."

I swing my head toward Finn. Sincerity shines from his eyes. "Really?" I ask.

"It's crazy, I know." He grins at me.

We pick up our coffee mugs and sip the brew in comfortable silence. When I finish, I put my mug on the table and turn to him. A question has been on my mind since I saw his leg. I rub the spot over his pants. "How did you get the scar?" There's so much I don't know about Finn. I want to catch up on everything I've missed.

Shifting in his seat, he places his mug next to mine. "Doing something stupid."

I frown. "What did you do?"

For a moment, he stares at the floor.

Maybe this is something he doesn't want to talk about. I shouldn't have brought it up. "I'm sorry. You don't have to tell me," I say.

He pulls in a deep breath. "That's okay. If you're being open about your past, I can too."

I avert my eyes away for a second. I hate that there's more to tell him. How can I? It will destroy his relationship with his father.

"The day of your wedding, I came to see you."

I snap my head up with a gasp. "You did? No one told me. Why did you come?"

"I wanted to talk to you. Change your mind. He was nearly as old as my father. There had to be a reason you married him." Finn rubs his forehead. "Your parents came to the door. They wouldn't let me inside. Told me you'd made your decision. You were the happiest you've ever been, and I needed to accept it. When I think back, they couldn't look me in the eye. They couldn't look me in the eye because they felt guilty for prostituting their daughter for money."

God, if I'd seen him that day, there was no way I could have gone through with the wedding, no matter the consequences. My throat clogs with emotion.

"I called out to you. I didn't even know if you were in the house. But I yelled and tried barging inside. Security guards at the door had to drag me away."

Tears slide down my cheeks, and I swipe them away. How could the people I thought loved me more than anything in the world have done something so horrendous—to their only child...to Finn? Just to get themselves out of trouble?

"After they kicked me off the property, I sped away in my car and wrapped it around a power pole. It was a miracle I survived the accident. I spent weeks in the hospital."

Feeling ashamed for what I caused and needing to comfort Finn, I place my head on his chest. Finn wraps his arms around me. I'm so grateful he doesn't reject me. "I'm so sorry for the pain I caused you. No one told me about the accident." If they had, there was no way they could have kept me from him.

Finn places a finger under my chin and tilts my face up. "It's in the past. Let's forget about it."

Hope springs into my chest. "Does this mean you've forgiven me?" He grows still. I stop breathing as I wait for his answer.

"I...I'm trying."

I exhale with regret. Of course it's not going to be so easy. He's spent years hating me. Years thinking the worst of me. He'd stopped loving me. Feelings can't come back with the snap of his fingers.

He must have sensed my disappointment, because he says, "We're friends, right? That's a good start. It's a lot to absorb. Give me time."

"Okay." I nod. But I don't have time. He'll be gone in a few weeks. His life will go on without me.

I'll be forgotten.

Chapter Twenty-One

FINN

My eyes pry open to the dim light of morning filtering through the thin curtains. I wince as I try to move. There's a crick in my neck, and a warm body lying on top of me. A little disoriented, my eyes scan the room. I'm in Harper's apartment, and she's the warm body lying on my chest.

We spent hours last night talking about our old lives and laughing at some of the shit we got up to. Not once did we mention anything after the breakup. We already covered what happened. No point hashing it up again. It's like we didn't want those memories tainting the good ones.

I wasn't planning on telling her about begging to see her at her house or about the accident. It was the lowest moment of my life. Once I started, something loosened in my chest. Like all the pent-up resentment I'd been clinging to was dissolving. Making me feel lighter...freer. She'd asked if I'd forgiven her. I wasn't lying when I said I needed time. Yet maybe I won't need as much time as I thought.

I don't remember falling asleep. I must admit, it feels good having her in my arms like this. Is this how friends behave? Probably not. This being 'friends' idea might be easier said than done. It's taking a herculean effort not to run my hands over her body and wake her up with a good-morning bang.

Harper stirs. Tilting her face up to me, she smiles. "Good morning." Her voice is husky from sleep and sexy as hell. Then her eyes widen. She looks down at my chest and back up at my face. "Why...how... We fell asleep! I'm sorry." She scrambles into a sitting position on the edge of the sofa.

"Don't be sorry. I'm not."

"You're not?"

"It's the best sleep I've had in years." It's true. Apart from a stiff neck, I haven't felt so relaxed. I stretch and sit up.

She glances at her watch. "Oh crap! I have to get ready for work. Help yourself to coffee while I get dressed." She shoots from the seat. I grab onto her wrist, stopping her from racing away.

"Don't rush. I can take you to work." My thumb brushes along the smooth skin of her wrist. *Or take you to bed.* Fuck, stop it. We're friends. That's it.

"Thanks for the offer, but I'll catch the subway."

"We're going to the same place. It makes sense I take you."

She pulls her wrist free and tucks her hair behind her ear. "No one can know we spent the night together."

I don't care what anyone thinks, but I ask, "Why?"

She pulls a face like I asked a dumb question. "I don't want anyone to know that I slept with the boss."

"We didn't have sex."

She rolls her eyes. "Not here, but we have. I don't want them talking about us."

I don't have the heart to tell her that Bianca probably already told half the office about our time in the trailer. With a shrug, I get to my feet. "There's nothing wrong with giving you a lift to work."

"I know…but—"

"Don't overthink it. If anyone says anything, I'll deal with them."

"You have to go home and change. I don't want to be late."

"I have clothes in the office. We can go straight to work."

She nibbles her bottom lip, thinking. "Okay, thanks. I won't be long." With that she dashes into the room.

I drop to the sofa, tilting my head on the back of the seat, and let out a long breath. Why do I always feel like I need to save the day for Harper? Why hasn't my protectiveness over her disappeared? How do I forget about how strong our bond was?

The answer comes quickly. I can't forget. Harper is unforgettable.

Chapter Twenty-Two

HARPER

My legs jerk up and down as I sit in the front seat of Finn's Porsche as we approach work. As we get closer to the building, I abruptly say, "Pull over!"

Finn's head swings toward me. "Why?" he asks before focusing his attention back on the road.

"Just pull over. I want to get out here." Far enough away from the Alessi building so no one sees me in Finn's car.

Finn twists in the seat, giving a quick glance over his shoulder. "There's nowhere to stop."

"Double-park. I don't care. I need to get out."

"Is this because you don't want to arrive at work together?"

I blow out a frustrated breath. Why isn't he stopping already? "Yes."

Finn pinches the bridge of his nose. "You're being ridiculous. But if you're so worried about it, from the garage we can take separate elevators to the office."

I bite the side of my cuticle. That could work. "Fine."

We pull into the parking garage. As we're getting out of the car, Hayden pulls up beside us. I drop my head. Crap! Will he know we've spent the night together? We haven't entered the office yet, and we're already getting busted.

"Good morning," Hayden says as he steps out of the car. His gaze travels over Finn and then me. When he looks back at Finn, he raises an eyebrow. I don't miss the hidden question in his expression. He's onto us.

"I thought Lily was sick and you were working from home today," Finn says, ignoring Hayden's surprise at seeing us together.

Walking to the elevators, Hayden shakes his head and rolls his eyes. "I found out she didn't want to go to school because her teacher, Mrs. Sharpe, is away at a conference for the day, and she hates the substitute teacher. Thought if she said she was sick, she'd get to stay home. It nearly worked until I found her dancing to Katy Perry in her room this morning. She didn't talk to me all the way to school." He pulls a frustrated face.

Finn laughs. I smile. I didn't know Hayden had a daughter. Is he married?

When the elevator doors open, Finn and Hayden step inside. I stay standing where I am. "Are you coming?" Hayden asks.

"She wants to take the next one. Doesn't want to arrive with her boss in case people talk." Finn gives me a cheeky grin.

The doors start to close, but Finn slaps a hand between them to keep them open.

"Do you have a problem arriving with two bosses? Give the team something to *really* talk about," Finn jokes.

I can see how ridiculous I'm being, and I step into the elevator and shuffle as far away from Finn as possible. I ignore the knowing mirth in his eyes.

I haven't seen Hayden in years, and I wonder what he thinks of me working at Alessi's and being around Finn. Is there hostility? I can't imagine he'd like me back in his brother's life after what I put him through. How much has Finn told him? God, I hope not everything.

After a moment of uncomfortable silence, I ask, "How old is your daughter?"

When he doesn't answer right away, I assume he's ignoring me. Embarrassment pinches my cheeks. Then to my relief, he says, "She's six going on sixteen." Even though moments ago he sounded frustrated at her antics, I can see the love and pride for her shining from his eyes.

"Do you have any more children?" There's so much about the Alessis I don't know. They'd all gone on with their lives while mine felt stagnant.

He shakes his head. "No."

He's not exactly chatty. Although I don't blame his wariness toward me. The doors ping open before I can ask any more questions.

"I need to see you in my office when you get the chance," Hayden says to Finn. "See you around, Harper."

I watch him amble up the hallway into his office. Our exchange was brief, but I can tell there's no fuzzy, warm feelings toward me. Why would there be? I'd caused a ton of trouble.

"Do you think he knows we spent the night together?" I link my fingers.

"Absolutely," Finn answers.

I palm my forehead. "Oh God. That's exactly what I want to avoid."

Finn rubs a finger against my jaw. "Hey, don't worry. He won't say anything."

"Finn!" Bianca snaps behind me.

Finn snatches his hand away. I take two gigantic steps back from Finn. Crap! That's all I need. Bianca witnessing Finn showing me a moment of affection. Why does Bianca always have the habit of sneaking up behind me?

With wide, shocked eyes, Bianca scans Finn from head to toe. "Is that the same suit you were wearing yesterday?" Her gaze flicks over to me. I know the second Bianca connects the dots. Her eyebrows shoot into her hairline.

"Excuse me, I'm going to start work." I scurry to my desk, throwing my bag in the drawer. Before I have time to breathe, Bianca is standing in front of me, giving me the deadliest look.

"What do you think you're doing?" Bianca says with a sneer, crossing her arms over her chest.

"Umm...getting ready for work?" But I know she's referring to what she witnessed with Finn. The reason I didn't want to arrive together. If he had just let me get out of the car and walk, I wouldn't be having this conversation right now.

"Don't play dumb. What are you doing with Finn? Do you think sleeping with him is going to help you climb the ladder around here? Or better yet, snag another rich husband?"

I gasp. How did she know about Derek?

"I know your wealthy husband died, leaving you nothing." Bianca smirks.

"How did you—"

"I'm friends with one of his many mistresses. She was happy to fill me in on your pathetic life. I've been Finn's assistant for years, and I know what he wants. He only fucks women. It's never serious. No attachment. So don't get your hopes up."

My body is shaking. I'm not sure if it's because Bianca knows about my life or her warning me about Finn. Probably a combination of both. "I'm here to work. Nothing more. What I do in my private life is none of your business." I'm surprised to hear my voice sounding firm and not wavering like my insides feel.

Bianca stiffens. "I'm giving you a friendly warning." There is nothing 'friendly' in Bianca's twisted smile.

"What have you got for me to do today?" I want to focus on work, so I don't have to think about Bianca's cutting words.

"Check your email." With that, Bianca saunters away from my desk.

I blow out a long breath and sink onto the chair. Propping my elbows on the desk, I drop my head in my hands.

Bianca has never been easy to work with. Now that she suspects something is going on between Finn and I, I dread what the day will bring.

Chapter Twenty-Three

FINN

I BARELY STEP INTO Hayden's office when he shoots his question. "Are you and Harper back on?"

Pulling out a chair, I sit opposite Hayden at his desk. I hook an ankle over my knee. "No, we are not 'back on'."

"You spent the night together." Hayden points at my suit I haven't changed out of yet. I'd come straight to Hayden's office before mine. I knew this conversation was coming. Better to get it over with before I start my day.

"I could have picked up Harper on her way to work," I say.

"What's going on?" Hayden doesn't buy my bullshit.

"Nothing's going on. We've decided to be friends." My foot jiggles on top of my knee. Asking her to be friends is something I never thought I'd do in this lifetime. Will it be that simple? Or have we already complicated it with sex?

"You're sleeping with her." It isn't a question. "What the fuck, man? After everything she's done to you. I watched you lying in a hospital bed, praying you'd wake up. All because Harper fucked you over."

The anguish on Hayden's face is hard to watch. "You're the one who told me I should talk to her. To get closure or some shit."

"Yeah, *talk*. Not fuck. Have you forgotten how she tossed you aside like garbage? She broke you, and I don't mean physically."

"I haven't forgotten. I know what I'm doing." Do I? Whenever I'm with Harper, I have *no idea* what I'm doing. Maybe Hayden's right to be concerned. I don't think clearly when I'm with her.

Hayden leans back in his chair. "Really? She's been back in your life for five minutes and you're already looking at her like a lovesick puppy."

My back stiffens. "You're making me sound like a pussy."

"Pussy-whipped, maybe. You hated her. What's changed?"

I should tear Hayden down for the 'pussy-whipped' comment, but I ignore it for now. "She told me why she married Derek." What he did to her makes me sick to my stomach.

When I don't say any more, Hayden waves his hand for me to continue. "And…why did she marry Derek?"

I rub the back of my neck. "Derek was blackmailing her."

"What the hell?" Hayden exclaims.

"She was protecting her father…me." It still irritates me that she didn't come to me for help. We could have worked it out together.

Hayden plants his elbows on the desk. "What are you talking about?"

I give Hayden a quick rundown of the conversation I had with Harper about getting her father out of his gambling debt and protecting our company.

Rubbing his chin, Hayden says, "Shit. That's incredible! So after she spilled her secrets, you kissed and made up."

I scrub my palms over my thighs. "Things are...better. We've decided to be friends."

"I'd say spending the night together is a little more than 'friends'. Do you want something more?"

I shake my head. "No. Too much has happened. I know it wasn't her fault but..." I trail off. I have a sinking feeling something is missing from the story. Something Harper has left out. Unless I'm over-analyzing things and trying to find reasons not to trust her again. Once trust is lost, it's hard to get back, no matter the circumstances.

"But...what? You've been madly in love with her since the day you met. I never believed you ever stopped."

I jerk back. "That's not true. I stopped loving her when she married Derek." Or I tried convincing myself of that. I'd buried any feelings for her deep down, locking them up tight. If the chains were to break, I still wouldn't let my heart free. I can't go through that kind of trauma again.

Hayden throws me a disbelieving look. "I'm not sure how being friends is going to work. Just be careful."

I leave Hayden's office and head to mine. I pass Harper on the way, standing with her back toward me at the copy machine. Stopping, I take her in, Hayden's caution to 'just be careful' ringing in my ears. She grabs the copies from the machine, and she turns. When she sees me, she gives me a shy smile. All caution gets blown in the wind. Our gazes lock. My heart pounds. With her looking at me like that, I want to pull her into my arms and forget about everything and never let her go.

Someone up ahead calls my name. I shake myself from my thoughts, smile back, and hurry away.

I've finished work for the day, and I pull out of the parking garage. Heavy raindrops splatter the windshield, and I flick my wipers on. Standing in front of the building, sheltering from the rain, is Harper. I didn't see her when I left. God knows I searched for her. I've been watching her all day. Asking her to bring me multiple cups of coffee. Getting her to photocopy things I don't need. Anything to have her near.

I'm now buzzed on caffeine and probably won't be able to sleep for days. I'm so drawn to her it's fucking ridiculous. I'm not that naive twenty-year-old anymore. I don't obsess over women. Or so I thought. Soon I'll be back in London. Back to my old life. I'll focus on work; I won't have time to think about Harper.

Pulling over to the side of the road, I stop in a no-parking zone to get as close as I can to Harper. Sliding down the window, I call her name. She turns toward me. As soon as she spots me, her face lights up with a smile. A smile that sucker punches me in the chest, leaving me gasping for air. I can't get enough of her.

"Jump in. I'll take you home," I call out through the window.

Her hand slides up and down the strap of her bag. "That's okay, thanks. I'll wait for the rain to ease then make my way to the subway."

I tilt my head up to the sky. The dark clouds are low and heavy. "Looks like the rain is set in for a while. Come on, get in."

Lifting her face toward the sky to judge for herself, I can see her dubious expression. "I think it will stop soon."

Stubborn woman. "We can grab something to eat on the way."

A hand covers her stomach. Yep, she's hungry. If she loves food as much as I remember, I bet she won't turn it down. "Okay, thanks."

Bingo! I wasn't wrong. Maybe I still know her after all.

She rushes toward the car and jumps into the passenger side. She runs her fingers through her hair and shakes out the droplets clinging to the silky strands. A soft scent of apples from her shampoo and rain fills the car.

"Thanks for the ride," she says as she buckles her seatbelt.

"No problem. Where would you like to eat?" I ask as I pull out onto the busy street.

She shrugs. "Anywhere is fine with me."

I think for a moment. Where did she like to eat? Then it hits me. I know just the place. "Are you in a rush to go home?"

"No. Why?"

"You'll see."

Her eyebrows lift with curiosity, but she doesn't ask questions. Instead, she settles back into the leather seats. Trusting me. That gives me the warm fucking fuzzies. Okay, she's only trusting me with dinner. Not saving her life. It still means a lot though.

During the drive, I catch her up on the things I'd been doing over the years. She was curious about my work and living in London. I wanted to know about her life too, yet any time I asked her about it, she closed up. Telling me there wasn't much to tell because Derek had kept her from doing anything she loved. My fingers grip around the steering wheel. Anytime that bastard's name is mentioned I want to punch something. Knowing what I know now, he's lucky he's dead.

Finally, we arrive at our destination. Harper peers out of the passenger side window at Madison Square Garden. She swings her head toward me, her eyes wide with surprise. "What are we doing here?"

"Going to see the New York Rangers smash Tampa Bay Lightning."

"Really?" She giggles with excitement.

"Yes." I drive to a nearby parking garage. The rain has stopped, and we walk to the arena.

Harper tugs at my arm. "I haven't been to a game in years! I can't believe I'm here."

A knife twists in my gut. She hasn't been to a game because her asshole husband wouldn't let her. I buy tickets—I have a box seat we could sit in that provides a gourmet banquet and the best wine and champagne, but I remember how much Harper loves being among the crowd. After we buy slices of pizza, popcorn, and beer, we make our way to our seats. As the teams warm up on the ice, Harper bounces on the chair like a child waiting to see Santa. It's so adorable.

Lights flash, music blares, and Harper is on the edge of her seat. When the New York Rangers skate onto the rink, she jumps to her feet and cheers, beer sloshing over the rim of her cup and onto her hand. She sucks the alcohol off her skin. The sight causes my balls to tighten. This was supposed to be an innocent night out. But just like that, I'm imagining her mouth sucking things on me.

I'm so relieved when the game starts, and I drag my attention to the ice. As the puck flies and hockey sticks clash, Harper is cheering them on. She screams along with the crowd when players get smashed against the Perspex glass and when fights start. I'm spending more time and having more fun watching Harper than I am watching the game. It's bringing me back to when we were young and carefree without a worry in the world. Just the two of us. Instead of the usual bitterness that comes with memories of Harper, joy fills me. I like this feeling much better.

It's the first break and the teams skate off the rink. Harper flops down on her chair with a sigh. "I'd forgotten how intense ice hockey is." She places a hand over her heart. "I can't take the anxiety."

I laugh. "Having a good time?"

Her face brightens. "Yes! Thank you so much. I miss this."

Does she mean she misses watching ice hockey or she misses watching it together? Laughter and cheering breaks into my thoughts, and I turn toward the screens suspended high above the rink. People in the crowd are on kiss cam. We sit watching the awkward and funny moments before couples kiss.

Then the camera spans to Harper and me. Like all the other awkward couples, we laugh uncomfortably and fidget in our seats. Here's my chance to do what I've wanted to do all evening—although, maybe not with a crowd of thousands cheering us on. I turn in my seat, cup Harper's face in my hands, and just before our lips touch, she lets out a gasp of surprise as she closes her eyes to receive it.

As soon as our mouths meet, I don't want to stop. My tongue skims her lips, wanting her to open to me. At the rowdy cheer from the crowd, Harper pulls away and gives a shy smile. Crap, even with an arena filled with people, Harper can make me forget where I am. If I think I can get this woman out of my system, I'm fucking lying to myself.

What the hell am I supposed to do about this? I can't go back to what we had...can I? No, we can never get that time back. Nor do I want to. Even though our past is filled with unforgettable moments, they're tainted. I know now it wasn't completely Harper's fault. But things just can't be the same. What about our future? I sit lost with thoughts as the game continues.

Harper's enthusiasm grows with each goal until she cheers with triumph as the New York Rangers win the game.

Throwing her arms around my neck, she hugs me. "This has been amazing! Thank you so much for taking me. I loved watching ice hockey again."

And I loved watching you. I keep those words to myself. "I'm glad you had fun."

On the drive home, Harper drifts off to sleep. I'm glad I don't have to fill the ride with chatter. Who knows what I'd say to her. Would I spill how I feel about her? I'm not sure I even know...or I'm not ready to admit what I'm feeling.

At her apartment, I gently shake her awake. She blinks with sleepy surprise at her surroundings. "I fell asleep."

I smile. "Yes, and you still snore."

She springs awake. "I do not!"

I chuckle. "Yeah, you do."

Harper scrubs her fingers over her eyes. "That's embarrassing." She unbuckles her seatbelt, picks her bag off the floor, and hooks the strap over her shoulder. Instead of getting out of the car, she turns to face me. "I had a great night tonight. Thank you."

"I'm glad." I want to tell her we should do it again. Is that wise? When I need to figure out what's going on in my head—heart.

"Would you like to come inside for coffee?"

Is this offer like the night before? Coffee as 'just friends'? Somehow the offer feels different. Do I want it to be more? Fuck yes! But Harper isn't a woman I can keep having sex with and have no attachments. "It's getting late. I should head home."

"Sure...yes...of course." She opens the door. "Thanks again. Goodnight."

"Goodnight."

She gets out of the car. Did I see a glimmer of disappointment in her eyes? Does she want me to come inside? It takes all my willpower to watch her enter the building and not follow her. If I go inside, we'll end up in bed. I know it. As much as I want her, I need time to sort things out. Being friends is more complicated than I thought.

Chapter Twenty-Four

HARPER

I walk into the dark apartment. Alyssa must be asleep already. I know she isn't working tonight at the club, because she has an early class in the morning and likes to get her eight hours sleep when she can. In my bedroom, I kick off my shoes, strip out of my skirt and blouse, and flop down on my bed.

Tonight was wonderful. The best night I have had in years. Finn couldn't have picked a better place to take me. Greasy pizza and cold beer while watching ice hockey is my vibe. It felt like my skin was tearing off my body, and the old me was breaking free. The old me who didn't have to watch what I said and could behave any way I wanted. I miss her. I like her. I like her with Finn. The moment he kissed me on the kiss cam, even though it wasn't a private moment, felt like home. This is us. Fun. Happiness. Love. All rolled into one.

Heading into the bathroom to shower, I turn the water on and wait until it's warm. As soon as it reaches the temperature I want, I dash under the spray and quickly wash myself before the hot water runs out. I wanted Finn to come into the apartment. After the way he kissed me, I thought he would. I hoped he wanted me like I wanted him. It looks like he's sticking to being friends.

I step out of the shower and wrap myself in a towel, brush my teeth, and make my way back to my bedroom. Dressing into my pajamas, I slide under the covers of my bed.

Is there a chance we can be more than friends? You don't kiss your friend the way Finn kissed me. Or am I holding onto hope?

The next day, I arrive at work. Tamara, with a steaming cup of coffee in her hand, greets me as she passes me in the hallway. "Morning!" she sings and blows into her mug.

"Good morning." I smile. Her outfit today is a tight, red pencil skirt that reaches her calves and a black, off-the-shoulder top. The glasses perched on top of her head are yellow.

"What are you doing for lunch today? Want to try the new sushi restaurant across the street?" she says before sipping her coffee.

I search down the hallway to Finn's office. Is he here yet?

"Sure, sounds great," I say absentmindedly. I look at Bianca's office. The door is closed. Is Finn inside?

"Finn's not here," Tamara says like she can read my mind.

Shaking my head, I say, "I wasn't... I'm not..." Tamara gives me a knowing smirk. I sigh, and my shoulders slump. "Okay, I was looking for Finn."

Tamara turns her head from side to side to look around, latches onto my arm, and drags me into her office, closing the door behind us. "Has something happened between the two of you? I've noticed these past couple of days he isn't shooting heat-seeking missiles at you from his eyes."

My heart warms. I'm so grateful that Finn doesn't hate me anymore. "I explained things, and he finally listened. He wants to be friends."

The phone rings on Tamara's desk. "That's wonderful. I want to hear more about this. I'll see you at lunch, yes?"

"Sure."

She picks up the phone, and I give her a wave goodbye as I leave her office. I make my way to my desk, again searching the area for any signs of Finn. We might be friends, but it doesn't stop my heart from fluttering whenever I think of him, and that turns into a stampede of elephants whenever I see him. I need to calm down. If what we have isn't moving beyond friendship, I have to stop feeling this way.

Bianca sails past my office and drops a stack of fabric samples on my desk. "These need to be categorized and taken to the fabric department." *Good morning to you too!* She saunters away, pauses, then spins back around. "By the way, Finn will be in meetings most of the day. You are under no circumstances to disturb him." She pins me with a fierce expression.

"He likes me to make him coffee," I say.

"I'll take care of it." She spins on her heels and heads to the boardroom. That must be where Finn will be when he arrives.

For the rest of the day, Bianca has me stuck in the fabric room, sorting out swatches and reorganizing. It wouldn't surprise me if she's giving me this job to keep me away from Finn. I meet Tamara for lunch and give her an abbreviated version of what's going on between Finn and me. Whether she knows I left a monumental part out of the story, she doesn't let on.

Back at work, I see Finn. But he's so focused on what he's reading in a folder as he walks from his office to the boardroom, he doesn't notice me. Here I am scanning the office every time I hear a door open, footsteps, and chatter, just to get a glimpse of Finn, and he doesn't give a glance at my direction at all. Isn't that what I want? To give my colleagues no reason to gossip about us?

At the end of the day, I find myself once again waiting for the rain to ease so I can make a run for it to the subway. Why didn't I remember to bring an umbrella? As I'm waiting, a familiar car pulls up in front of me and the window slides down. It's Finn.

He flashes me his killer smile. "Waiting for me?"

Oh no! Would he think I'm here on purpose? "No...I'm...the rain..."

He chuckles. "I'm joking. Jump in."

This time I don't hesitate. I've been wanting to see Finn all day. If I can get a few minutes alone with him now, I'll take it.

Once I'm in the passenger seat, he pulls out onto the road. "Are you hungry?"

Lately, I'm always hungry. Hungry for food. Hungry for my new life. Hungry for Finn. It's like my freedom has awakened my appetite for everything. "I can eat."

He flicks me a glance. The light of the dashboard illuminates his beautiful face. "Any requests?"

I nibble my bottom lip. "I've had a massive craving lately for something I haven't had in years."

"Oh yeah? What is it?"

"I don't think you're going to like it."

He slows down and stops at a red light and turns to face me. "Whatever you want is fine with me."

"Okay...I'd love McDonald's."

Finn's eyes widen. "McDonald's? Really?"

I nod and giggle at his shocked expression.

"I can take you anywhere. Are you sure?" The light changes to green, and he navigates through the traffic.

"Yes."

He chuckles. "Okay."

When he finds the nearest McDonald's, he pulls into a parking spot on the side of the road. The rain has eased, and we dash the short distance to the restaurant. After ordering we take our meals to a table.

"I still can't believe this is where you want to eat." He shakes his head with disbelief.

"Do you think the burgers and fries taste the same in every country?" I ask as I pop a fry into my mouth.

Finn frowns at his burger. "I don't know, and I don't care."

I giggle at his disgruntled expression. "It's delicious. Here..." I reach over the table and hold out a fry for him to take. "Try it."

Instead of plucking it out of my hand with his fingers, he uses his mouth. His lips cover my fingers, giving a little suck as he draws his head back. When I go to pull my hand away, he clasps my wrist, brings my hand to his mouth, and licks my fingers. "Delicious."

The tugging of his mouth pulls through my stomach, and heat pools between my legs. I squirm in my seat. Clearing my throat, I say, "See, I told you it's good. Another great way to eat your burger and fries is to lift the lid of the bun and layer the patty with fries." I go on to demonstrate. I have to think about something other than Finn's mouth and tongue. We're in a restaurant with young families. We must keep it PG.

After we finish our meals, Finn relaxes back in his chair. "That was really good."

I point a finger at him and playfully say, "See! I told you. You've gotten too fancy in your old age Mr. Hotshot Fashion Mogul."

He chuckles at my comment. Then his smile drops. "You were going to be a hotshot fashion mogul too. Ever think you'll go back to school? I remember you loved it."

Crumbling my napkin, I toss it in the empty burger box. "Sometimes. Yes, I loved it. Maybe one day I'll look into it.

So much has happened these past few weeks. I need to get my head around one thing at a time." I'd called Tamara's sister, the therapist, and it's something we've discussed. I need to focus on getting back on my feet, not trying to bombard myself with too much at once. I've only had one session with her, and the tools she has given me have already helped.

"Well, if you ever need any help with getting started again, let me know."

In just a few days, we have come so far. Finn's gone from hating me to wanting to help me. I can't ask for a better outcome. Well, I could. We could be romantically involved again, but I'll take whatever I can get. Having his friendship back means the world to me.

After dinner, Finn takes me home and parks outside of my apartment. Once again, we sit in the dark interior. "Would you like to come in for a coffee?" I ask.

His head drops back on the seat's headrest. It's like I've asked him the most difficult question in the world. From the way his face is screwed up with indecision, I'd say he's struggling with an answer. I hold my breath in anticipation. Will he say yes?

Finally, he says, "I should go." Finn clears his throat. "I'll see you tomorrow at work."

I let out a disappointed exhale. I keep hoping for something that will never happen. The smile on my face stiffens. "Okay. Thanks for dinner and the ride. See you tomorrow." I fumble with the doorhandle and rush from the car and into the apartment.

God, what was I thinking? He's told me we can only be friends. Why won't I listen? I need to stop living in fantasy-land and believe him. But when he kissed me—even for a silly kiss cam—I felt it down to my toes. The way he licked my fingers and looked at me with his smoldering gaze, my stomach summersaulted. Friends don't do stuff like that, do they? Kicking off my shoes, I sit on the edge of the bed. I'm reading too much into it. Confusing our past with our present.

Walking into the bathroom, I go through my night-time routine. Alyssa is working, so I won't see her until the morning. So when I finish taking a shower, I walk into the kitchenette wearing only a towel.

At the knock on the door, I pause, holding the glass of water I was taking to my room. Maybe Alyssa forgot her key? I look at the clock on the wall. No, she's not due home for another two hours. Someone knocks again.

I place the glass on the counter, tighten the towel around me, and pad to the door. "Who is it?"

"It's me," a deep voice answers. One I'd recognize anywhere.

I open the door. My heart trips.

Finn.

Chapter Twenty-Five

FINN

After watching Harper walk into the building, I sit in my car staring at the doorway, desperately wanting to follow her. When I'm with her, past hurt pales compared to the longing I have for her. I can't keep holding on to what happened. It was eating away at me. Little by little it was sucking the joy from everything. Slowly killing me.

During the last few days, Harper has made me feel alive again. This woman who yells at ice hockey games and eats McDonald's like it's the best meal she's ever had, consumes my body and soul. My heart, which was once cold and dead in my chest, has been zapped back to life. I want to take what I want, and fuck all the reasons that have held me back.

I want Harper.

Getting out of the car, I walk to her door. My hand hesitates for a second before I knock. Was her invitation for coffee really just that, or was she asking for more? After I insisted we could only be friends, maybe I read her wrong? No. She looked disappointed when I declined.

Fuck! When have I ever been so nervous about knocking on a woman's door? It's because it's Harper's door. If I do this, there's no turning back. There's no 'don't call me, I'll call you'. This isn't a quick fuck to pass the time. Or a woman to bury myself in to help me forget about Harper. This *is* Harper. She isn't just any woman.

I knock, my heart hammering. When she opens the door, the air in my lungs gets sucked from my body. She's standing in the doorway with a pale blue towel wrapped around her. Damp hair sits on top of her head in a messy bun. I almost swallow my tongue. She's fucking the sexiest woman I have ever seen. Traveling my gaze over her, I drink her in. Too caught up in her beauty to move or say anything.

"Finn. Is everything okay?" Harper asks as she tightens the towel across her chest.

Before I step inside, I say, "I want to kiss you. Will you let me?"

Her eyes widen with surprise. "You want to kiss me?"

I nod. "More than I fucking need to breathe."

A bright smile lights up her face, but she hasn't answered my question.

"I'm dying here. Will you let me kiss you?" My body is wound up so tight, I can barely stand here a moment longer.

She answers by throwing her arms around my neck and pulling me to her. Our lips collide. I wrap my arms around her waist and pick her up. I take two steps into the apartment, she hooks her legs over my hips, and I kick the door closed, all without breaking our connection. We kiss until I can barely breathe. What a way to die!

I break away, sucking in deep breaths, to ask, "Where's your bedroom?"

She points her finger in the direction as she nibbles and licks my neck. In her room, I gently place her on the double bed. During our walk to her room, her towel fell off, and she is sprawled out in all her naked glory, staring up at me with fire blazing from her eyes.

"Do you want this? Not just the sex. This is more than sex now. Do you want...us? Trying to be friends is bullshit." I fought it from the moment I touched her.

Her lip trembles, and her eyes glisten. Nodding, she whispers, "Yes. I want this. I want *us*."

My chest rises and falls. I join her on the bed and thread my fingers in her hair, kissing her long and deep. Pouring my heart into her. Trying to say the things I can't yet say out loud. These past few days haven't been easy. One step at a time.

The kiss deepens, and her hands skim over my shoulders, down my back, clamping on my ass. Her body thrusts against mine.

"Not so fast, baby." Pulling away, I get to my feet and stand at the end of the bed.

She scowls at me. "What are you doing?"

"With you laying buck naked, you didn't think I wouldn't make the most of it, did you? I want to see every inch of you. Spread your legs."

Understanding flashes across her face. She props herself up onto her elbows. My mouth waters at the sight of her tits bouncing at the movement. "If I have to do something for you, you need to do something for me first."

I arch an eyebrow. "Oh really? What is it?"

"Take off your shirt."

I yank the shirt off and toss it on a stool in the corner of the room. The sooner I do as she says, the sooner I get my hands on her.

"Now it's your turn. Spread your legs," I demand.

With slow, torturous movements, she does as she's told.

"Good girl."

"Lose the pants," she insists.

I kick off my shoes, then slide my pants off. They too get tossed on the stool.

"Bend your knees and keep your legs spread," I instruct her.

Slowly, her legs rise, and her knees fall apart. My eyes zone to her pussy. It takes all my willpower not to dive onto the bed and lap her up.

Her chest is rising and falling. She's turned on just as much as I am. "Take off your underwear," she says.

Done.

It's my turn, I'm making it good. "Touch yourself."

With hooded eyes, her hands skim over her heaving breasts, massaging them for a moment and plucking at her nipples. I lock my knees before they give way and I collapse on the floor. She gives me a sexy smile as her hands caress her stomach and head lower, rubbing her fingers across her sex. I clench my jaw. It's taking all my effort not to join her on the bed to replace her hand with my mouth.

"Your turn to touch yourself," she says.

I do as I'm told and clutch my cock in my hand. Slowly stroking myself as I watch her fingers slide between her wet folds. Her tongue darts out to lick her bottom lip. Fuck me! She's so sexy.

"On your knees." My voice is deep and husky. "Take over."

She quirks an eyebrow. "That's two demands."

"Are you complaining, Ms. Madden?" I give her my stern I-don't-get-questioned voice I use at the office.

"Of course not, Mr. Alessi." Her lips twitch with a smile.

Shuffling onto her knees, she grabs hold of my cock, stroking me from root to tip. When she tightens her grip, my head drops forward and I thrust in her hand. Then she replaces her hand with her mouth, and my knees buckle as her tongue glides over my hard length. Her mouth opens wide to take me deep into her throat.

Fisting my hand into her hair, I thrust between her wet lips to keep up with her rhythm. "Fuck, Harper. This feels good."

She keeps sucking, licking, and squeezing until I feel the pressure of my release rising. As much as I'd like to come in her mouth, I need more of her. Stopping before I spill my load, I slightly nudge her shoulders, pushing her so she lands on her back. Crawling over, I hover above her. My erection branding hot on her inner thigh. Lifting her hips off the mattress, she encourages me to enter her. I don't give her what she wants. Not yet. I'm not ready for this to end.

"I haven't felt this horny since we were teenagers. What are you doing to me?" I may have slept with dozens of women, but no one has made me feel the way I do when I'm with Harper.

Harper giggles as she squirms under me. "I know what you mean."

My mouth covers her left breast, and her giggles turn into a long moan as I suck and nip at her soft skin and flick my tongue over the peaked nipple. I trail my lips to the other one, giving both sides equal attention. "Your tits have grown. I fucking love them."

With slow, open-mouth kisses, I leave them for something else I want my mouth on, and I make my way south. The flat of my tongue slides over her folds, and her body jerks. I pull my head back to make sure this is what she wants. But her fingers are already tangled in my hair, guiding me back. With pleasure, I lave her up.

Harper's back arches off the bed as she pants, "Oh, Finn...yes!"

I love how sensitive and responsive her body is. I could do this all day. Her hips lift higher as I fuck her with my tongue. Her body is pulsing. She needs more. I add a finger inside her and then another, thrusting slow and circling her clit with my thumb.

"Finn...this...is...too...much..." She's on the verge of coming. Her body is tightening, ready for release.

"Not so fast, baby. I'm not done." She half-moans, half-sobs. I love how I'm driving her crazy. Now she knows how I feel every time I look at her.

She tugs at my hair, pulling me up along her body. Nudging at my shoulders, she pushes me so I fall flat on my back. She swings her legs to straddle me. "I can't wait a moment longer. I need you inside me now!"

That was fucking hot. "Who am I to argue with a determined woman?"

She lifts slightly, clasps my cock, and slowly slides down, taking every inch of me until I'm buried to the hilt. We both suck in a gasp. Her head falls back. For a second I squeeze my eyes shut. She's wet and tight, and I don't know how much I can take. When I get myself under control, I grip her hips and urge her to rock against me. She doesn't need any encouragement; her body is in tune with mine, and our rhythms are in sync.

I snake a hand around her neck, pulling her down for a kiss. The urgency between us is building. I rise from my back to suck her nipples. Holding my head to her chest, she thrusts against me. My fingers trail down her spine and clasp at the curve of her ass. I urge her on to ride me harder and faster. Our sweaty bodies are slapping against each other. We're gasping, moaning. Words are mumbled. The urgency is building.

Harper's body quivers, she's nearly there. "Come on, baby!" My hand slides between our bodies, and I press her clit.

"Yes, Finn!" she cries as an orgasm shatters her.

I grip her hips and pound into her. I throw my head back and grit my teeth. Groaning long and low, my body jerks and bucks off the mattress until I have spilled everything I have in her. Harper collapses with sated satisfaction on my chest. With my heart pounding at a feverish speed, she can probably feel it against her cheek.

"That was amazing," she pants and fists a hand on my pec to rest her chin on it. With her eyes half-closed, she gives me a lazy, satisfied grin.

It was *fucking* amazing!

Her eyes lower and she gently plucks at the hairs on my chest. "Finn, when you said you wanted...us. What *exactly* did you mean?"

Placing a finger under her chin, I tilt her face up. "I want to put the past behind us. I want to start again. You are all I think about. All I've ever wanted. It's pointless trying to fight it."

A tear slides down her face. I brush it away with my thumb. "You are all I think about. All *I've* ever wanted," she repeats my words. "Can we really do this? Can *you* really forget the past?"

There's no other option. It's that or not have Harper in my life in every way I want her. "Yes."

Harper's face beams with a bright smile. "You've made me so happy. I never thought I'd ever feel this way again!" She slides her arms around my neck and kisses me deeply.

I never thought I'd feel this way either. I want her in my life. *Need* her. Even though I'm feeling euphoric at our rekindled connection, why is there a niggling voice in the back of my mind whispering to be careful?

Chapter Twenty-Six

HARPER

Early the next morning, I lay in the tangled sheets of the bed watching Finn dress in the wrinkled clothes strewn on the floor. His hair is tousled from the many times my fingers tugged at his dark locks. Before he buttons his shirt, I see a red mark on his collarbone. I did that. I smile with satisfaction.

"If you keep looking at me like that, I won't make it to my breakfast meeting. I'm already late because I have to go home and change. Who fucking cares?" He tugs the tie hanging from his shoulder and tosses it on the bed. "They can wait," he says as he crawls on top of me.

I stop him getting any further with my hand on his chest. "As much as I'd love to do what is obviously on your mind, I have to get ready for work too."

Dropping his head, he blows out a frustrated breath. "Let's call in sick and spend the day in bed."

The sheet covering my body slips down. Finn zeros in on my breasts. His tongue licks over my nipple. Biting my lip, I squeeze my eyes shut, enjoying the heat bursting through my body. I pull my mind out of the lust haze that's clouding it. "We can't. Well...*I* can't."

He travels to my other nipple and sucks it into his mouth, his tongue twirling around it. God, it's hard to concentrate while he's making my body hum.

"I'm your boss. I'm demanding you take the day off." His hand slides between our bodies and heads south. I know what he's aiming for.

Wet heat pools between my legs, but I can't let him continue or I'll never get to work on time. I clamp onto his wrist, stopping him from going any further. "Finn. Stop."

Finn pulls his hand away and drops his head on my shoulder. "We're picking this back up tonight." His hot breath fans my neck, sending goosebumps over my skin.

"Okay." Like I'd say no.

He finishes dressing, and I enjoy watching every movement. This man is mine. I want to scream with happiness! Not in a million years did I believe Finn would want me back. My heart wished for it, but it was only a distant dream. A dream that has come true. Now, I'm not rushing out to pick a wedding dress; I know we have a long way to go. But hearing him tell me he wants us were the best words I'd heard in years. We're heading in the right direction. Happiness wants to burst from my body.

After all the amazing orgasms Finn gave me until the early hours of the morning, my body is too languid to move right now. He bends over me and gives me a kiss that makes my toes curl. Making me rethink Finn's idea of calling in sick.

"See you at work after my meeting." He smiles.

All I'm able to do is give him a finger wave.

He chuckles, clearly knowing he's turned my body and mind into mush.

I don't have the luxury to lounge around all morning, and I drag myself from bed. After a quick shower, I dress and head into the living room to leave for work. Alyssa has her feet propped up on the coffee table with foam separators between her toes, painting her nails black.

"Do you ever wear any other color?" The black polish matches the black cargo pants and black crop top she's wearing. Add the chunky biker boots she favors, and she looks like she would be more comfortable on a motorcycle than on stage in pink tights and a tutu.

"Nope," she says, brushing on another coat. "So…your ex stayed the night. What's going on? Well, apart from the mind-blowing sex you were having."

My face heats. "You heard us?"

Alyssa blows at her toes. "I think the apartment block across the street heard you."

I slap my hands on my fiery face. "Oh God. How embarrassing!"

Alyssa waves the brush in the air. Small drops of black polish splatters on the already stained coffee table. "Don't worry. I fell asleep as soon as my head hit the pillow. I didn't hear much. I'm only teasing you."

I sag with relief. Although, I'm still horrified she heard even a second.

"Are you and Finn back together? The last time we spoke, he didn't want to have anything to do with you. Though you looked pretty happy together the other night when I hurt my ankle and he carried me like a superhero into my bedroom." Concern lines her face. "I hope he isn't using you." With Alyssa's late working hours and busy dance schedule, we keep missing each other lately, and I need to catch her up on the past couple of days.

"We've talked and spent some time together. He wants to be more than friends." My heart flutters. I still can't believe he's forgiven me.

"Really?" Alyssa doesn't look convinced. "He said that?"

"Yes. He wants to put the past behind us and move on."

Alyssa fans a magazine above her feet. "You believe him?"

"Yes. Is there a reason I shouldn't?"

"No. I'm just worried that it's all happening so quickly. Didn't you say he's going back to London soon? What happens then? Is he moving on with you only while he's here, then it's over when he goes back?"

I sink onto the arm of the sofa. "We haven't discussed that." Surely, when he said he wanted 'us' he meant wherever he is.

"I'd hate for you to fall back in love with him and then he leaves you in limbo. Oh crap..." Alyssa stops fanning her toes and drops the magazine on the table. "You already love him."

"I never stopped."

"Forget everything I said. I'm sure you'll work it out. I'm rooting for you. You deserve to be happy."

I love Finn. Always have. Once he loved me too. Now he's telling me he wants us to be together again, but he never said a word about love. Does Finn love me?

Only time will tell.

In the office, I'm busy reading over Bianca's numerous emails. I haven't spoken to her all morning, which I don't mind; I'd rather the silence then her snapping at me. I feel someone come up from behind me. The scent of woodsy cologne surrounds me, and I know exactly who is standing there. Finn places a hand on the back of the chair and leans down so our faces are at the same height. Scanning the room, I breathe a sigh of relief to see everyone busy on the phone or computer. Not paying us any attention.

"What can I do for you, Mr. Alessi?" I keep my tone formal. Anyone close by could be listening.

He points at the computer screen, pretending to show me something. In a low, deep voice, he says, "Come to my office."

I tap my finger on my chin like I'm taking in the 'work' he's showing me on the screen. I know exactly what he wants. "No."

Turning his head toward me, he cocks an eyebrow. "No?"

I push my chair away slightly, pick up a folder and hand it to him. Opening it, he scans the document inside. "Why not?"

"We're at work. Dozens of people come and go from your office or walk past it." Alyssa's comment about overhearing us last night comes to mind. That can't happen here. "It's not the time." Even if I wanted to follow him into his office, he has a meeting with another fashion house in ten minutes. Bianca told me to make coffee for it in one of her emails.

Finn snaps the folder shut with a huff and places it neatly on top of the pile of other folders. I touch it so it's slightly askew. I'm getting better at things being neat and in their place. Sometimes the habit of messing things up creeps back.

"Fine. Come to my office after work. I'm going to bend you over my desk and fuck you from behind. Be prepared." With that, he spins on his heels and strides into his office, closing the door behind him. My mouth drops open. I give another quick glance around the office. Thankfully, no one heard. Five o'clock can't come fast enough.

Ten minutes later, I'm in the boardroom getting coffee ready for the meeting, when Finn, Hayden, Lucas, Juliette, and Bianca walk in. Following behind them is a man I recognize. "Matteo?"

Matteo Blanchett turns to me and gives me a huge smile. Matteo is one of Derek's old friends. I use that word lightly, because Derek never had any real friends. I never knew why Matteo was involved with Derek; he'd expressed on multiple occasions he couldn't stand him. They must have had some business between them, or Derek was blackmailing him too. Whatever the reason, when I saw Matteo, he always treated me with kindness.

"Harper, it's so good to see you." He strides toward me and envelopes me in a warm hug. He pulls back but keeps his hands on my arms. In his late fifties, Matteo's auburn hair has silver streaks at his temples. His build is solid, a result of regular visits at the gym, and creases fan from his blue eyes as he smiles at me. "How have you been?"

Before I can answer, a throat clears behind me, and I break away. "How do you two know each other?" Finn glances at us, a frown creasing between his brows.

Matteo gives me another smile. "We saw each other often when she was married to Derek. She was the only reason I suffered through his boring dinner parties." Matteo chuckles.

Finn doesn't appear to find his comment amusing. He pins Matteo with a hard glare. Uncomfortable tension pinches the back of my neck.

Turning to me, Matteo says, "I'm sorry I missed Derek's funeral. I was out of the country. I wish I could have been there for you." He rubs a comforting hand along my arm.

Finn's glare grows more dangerous. I step away and ask, "Coffee anyone?"

Without waiting for anyone to answer, I rush to the coffee station, turning over cups. They shake in my hands and rattle on the saucers. When everyone is seated, I serve them. Thankfully, with no one getting scorching coffee spilled in their laps. After asking if anyone needed anything else, I excuse myself and make my way from the office.

Before I reach the door, Matteo calls my name. I turn to face him. "We'll have to meet for dinner soon and catch up."

I give a quick nod so I don't appear rude turning him down in front of everyone and hurry from the room.

Chapter Twenty-Seven

FINN

My fists clench on my lap under the table. Why the fuck is Harper so friendly with this piece of shit? Anyone who associates themselves with Derek can't be trusted.

Matteo Blanchett, of Blanchett Fashion House, has always rubbed me the wrong way. The only reason we're holding this meeting is because our father asked us to. Dad said Matteo might have something to offer. I've seen Matteo's work lately, and there's nothing I'm interested in.

As Matteo drones on and on about collaborating with a collection he believes will blow our competitors out of the water, all I can think about is whether Harper will meet Matteo for dinner. He's roughly the same age as Derek. Runs in similar social circles. Is he someone she'd be interested in? *No! Stop thinking of Harper that way. That's not her.* I told her I can let the past go.

"Well, what do you think? I'll have my head designer bring you samples, and we can build them from there with Juliette's input." Matteo looks at me and my brothers expectantly. Like he's come up with a brilliant idea.

I lean back in the chair, placing my forearms on the armrests. Steepling my fingers, I give a quick glance at Hayden, Lucas, and Juliette for their reaction, already knowing what's on their minds. The man has rocks in his head.

Hayden speaks up, asking questions regarding the financial side of things. I know he's only trying to be polite and not toss him out the door with a don't-bother-us-again boot to the ass.

Holding up my hand, I stop Matteo in the middle of his financial spiel. I'm not as polite as Hayden. "Juliette's designs on their own will blow our competitors out of the water. We don't need to collaborate." Without looking at Juliette for her reaction, I know she'll agree.

Matteo's mouth opens and closes in surprise before he says, "This is an amazing opportunity. Aren't you even going to discuss it? You'd be foolish not to agree."

Shrugging, I say, "We don't need to discuss it. Hayden, Lucas, Juliette, and I are anything but foolish. Our work is at the top of our industry. What would be foolish is if we collaborated with you." I sound harsher than I'd normally be. Blame it on the fact he had his hands on Harper.

Matteo sucks in an offended gasp. "If this is what you want, don't come crawling to me when Alessi's is no longer the talk in the fashion industry. You might be on top now, but it only takes one mistake to plummet to the bottom." Rising from the chair, Matteo straightens his jacket before marching from the room.

"What was that about—"

I cut Lucas off with a wave of a hand. I know he's wondering why I was being such a prick, but I don't have time to talk to him. Rushing from the boardroom, I need to see if Matteo speaks to Harper. He's standing at her desk, smiling down at her. She nods at something he's saying, rises, and gives him a quick hug before he turns to leave.

A burning sensation like something I've never felt before rushes through my veins. A mix of jealousy and anger battle it out. The two of them seem awfully friendly. Did she fuck this man behind her husband's back? And lie to me about never sleeping with another man? Was her story about Derek and the blackmailing a bunch of lies? Have I fallen for them?

Stop it! This is not letting go of the past. I believed her story. You can't fake that kind of sadness and emotion. She was genuinely upset and broken by her past. Still, I hate how friendly Matteo behaved around her. Hated that he touched her.

Later that day, when everyone has gone home, Bianca knocks on my door and walks into my office. "So much has happened today, let's go for a drink and I'll debrief."

"Sorry, not tonight. I'm working on something. Schedule a time in the morning." I open a file and pretend to read its contents.

"Anything I can help you with?"

"No, thanks. See you tomorrow."

"Oh, okay." She hesitates at my desk for a second then says, "Bye."

A few minutes after she leaves, there's another knock at my door before Harper enters the room. "Finn, have you finished work?" I'd forgotten I told her to come to my office so I can bend her over the desk. I've been so preoccupied with her and Matteo.

I lean back in the chair, hooking a leg over my knee. "You and Matteo looked friendly."

Harper's eyes widen at my harsh tone. "We haven't seen each other in months. It surprised me to see him."

"Did you fuck him?" I know I shouldn't have said it the second the words passed my lips. I know she hasn't. I'm a dick for asking. "Harper, I'm—"

She jabs a finger in my direction. "Who the hell are you to ask me a question like that? Especially someone who screwed so many women after we broke up. You're unbelievable! I've told you the truth. You said you can get over the past. If you don't trust me, that's on you." She waves a hand between us. "I lived with a controlling man for nine years, and I will not put up with another." Spinning on her heel, she marches toward the door.

Christ! I'm such a bastard. Rushing behind her, I slap a hand on the door above her shoulder, stopping her from opening it. She whirls around, giving me a deathly glare.

"I'm sorry. Seeing his hands on you drove me crazy. I've been without you for so long, jealousy gripped at my gut. I trust you." I cup her face in my hands. Her eyes soften. "I'm sorry."

"I can't be worried how you're going to react every time I talk to a man."

"I know. It won't happen again."

"Are you sure? I know you said you can move on, but maybe you can't." Her eyes turn sad.

"Maybe it's going to be harder than I thought. But believe me, I want to make this work."

Harper pulls back and steps away from me, hugging her arms around her waist. "You're leaving for London soon. How will we make it work?"

I slide my hands into the pockets of my pants. I want so much to touch her. I'm not sure she wants me to. "Maybe I can work from New York, or you can come to London."

"You'd want me to go to London with you?"

"Of course. You *are* my girlfriend. Will you come with me if I go?" I say, hoping she wants the same thing.

Harper giggles. "Calling me your girlfriend sounds like we're teenagers again."

"Are you going to make me wait two days for an answer like you did when I asked you to be my girlfriend the first time?" I smile playfully, but deep down, her answer is important. I need to know we're on the same page.

She giggles again. "I made you wait, didn't I?"

"I remember you were such a prick tease." I cross my arms over my chest and lean a hip on the desk.

Harper chokes on a laugh. "I was not! *I* remember you had me naked on our first date."

"But you wouldn't have sex with me. Prick tease," I joke.

Harper's cheeks turn pink. I love that even after everything we've done together, she can still get embarrassed. "God, I really wanted to. I promised myself I wouldn't be that kind of girl."

"It didn't take you long to *be* 'that kind of girl'." I grin.

"You were too good with your hands for me to resist."

I reach out and clasp onto Harper's hand, tugging her toward me to nestle between my legs. "Are you going to need two more days to answer me?" I need to know if she'd be willing to move to London. If she's truly committed to this relationship.

Hooking her arms around my neck, she says, "Maybe I'll waive the two-day period if you show me again how good you are with your hands first."

I place my lips at her ear. "You already know how good I am with my hands. How good I kiss you—everywhere. You already know how good I fuck you." Harper bites her bottom lip. Her body is trembling in my arms. "If you need reminding, I promised you I'd fuck you over my desk."

Harper glides a finger across my lips. "Yes, please. Remind me."

Cupping her face in my hands, I cover her mouth with a firm, quick, possessive kiss. *Mine.* Harper belongs to me. And she owns every part of me. She is it for me.

My erection is painfully hard against the zipper of my pants. I don't have time for foreplay. Needing to be inside Harper now, I spin her around, splaying her palms flat on the desk, bending her over. With my foot, I nudge her legs apart.

Harper glances over her shoulder as I unzip my fly and release myself. Her gaze zones onto my cock as I fist it and slowly stroke. The heat shining from her eyes and the lick of her lips tells me what she's thinking. She wants to kneel in front of me and take me into her mouth. I'd love so much for her to do that. But it's going to have to wait. "Another time, baby. I need you now."

The need to brand her as mine is strong. So barbaric. I don't care. Lifting her skirt around her waist, I groan at the sight of her ass in a black, lacy thong. Like she knew this was going to happen today, she's come prepared. Palming her cheeks, I then run my hand up her spine. Her back arches like a cat. My cock is so hot and heavy I can't wait any longer. To be sure she's ready, I slide two fingers inside her warm center. They come out dripping wet. Oh yeah, she's ready.

Pushing her thong to the side, I grip her hips and slam inside her. Burying myself deep. Harper cries out, her sex clutching around me. "You're mine, Harper," I groan as I thrust in and out. "Tell me you're mine."

"I'm yours," she pants. "I'll always be yours."

Her words slam into me, making me harder than I ever thought possible. Clutching at her hips, I drive into her harder, faster, until I feel her orgasm build. I pick up speed, hammering into her. Not caring about finesse. She presses back on me, and with a long groan, her body spasms. Oh God, she feels good. Seconds later, I pour my release into her. When I get my breathing under control and my body stops trembling, I pull out of her and adjust her thong and skirt.

She turns around. Pulling me in for a kiss against my lips, she says, "Yes. I'll move to London with you."

Chapter Twenty-Eight

HARPER

When I arrive at work the next morning and step from the elevator into the office foyer, my colleagues, who are focused on the elevator doors, all slump with disappointment. "Wow, don't look so excited to see me," I joke.

They give me a quick hello and focus their attention back on the elevator.

I see Tamara walking out of her office and stop her before she hurries off. "Why is everyone staring at the elevator? Is the King of England arriving?"

Tamara clasps her hands under her chin and beams. "Better than the king. Portia Livingstone is on her way."

"The movie star?"

Tamara's orange glasses propped on the tip of her nose almost fall off her face as she nods with excitement. "Yep."

Portia Livingstone, featured in multiple blockbuster movies is Hollywood's highest-paid female actor. I can understand why everyone is so excited to see her. I wouldn't mind getting a glimpse of her too.

"Why is she coming here?" I ask.

"Juliette has designed her Met Gala outfit. She's here for a final fitting."

"Wouldn't such a huge actor have her designer go to her?"

Tamara gives a snort of laughter. "Juliette goes to no one."

As we wait for Portia Livingstone to arrive, I get caught up in the office excitement and stare at the elevator door. As it dings its arrival, excited gasps and whispers of, "she's here" echo around the room. The doors slowly slide open and out steps Portia Livingstone. Tall, slender, with dark blonde hair that hangs in silky waves to her waist. Wearing tight, black leather pants, an oversized white t-shirt, and gold accessories. She's more beautiful than on the big screen. Her entourage steps out from the elevator behind her.

Flora, the receptionist, picks up the phone and says to Portia Livingstone, "I'll let Mr. Alessi know you're here."

At the mention of Finn's name, my heart gives a little leap. Will that ever stop? With the actor here, there's no way I can sneak into his office for a quick kiss.

"Thank you," Portia Livingstone says. While she waits for Finn, she glances around. Surely she must be uncomfortable with everyone standing around staring at her. They aren't even pretending to be busy doing something. Portia smiles, waves, and greets everyone with a sincere nature about her. It doesn't look fake or forced.

A moment later, Finn saunters from the office to greet her. My heartrate kicks up a notch. This man gets me more excited than any famous actor ever could. Finn smiles at Portia, places a hand on her waist, and kisses her cheek. Propping a hand on his shoulder, she giggles at something Finn says to her. After their greeting, Finn rests his hand on the small of Portia's back and guides her to his office, closing the door behind them. All without glancing at me for a quick, secret smile. Anything to let me know he's aware I'm around. Now he's alone with a beautiful woman, and I'm out here like I'm part of her entourage. Now that I've gotten him back, I never want to lose him again!

What am I thinking? He wants me to move to London with him. This is just work. Nothing more. Although, they looked rather friendly.

"If you keep staring at Finn's door, you're going to burn a hole through it," Tamara says from my side. Her words startle me, because I'd forgotten she was there. "Come with me." She clasps my bicep and tugs me into her office.

"Take a seat," she says, pointing to the chair opposite her desk. Tamara takes her seat. "How are you? I've been so busy with work lately I haven't had time to check in with you."

"I'm good. Things are getting better. I'm feeling better." And it was true. Normally, I had to pretend that my life was wonderful and joyful, when inside it festered with sadness and loneliness.

"I'm glad to hear it. Have you talked to my sister? Or anyone? You don't have to answer that if you don't want to. You can tell me to mind my own business," she says, pushing her orange glasses up on her nose.

I know Tamara isn't being nosey. She genuinely cares about my welfare. "Yes, I've given your sister a call, and we've spoken a couple of times. She's great. Thank you so much for giving me her number. She's helped me a lot."

"I hope she's given you the friends-and-family discount, otherwise I'll kick her ass," she says with mock seriousness.

"She's been very generous. Thank you." I'll always be forever grateful for Tamara's help.

"You're welcome. Now—" She taps her hand on the desk. "What's going on between you and Finn? Again, you can tell me to mind my own business."

I tell her about how we've been spending time together and that we have talked. That Finn's forgiven me, and we've made up and are giving our relationship another chance.

"I'm so happy for you. I hope it all works out."

"Thank you." I hope so too.

"Oh, you haven't started work yet and you're already taking a break." Bianca's sarcastic tone slices through the room.

I rise from the chair. "Sorry."

"She was helping me with something," Tamara lies. I smile my thanks.

"Well, she's needed in Juliette's office."

Great. Another day starting off with Bianca already pissed at me. I say goodbye to Tamara and follow Bianca.

When we reach my desk, Bianca says, "Go to Juliette's room. After Portia's fitting, her stylist will meet you there to pick up the gown. You'll need to dress it on a mannequin and place it into the box that's there. Wear gloves. Do *not* mark it. Do *not* crease it. Don't even *breathe* on it. Understand? God, I don't know why I'm letting you do this."

If she's so worried, why doesn't she do it herself? "If you don't trust me, maybe you should pack the dress."

Bianca tosses her head back like she's offended that I can give her an order. "I don't have the time. Hurry, they haven't got all day to wait for you." With that, she leaves me at my desk and enters her office.

I glance at Finn's closed door. Is he still inside with Portia Livingstone? If so, what are they talking about? Is he bending her over the desk like he did with me last night?

Oh God! What is wrong with me? I've never had this jealous streak with Finn before. Maybe it's because, at one point, I was the only woman he'd ever been with. Things changed, and I need to get used to it.

After putting my bag in the desk drawer and hanging my coat over the chair, I race down to Juliette's design room. I stop short in the doorway. Portia Livingstone is perched on top of a dais. Finn is circling around her, his gaze roaming from her head to her feet. My heart squeezes. It was only last week I was standing there with Finn's eyes on me wearing one of Juliette's gowns. Portia Livingstone is a vision in white. The bodice of the dress is sheer, tight, and lined with pearls that wrap around her neck.

The skirt of the gown flares out from under her hips in layers of sparkling fabric lined with soft strings of feathers.

"Amazing! One of your best designs yet," he says, smiling at Juliette.

Of course, Finn was checking out the dress. Not Portia. I breathe a sigh of relief.

Juliette waves her fan in front of her face, pretending to be embarrassed by Finn's compliment. "Oh, darling, stop. I'm blushing. But yes, it's fabulous if I say so myself."

"He's right. This is gorgeous. I feel privileged wearing it," Portia says as she admires her reflection in the tall, arched mirror propped against the wall. She swishes from side to side like a little girl wearing her first pretty dress.

I stop hovering in the doorway and enter the room. "It looks stunning on you, Ms. Livingstone."

Turning to me, she smiles. "Thank you...what's your name?"

"Harper," I answer, feeling a little giddy that she's talking to me!

"Thank you, Harper. I love Juliette's designs." Again, she swishes her skirt.

You hear stories about a lot of actors being stuck up and horrible, but she genuinely seems lovely.

Juliette snaps her fan closed. "All these compliments are going to give me a big head."

"You already have a big head." Finn laughs. Turning to me, he says, "Do you need me for something, Harper?" I'm relieved to see a gleam of mischief shining from his eyes. Portia and Juliette are too busy fussing with the gown to notice.

We are at work; I need to stay professional, especially with the head designer and a famous client in the room. "Bianca wants to me to pack the gown for Ms. Livingstone's stylist to pick it up."

Juliette points to a corner with a mannequin and a huge, white box. "Everything you need is over there. I'll help Portia get this off and you can have it." Juliette helps Portia off the dais, and they head behind a privacy screen. I can hear chatter and the rustle of fabric.

Stepping closer to me, Finn's warm breath fans over my neck. "Meet me in my office when you're done here."

My head snaps back, and I glance at the privacy screen, hoping the women behind it didn't hear Finn. I lower my voice and say, "I told you we're not having sex in the office during work hours."

"Ms. Madden, I'm shocked that you would think such a thing. I have a job for you to do." His faux innocent expression isn't fooling me. I know exactly the kind of *job* he wants. I pull an I-don't-believe-you expression. I'm keeping clear of his office just in case I succumb to temptation.

Tapping my nose with his finger, he gives me a sexy grin then leaves the room. A few minutes later, Portia and Juliette follow. I'm left with packing the garment, taking extra-special care not to damage it. By the time the stylist arrives to pick it up, my nerves are a jittery mess and sweat trickles down my spine.

I can't wait to see Portia arrive at the Gala. This gown is going to be the talk of the evening.

Chapter Twenty-Nine

FINN

At the end of the day, I stand at my office door watching Harper at her desk. She shrugs into her coat then checks her phone before putting it into her bag. She's so beautiful and distracting, I'm finding it hard keeping my hands to myself.

I walk to her desk. "Are you ready to go? I'll give you a ride home."

She gives the area a quick scan. The office is empty. Seemingly happy we're alone, she steps closer and straightens my tie. "That would be great. Thanks."

"We can stop somewhere for dinner—not McDonald's," I quickly say before she can suggest it. "Then I'll take you back to your place and have *you* for dessert." My hotel would be more comfortable, but I don't want to take her to my suite where I fucked another woman a couple of weeks ago.

Her hands hook around my neck, and she presses her breasts against my chest. "How about we skip dinner and head straight for dessert?" She places kisses along my neck.

A throat clears behind us. Harper springs away, her face flaming red. My father is flicking his gaze between us with a shocked expression on his face. Shit! This is not the way I wanted him to find out about Harper and I.

"Hey, Dad," I say. "What brings you to the office this late? Everyone's gone home."

"Not everyone." He pins Harper with a hard stare.

I can feel the tension vibrating from him toward Harper. I know it was hard for him to watch my destruction after she left. Being in the same room with her can't be easy. We'll have to take it day by day, and hopefully, he'll come around and see that Harper isn't the villain he believed she was.

I rub a hand up and down Harper's arm. "I need to speak with Dad in my office. Don't go anywhere. I won't be long."

With wide eyes, she nods. Color has drained from her face, and she looks ready to bolt. Is she worried about getting caught together or if my father is going to have harsh words to say to her for what she did to me? I won't let that happen. She's been through enough. Once he knows the truth, he'll understand.

"Don't leave," I say again. Harper sits on her chair. Satisfied that she won't leave, I lead my father into my office.

As soon as the door closes behind us, my father's face turns thunderous. "Why is that bitch still here? More importantly, what are you doing with her? Are you back together? Do you remember what she did to you?"

I hold up my hands to calm him down. "Dad, relax. It's okay."

His eyes practically bulge from his head. "Relax? Relax? How can you tell me to relax? She left you for money. While I was by your hospital bed, not knowing whether you'd live or die, she was marrying another man." My father jabs a finger at me. "She almost killed you!"

"*I* almost killed myself. It wasn't her fault. None of it was. She had her reasons for marrying Derek. He blackmailed her."

My father gives a mirthless laugh. "Is that what she told you? She was *blackmailed*? She wanted money. Don't believe a word from her lying mouth."

I have to take a deep breath to calm the anger building inside me. I hate the way he's talking about Harper, but I know it's coming from a place of concern for me. "It's true. She did it all to help her family…us."

He jerks his head like I slapped him. "What are you talking about?"

I explain about Harper's father's gambling debts, Derek using her family for his political campaign, and about the fire he'd set in our Paris building when she tried to leave him.

"That son of a bitch did us all a favor when he died," he says, scrubbing a hand behind his neck.

What does that mean? The hairs on the back of my neck rise. "Did you have any dealings with Derek?"

He waves a dismissive hand at my question. "No. I know his reputation. He's a snake and used anyone to get what he wanted."

"Exactly, and he used Harper. She paid the price for nine years."

He gives me a skeptical look. "You believe her story?"

I nod. "I do."

"Then you're delusional. If he left her with nothing, she's here for money. Getting back with you is the way to do it."

I scrub my hand through my hair, frustrated that he won't let this go. "Dad, enough. It's not like that. I know it was tough seeing me in the hospital. I understand your concern, but she's in my life again. I'm not expecting you to welcome her with open arms, but please be civil toward her. That's all I ask."

"Stay away from her. I don't care what bullshit story she's spun, I don't trust her." A vein ticks at the side of my father's temple.

"Dad, I don't want to hurt you, but this is my life, and Harper is a part of it again. You're going to have to get used to it."

He narrows his eyes at me. "Fine. But if she hurts you again, she'll be dealing with me." The fierce expression on his face tells me he means every word.

To change the subject, because talking about Harper is only making him tense, I say, "What brings you to the office?"

"I was nearby, having drinks with a friend. Thought I'd stop in to see if any of my boys were still working. I wanted to say hello."

"What are you doing next Sunday? We haven't played golf in a while. If you're available, I'll tell Hayden and Lucas to join us."

"Sounds good." My father smiles for the first time since coming into the office. "I should go. I'll see you Sunday."

I step in front of him to lead him out of the room and also to buffer Harper from any confrontation that may occur. When I open the door, she's not at her desk. I give a quick glance around the office.

She's gone.

Chapter Thirty

HARPER

Back in my apartment as I'm pouring coffee into a mug, someone knocks on the door. I have a sneaking suspicion I know who it is. Finn asked me to stay in the office while he spoke with his father, and I didn't listen. After hearing mumbled parts of their conversation, I couldn't stay and face Marco. Not when I know what he did to his wife. How could he choose his mistress over his wife? She laid in the hospital for hours before she died. Were they not in love and their relationship was for show?

Still, he should have been there for his sons. That man is the reason I can't tell Finn the whole truth. Because if Finn knew his father had cheated on his mother while she lay dying in a hospital bed, Finn would lose his mind. Marco was a piece of shit, but he'd always been a good father to his sons. Always in their lives, supporting and loving them. This news would crush Finn. Crush his brothers. He'd cut his father from his life.

After hearing him tell Finn to stay away from me, I wanted to storm into Finn's office and confront Marco. Expose him for the man he really is. It took an enormous effort to stop myself. That's why I couldn't stay. I didn't want to be responsible for ruining their relationship.

I open the door. Finn is leaning on the doorjamb. His jacket is gone. The top three buttons of his navy shirt are open, and his hair looks tousled, like he'd run his fingers through it. He's so handsome he takes my breath away.

"Can I come in?" he asks.

I move aside so he can enter and close the door behind him. "I'm making coffee, would you like a cup?"

"No, I'm good, thanks." He slides his hands into his pockets. "You left the office."

I lace my fingers together in front of me. "Yes."

Finn frowns. "I told you not to."

"I know."

"Why did you leave?"

Not wanting to tell him the real reason, that I wanted to expose Marco, I keep quiet. God, I hate keeping this secret from him. We're starting over. Things should feel fresh and new, and yet, it feels like I'm carrying a heavy load on my shoulders.

Finn sits on the armrest of the sofa. "You heard me talking to my dad about you, didn't you?"

That is the truth. I nod.

"He's not happy we're back together," Finn says.

Probably not for the welfare of his son but for the secret I can expose.

Holding onto my hand, Finn guides me to his lap. When I sit, he wraps me in his arms. "Don't worry about Dad. I've told him what Derek made you do. Once he calms down, he'll see it wasn't your fault. He'll come around."

There is no way Marco will 'come around', not with such a dangerous secret hanging over his head.

"Maybe I should give him space for a while. He almost lost you. Blamed me for your accident. Seeing me will only bring back those memories." It will also stop me from blurting out the truth to his face.

Finn frowns like he doesn't like the idea. "Sure, when you're ready we'll work something out." Probably sensing my tension, he rubs his hand along my arm. Ducking his head to look right into my face, he asks, "Are you okay?"

How can I be? If things work out between us, Marco will always be in our lives. Every time we're in the same room, I'll never be able to look at him with nothing but disgust. Surely, Finn will pick up on the animosity. I'm so conflicted. If I keep the secret and Finn finds out, I'll risk losing him again. If I tell him, his relationship with his father might end.

It's too much for me to think about right now. All I want to do is savor the feel of Finn's warm, strong arms holding me. Pressing myself against him, I take comfort in his embrace. "I am now. I don't want to be anywhere but in your arms."

"I'll always hold you." He kisses my temple.

Please, let that be true.

We lay naked on my bed among the tangled sheets. With my head propped up on Finn's chest, I snuggle as close as I can get to his body. I listen to the rapid beating of Finn's heart. Only moments ago, we were as close as two bodies can get, and yet, I still need to be glued by his side. Being together is a dream come true. I can't do anything to ruin it again. That might mean keeping Marco's secret. Can I really do it?

Finn's fingertips ghost up and down my spine. "You're quiet."

I tilt my head up to look at him. His eyes are half-mast with after-sex sleepiness. A slight dark stubble is breaking through his jaw. A lock of hair has fallen over his eyes, and I reach up to brush it back. My heart swells with love for him. "Just enjoying the moment." And I was, until dark thoughts crept into my mind.

"Happy?" His finger glides over my bottom lip.

When we're together? Always. "Yes. Are you?"

Finn hesitates for a beat. Tucking a lock of hair behind my ear, he says, "Never did I think I'd be truly happy again. Things in my life made me content. That was good enough for me. Then you stumbled back into my life. For years I thought I hated you. Tried hard to hold on to that belief. But when you look at me...touch me... I know I've been lying to myself. You make me happy. You always have."

Tears burn the backs of my eyes. God, I love him. I want to tell him so. Although he's saying all the right things, our relationship is too new to sprout words of love. What if he's not ready to hear them?

So instead, I cup his face and pull him down for a kiss. Pouring all the love I have for him into that moment. I never want to hurt him again, even if it means keeping Marco's ugly secret to myself. A fist-sized knot twists in my gut. In time, I hope I'm doing the right thing.

"Morning!" I say as I meet Alyssa in the living room on my way out to work. Her hair's tied up in a sleek bun. A dance bag is slung over her shoulder. "Got a class?" I ask.

"Yep. Ballet and then tap."

I can't believe the amount of dancing Alyssa does in a week. It makes me exhausted just thinking about it. At the coffee machine I fill up a travel mug to take to the subway.

"You look happy. Sleep well?" Alyssa asks with a knowing grin. She knows Finn's been staying over the last few nights. I'm getting used to waking up in his arms. How can I not be happy?

"Like a baby," I reply. Finn had given me three orgasms, and I'd fallen into a sated, blissful sleep.

"Where is Finn?" Are you still doing the 'you go to the office first and I'll follow a few minutes later' routine?" Alyssa drops her bag on the coffee table and digs inside.

"He needed to get to the office early for a meeting. I think we can stop with the act now."

At my comment, Alyssa stops rummaging through her bag. "Things are going well?"

I want to hug myself and twirl around. "Yes. Things are wonderful." Finn's words the other night was music to my ears.

"That's amazing." Alyssa beams.

It would be even more so if the secret I'm keeping didn't poke me in the ribs.

Flinging the dance bag over her shoulder, she starts to leave, then pauses at the door. "After work, if you're not too busy with Finn, let's order pizza and drink wine while we watch the Met Gala. We can rate their outfits."

I tuck my phone into my bag, follow her out of the apartment, and lock the door behind us. "I would have loved to, but we're staying back at work to watch it. Portia Livingstone is wearing a Juliette Monet design."

"Oh wow! I bet she's going to look amazing."

"I saw the final fitting, and it's stunning. I can't imagine anyone looking better."

Saying our goodbyes, we head off in opposite directions. Once at work, I go straight to my desk. The temptation to find Finn is strong. It takes a lot of self-control to walk past his office and not duck inside. Not bothering to ask Bianca what today's duties are—she'd only tell me to check my emails—I sit at my desk and log onto the computer.

A few moments later, I feel Finn's presence behind me before he places a kiss on the side of my neck. "Good morning."

Normally, I'd freak out about who can see us, but now, I don't care. I scan the room and notice a few curious eyes on us. "I don't think we can hide our relationship anymore. You just announced it to the entire office."

Finn leans against the desk and grins. "I'm not sorry."

Shaking my head with mock sternness on my face, I say, "They're going to gossip."

Finn leans toward me. "Let's give them something to gossip about."

I want him to kiss me so bad, but it's not the time or place. I push my chair away. "Behave."

Blowing out a breath, Finn lifts from the desk. "Fine," he grumbles with a disgruntled expression on his face. "You're going to pay for it tonight."

I giggle. "I can't wait!"

Before Finn leaves, a courier carrying a huge bouquet of flowers walks to my desk. "Are you Harper Richardson?

God, I hate that name. I flick a glance at Finn, a vein is pulsing at his jaw. He hates it too. "I was, I go by Harper Madden now."

The courier gives me an 'I don't care what you go by, I just want to deliver the flowers' look and plonks them on the desk. I sign his clipboard and he leaves. With the courier calling me Richardson, I'm assuming Finn didn't send them. Who did? I pluck the card from the foliage.

Dear Harper,

Loved seeing you again. Looking forward to catching up.
Matteo

Why is Matteo sending me flowers? I stare at the card with confusion.

"Nice flowers." Finn's tone is clipped. I know he's read the card. A thunderous expression covers his face. "I didn't realize you and Matteo were so close."

"We're not."

Finn raises a dubious brow and points to the bouquet.

"I don't know why he would send me flowers. Maybe because he missed Derek's funeral."

Finn's eyebrow rises even further. He's not believing that for a second. What else can it be?

"It's more than that. That man wants you. I saw it the moment he laid eyes on you." He folds his arms across his chest. "Are you going to *catch up*?" His face twists like he's eaten something bad.

I rise from the chair and step closer to Finn, not caring if my colleagues are watching. I rest my hands on his shoulders. "No. I'm not going to *catch up*. I have no reason to. He was an associate of Derek's. I want to cut every part from that time out of my life."

Finn's face softens.

Stepping closer, I place a kiss on his mouth. "Are we okay?"

He nods. "Yeah, we're good. Although, you're still going to pay for it tonight."

For the rest of the day, my co-workers are giving me side glances or whispering to one another behind their hands. In one way, it's making me a little uncomfortable, and in another, I want to shout about our relationship from the rooftops. Although, there's one person I don't want to express my feelings too—Bianca. She hasn't been trying to hide her baleful glares thrown my way. Well, she's just going to have to get used to Finn and I being together. Hopefully she'll get over it and not make my life at Alessi's harder than she's already making it.

That afternoon, Finn, Hayden, Lucas, Bianca, and a few other staff are gathered in the boardroom. A huge TV on the wall is tuned onto the Met Gala. We watch celebrities and fashion designers arrive, stopping with journalist to talk about their gowns and who created them. There are many beautiful designs, yet nothing has wowed me as much as seeing Juliette's gown on Portia. All eyes in the room are glued to the screen, waiting for Portia to arrive. I too am feeling excited. All I did was pack it for Portia's stylist to pick up, and yet, I feel like I have a little bit to do with the grand moment.

Celebrity after celebrity make their way up the stairs. Then one celebrity makes everyone in the boardroom gasp. A white vision. Layers of glittery fabric with feathers and pearls. Juliette Monet's gown is a showstopper. The most beautiful creation anyone has seen so far. The media are nudging each other to get a closer look, wanting to be first to snag the interview. The gown and headpiece are so stunning and ethereal, the actor looks like she's floating on air. The problem is…it's not Portia Livingstone wearing it. The room grows deathly still as Raquel Addaman speaks to a journalist. Standing next to her is Matteo Blanchett, beaming with pride and boasting about the gown and headpiece *he* created.

Finn explodes from the chair with such force it tips and crashes onto the floor. "What the fuck!" His voice roars through the room. Everyone jumps. Hayden and Lucas both bound to their feet. "How the hell is Raquel Addaman wearing Juliette's dress?" he yells to no one in particular. With nostrils flaring and eyes bulging with anger as he glares at the TV, he barks, "Bianca, contact Juliette's team. Stop them from getting on that carpet."

Bianca picks up her phone from the table and begins dialing.

Hayden sidles up to Finn. "How did this happen?"

"I don't fucking know. I'm going to kill whoever did this!" Finn says through gritted teeth.

"He was here a few days ago—do you think he somehow got a look at the design?" Lucas asks with eyes still filled with shock.

Finn clenches his jaw so tight I'm worried he'll crack a couple of teeth. "Maybe."

"But how can he work so fast?" Lucas asks.

"With a big enough team working day and night, it's possible," Finn says.

Making my way to Finn, I place a comforting hand on his arm. "What can I do to help?"

He gives me a brief glance. Instead of answering, he snaps at Bianca, "Have you got ahold of anyone yet?"

Bianca shakes her head. "No."

"Fuck!" He slaps a hand on the table. "Keep trying. Portia cannot get on that carpet." Finn shakes my hand off his arm and begins pacing the room. I try not to feel offended by the rebuff. This is a stressful situation. I can't imagine how he must be feeling.

With his hands on his hips, Finn turns his back to the TV and stares out the window. I want to go to him, wrap my arms around his waist and tell him everything will be okay. Yet, how can it be? A design from Alessi Fashion was stolen. Who could have done such a thing?

After a moment of tense silence, another gasp fills the room. Glancing at the TV, my heart sinks to my stomach. Nothing can make this situation better, but something can make it ten times worse.

Finn's back is still turned away from the TV, and he hasn't seen the new arrival.

"Arrh, Finn. Portia has arrived." Hayden almost sounds too fearful to tell him. I don't blame him. The black rage on Finn's face as he spins around is enough to scare the hell out of anyone.

Once again, the media is going wild. Has there ever been a duplicated design in the history of the Met Gala? By the way the media is swarming around Portia and Juliette, I don't think so. At first, the women look pleased with the media attention, but as they throw questions at them, you see by their shocked expressions when it dawns on them that something is amiss.

When Juliette is asked if she copied Matteo Blanchett's design, she leans close to the microphone, stares into the camera with eyes like deadly missiles, and says, "I am *Juliette Monet*. What a ridiculous question. Maybe you should be asking that question to Matteo Blanchett." She hooks her arm through Portia's and pulls her away from the reporters.

Someone switches the TV off, and the room falls silent. Finn's hands grip white-knuckle tight on the back of a vacant chair. "Everyone out," he says barely above a whisper, and yet, it's like a gunshot through the room. Everyone scuttles toward the door. "Bianca and Harper stay."

Hayden and Lucas have taken their seats again. They obviously know they're not being kicked out. Why did Finn want me to stay? Surely, this is something they need to discuss in private. Oh no. Did I give the dress to the wrong person? No, I was introduced to Portia's stylist. Although I can't stop wondering if this is my fault somehow. My legs shake.

Finn is still gripping the chair, staring down at the seat. "Who gave the design to Matteo?"

A cold shiver runs down my spine. Is he accusing me or Bianca? I look at Hayden and Lucas. They're staring at Bianca and I with unreadable expressions. Do they all think one of us stole the design?

"There must be several people who would have seen the gown and maybe passed on the design," I point out.

Finn pushes away from the chair. It ricochets against the table, causing a loud bang. I jump. "Who gave the design to Matteo?" he asks again.

Oh God. He really is accusing one of us. How can he think I'd do such a thing? I press my lips together. A terrible knot twists in my chest.

Bianca steps in front of Finn. "I've worked with you for years. I would never do anything like this to you or this company. I'm as shocked as you are." She places a soothing hand on his arm. "I'll help you find whoever did this." She tosses her head to the side and aims a harsh glance my way. It's clear who she suspects, and she's making it obvious to Finn. Not taking her hand off Finn—which I'd like to rip away—she says, "Why did Matteo send Harper flowers this morning? Was he thanking her for something?"

Finn swivels his head in my direction and narrows his eyes. Anxiety is expanding in my chest. "I didn't do this. You know I didn't." I place a hand over my heart.

"Don't you think it's a little suspicious that you receive flowers from Matteo Blanchett on the day of the Met Gala while his client is wearing our stolen design?" Bianca keeps digging me into a deeper grave. With a smirk twitching at her lips, I can tell she's enjoying herself. Finn keeps staring at me with a dark expression. Is he believing her?

After a moment of tense silence, Juliette and Portia barge into the room. "Someone needs to explain what the hell that circus was we were thrown into!" Juliette waves the fan at a rapid speed in front of her face. Portia, with tears streaking down her face, smearing her makeup, slumps into the nearest chair, still wearing the infamous gown.

"Portia, is there any way your stylist could have done this?" Hayden asks.

Finn clamps his mouth shut, and he hasn't taken his eyes off me. How can I prove this wasn't me?

"No. I had him sign a confidentiality agreement. I've worked with my stylist for years. He's one of my closest friends. There's no way he would do this to me."

"Well, someone had to have done it. Designs just don't fall into the competitor's lap," Lucas fumes.

"We all know who is most likely to have done this, yet no one wants to say it out loud." Bianca glares at me.

"Who?" Juliette and Portia both ask at the same time.

Finn is keeping quiet. My heart is breaking.

"How well do we know Harper? She gets a job here with no qualifications," Bianca says. My face must look surprised at how she knows this, because she continues on to say, "Yes, I've checked. We know there's history between Finn and Harper. Based on Finn's initial reaction to her, it's not great history. Could she be here for some kind of revenge? Is she punishing Finn for something?"

All eyes zero in on me. This is not looking great. Of course, I'd be the number one suspect. Especially with Bianca pointing the finger at me.

"I would never do this, Finn. Please believe me," I plead. I search his face for any sign of his trust. His expression is hard and cold. Dread flutters in my chest. "Finn, please." My voice cracks with emotion.

Turning his back to me, he says, "I need to think. You better go."

I bite my quivering lip and hold back tears that are threatening to spill. There's no point pleading my case. He won't give me the chance. His mind is made up. In his eyes, I'm guilty. Spinning away, I run to my desk to collect my things. Once in the elevator, away from prying eyes, I let the tears fall.

How can Finn believe I'd betray him this way? My heart skids to a stop at the answer. Because he doesn't trust me.

Chapter Thirty-One

FINN

I watch Harper's retreating back until the door closes behind her. A fist-sized knot is twisting in my gut. Juliette paces the room, fanning her face. Portia has her head in her hands, probably worried if this will ruin her career. Hayden, Lucas, and I stare at each other with a what-the-fuck-is going-on expression. A sense of shock and disbelief presses over us.

"What do we do now?" Juliette asks.

"Bianca, get hold of PR. We need to get a statement out fast." My phone has been buzzing in my pocket since Portia's arrival at the Gala. My brothers keep checking their phones every few seconds too. The media are circling. They want answers. "We can't let the fashion industry believe we're thieves."

Juliette scoffs and rolls her eyes. "I would rather be *dead* than copy anything from another designer. Especially one so inferior as Matteo Blanchett. Portia, I can't stand to look at that gown a moment longer. Go to wardrobe—someone will show you where it is—and find something to change into." Juliette points her fan at the door. Portia does what she's told and hurries away.

"Are you sure her people didn't do this?" Hayden asks me.

I shake my head. "I believed her when she said she could trust them. I know Portia is tight with her staff."

"What about your team?" Hayden looks at Juliette.

"No way in hell would they do this. They have been loyal to me for over twenty years."

"Then it's Harper," Lucas accuses. "We haven't seen her in years. Suddenly, she's working at Alessi's. Was it all a plan with Matteo?"

"Of course she's working with Matteo. You saw how close they appeared during the meeting. And today he sends her flowers. It can't be anyone else." Bianca looks at us like we're all dense and can't see this for ourselves.

Juliette slams her fan on the table. "Bianca, that's ridiculous. Harper did not steal the design. That girl is as innocent as a newborn lamb."

Bianca rolls her eyes. "Don't be fooled by her oh-so-sweet look. That woman was married to Derek Richardson, remember? He probably taught her everything he knew."

Anger simmers in my gut. My fists clench at my sides. That fucker's name always causes such a reaction.

"I have to say, it was a ballsy move on her part. Did she think she wouldn't get caught? Giving Matteo the design for the gown and headpiece was a stupid move, especially since we know they're well acquainted." Bianca gives a mocking laugh.

My body grows still. "Harper didn't know about the headpiece."

Bianca's eyes widen. "What?"

"The headpiece. You said Harper gave the design for the gown *and* the headpiece to Matteo. Only Portia's stylist, Juliette and her team, and us in this room knew what the headpiece looked like."

Bianca waves a dismissive hand. "Oh…I…just meant to say gown. Slip of the tongue." Color drains from her face.

"Pass me your phone," I demand.

"Why?" Bianca's gaze flicks around the room like she wants to make a run for it.

I hold out my hand. "Give me your phone. Now." I keep my voice quiet and controlled, belying the raging anger pulsing through my body.

"Finn, this is ridiculous. You don't think I had anything to do with this, do you?"

"The. Phone."

Bianca's gaze darts from Hayden, Lucas, and Juliette. "Tell Finn this is absurd." No one speaks up to defend her. Bianca's pleading eyes flick back to me. "Please, believe me." Harper said those same words and I let her believe I didn't.

"The phone."

"This is my phone. I don't have to give it to you." Bianca pulls her shoulders back, challenging me, although her voice trembles with fear.

"It belongs to the company, therefore it's mine. Give it to me now, or I'll call the police and you can give it to them."

Bianca stares at me, her face white, her eyes wide, and her chest heaving. Finally, with a shaky hand, she passes the phone to me. Hayden and Lucas flank my sides. Juliette sidles up close too. Swiping the screen open, I go straight to Bianca's inbox. When I can't find anything incriminating, I pull up the deleted messages. Bam! Message found. The name is saved as MB. Not exactly a great disguise. She probably never thought she'd get caught. Opening the message, I read their correspondence. There are also photos of the sketches and of the completed gown and headpiece.

With a gasp, Juliette covers her mouth with her hand. "How could you? This is my life. My baby. You have sullied my work and reputation. Why?"

I throw the phone on the table with such force it skids along the smooth surface and onto the floor. "I know you've given Harper a hard time from the moment she started working here. Over the years, I've put up with your jealousy—hoped you'd get over it. But doing this to our company—to Harper—you've gone too far."

Bianca points a finger at me. "Ever since she stepped foot here, you've been thinking with your dick not your head. She's bad news. Someone needed to put a stop to her before she ruined you!"

I slam my hands on my hips. "Your fucking dirty trick could ruin us! Grab your things and get out."

Bianca rushes toward me, grabbing my arm with pleading eyes. "I'm sorry. We can work this out. I'll do anything to make this better."

Flinging her hands off me, I scoff. "You can't be serious? I never want to see you again."

"You don't mean that." She tries reaching for me again but abruptly stops at the fierce don't-fucking-touch-me-again expression I throw at her.

"If you're not gone in ten minutes, I *will* get the police involved. You're lucky I haven't done so already."

At my warning, Bianca gives one last look at everyone in the room. Probably hoping someone will stand up for her. When no one does, with her head hanging low, she scurries from the room.

"What the hell just happened?" Lucas drops into a chair, and Hayden and Juliette do the same. I'm too agitated to sit. "I always knew she had a crush on you, thought her jealous streak was kinda funny, but...this? All because she's jealous of Harper. I never would have suspected Bianca."

"We never should have accused Harper without more evidence." Hayden rests his elbows on the table and shakes his head.

I link my fingers behind my neck. "I never accused her." But I made her think I did.

"She pleaded for you to believe her. You let her walk out of here without saying a word," Hayden reminds me.

It was so damn hard watching her leave. The sadness shimmering in her eyes was like a knife to my chest. But it had to be done. "I needed to let Bianca believe I accused Harper. I suspected Bianca all along. I just needed her to trip up. And she did." Now I can only hope Harper forgives me for what I put her through.

Chapter Thirty-Two

HARPER

I'm sitting on the sofa with an untouched glass of wine in my hand when Alyssa walks into the apartment. She throws her dance bag in the corner of the room and flops down next to me. "Hey! How did the Gala go? I ended up having to fill in for a teacher who got sick and taught classes, so I never got to watch it." She takes one look at my face and her smile drops. "Oh no. The dress bombed. Is Portia Livingstone going to be on the worst-dressed list? Is this bad for Alessi Fashion?"

"I guess you haven't seen the news?" I place my glass on the coffee table. "Raquel Addaman wore the exact same gown."

"What? How is that possible?"

I fill Alyssa in on what happened. Not leaving out the part where Finn believed I was involved.

"How can Finn think you'd do this?" she asks, baffled.

"He has good reason not to trust me." I fold my legs onto the sofa.

"Because you got flowers on the day of the Gala from some guy who was friends with your dead husband..." Alyssa scratches the side of her face. "Yeah, I can see how that might look. This is all a misunderstanding. At the moment, he's shocked and angry. Give him time, I'm sure he'll figure out you had nothing to do with this."

I hug a cushion to my chest. "I hope so." Hurting him is the last thing I want to do. I've only just gotten him back.

Someone knocks at the door. My heartrate kicks up a notch. Is it Finn? I jump up from the sofa and swing open the door. My shoulders sag with disappointment. "Oh...hi, Tamara."

Tamara gives a choked laugh. "Don't look so happy to see me."

"Sorry." I gesture for her to come inside. "I thought you were someone else."

"Like Finn?" Tamara sits on the wingback chair.

I nod and drop down next to Alyssa on the sofa again. "I hope you didn't come here to accuse me of stealing the design. I don't have the energy to throw you out, but I might get Alyssa to do it."

Alyssa folds her arms across her chest and feigns a fierce expression. "Don't be fooled by these skinny ballet arms. I can take you on."

Tamara giggles. "I bet you can." With seriousness, she says, "I'm not here to accuse you, Harper. No one should have done that."

"Finn did." He looked me dead in the eye and dismissed me after I tried pleading my innocence.

"Have you not heard from Finn?"

I shake my head with confusion. "No, why? I'm the last person he'd want to speak to."

Tamara rests her hands on her knees and leans forward. "You should have stuck around the office. Oh my goodness, the drama that unfolded."

I sit forward. "What do you mean?"

"After you left, something went on in the boardroom. Finn, Hayden, Lucas, Juliette, and Bianca all stayed inside. Then Bianca comes marching out. She packs up her desk, doesn't say a word to anyone, and security escorts her from the office. The word whispering around the office is Bianca is responsible."

I gasp with shock. "She accused me and *she's* the one who did it? Why? How?"

"I haven't spoken with Finn to get the details yet. You can imagine the chaos that's happening in the office. Anyway, he looked mad as hell. No one dared approach him. The last I saw of him, he was with Hayden and Lucas, talking with the PR team. They were preparing a statement for the media."

"This is so bad." I sigh. "What will happen to Alessi's reputation?"

"Hopefully, this will blow over soon. Although, I can see it being talked about at every Met Gala for a while. Alessi's reputation is too good to be destroyed over this. Their statement will clear things up. Alessi Fashion outshines Matteo Blanchett's designs. No one will believe Alessi's is the thief. Matteo's clothing range is getting bad reviews lately. Most celebrities who wear his designs are landing on the worst-dressed list."

I sink back into the cushion of the sofa. "I hope you're right."

Finn may have discovered Bianca was involved, but he assumed it was me first. Will he ever trust me? Every time something happens, will I be the first person he points a finger at? Can I work this way, worried that everything I do or see at Alessi's might make me end up in some scandal?

"I'm going to quit my job," I announce.

Alyssa exclaims, "What!" at the same time Tamara says, "You can't!"

I pick the glass of wine up from the coffee table and take a long swig. God, can I really do it? I don't think I have much choice. "Mixing business with pleasure is often a bad idea. If I'm not in the office, no one can accuse me of something like this again."

Tamara shakes a finger at me. "I'm not letting you quit. I'm in charge of HR, and I say no."

I chuckle at Tamara's stern expression. "My job is only temporary. Soon I have to find a new one anyway." Whether Finn wants me to go to London now with him or not.

"I can try to find something else for you in the company," Tamara offers.

I smile. Tamara has been a savior to me. "Thank you. That's sweet. But I think leaving is the right thing to do. Our relationship has caused this problem in the office to happen. It's better if I'm not there. I don't even know if Finn still wants me to be there."

Alyssa nudges my shoulder. "You're sounding like you and Finn have broken up. Bianca is gone. You're in the clear. All is good again…well, when this shitshow blows over, everything will be sunshine and rainbows again."

"Then where is he?" I fling out my arms. The wine in my hand sloshes over the glass, staining my blouse. Shit. I have to give this back to the clothing department when I leave. I can't afford to replace it. I put my glass on the table before I do more damage to the silk fabric.

Tamara pulls her phone from her pocket and waves it at my face. "He's working with the PR team doing interviews. He's busy with his brothers trying to fix this."

I deflate, cupping a palm to my forehead. "You're right. God, I'm so insensitive. Here I am moaning about my problems when he's got his company's reputation at stake. I'm the last person he'd be thinking about."

"Does that mean you're going to stay at Alessi's?" Tamara asks.

I shake my head. "I still think leaving is for the best."

Tamara frowns, not looking pleased with my decision. "What will you do?"

I shrug. The heaviness of not knowing if I'll be able to pay for rent or food weighs on my shoulders. The thought of having to go through job applications again makes my insides churn. "I'll start applying for jobs again." Hopefully, this time I'll have more luck.

"You have experience now, that will help," Tamara points out. "And I'll be happy to be a reference."

"Thank you. I appreciate that."

Alyssa taps my shoulder. "One of our bar staff at the club just quit. My manager is looking for her replacement. I can put in a good word for you."

"I have no bar experience."

Alyssa scoffs. "You had no experience at all, and you still landed a job at Alessi's."

"That's because of the bogus resume you sent and Tamara's kindness after I had a meltdown in her office." I inwardly cringe. God, I can't believe I did that. Thankfully, it all worked out.

"How hard is it to mix a few drinks? We'll google the popular ones and practice making them. Speaking of work, I need to get ready for my shift. I'll talk to my manager and let you know."

In my position, I can't be choosey. Jobs are scarce. I need something to keep me out of trouble until I figure out what it is I want to do with my life. What happened to my dream of becoming a designer? During the brief time I'd spent with Juliette, the designer had chipped away until my love of it reappeared. If I want to enroll in the course again, I'm going to need money.

"Thanks. I appreciate it," I say to Alyssa.

After Alyssa gets changed for work, we say goodbye and I lead her and Tamara to the door. "Thanks for filling me in on what happened after I left work."

"No problem. Let me know if there's anything else I can do for you."

I give Tamara a quick hug. "Thanks."

I open the door to let them out. Standing at the threshold, with his hand raised to knock, is Finn.

Chapter Thirty-Three

FINN

From the moment the door opens, I can't take my eyes off Harper. I barely notice Tamara and Alyssa scurrying past me to leave. With Harper's wary expression and hurt in her eyes, I can kick myself for putting that pain on her face.

"May I come in?"

Harper crosses her arms over her chest. Is she going to refuse? I don't blame her. Finally, she steps aside. "Sure." I walk into the room, and she shuts the door behind me.

"I'm sorry it's taken me so long to see you," I say at the same time Harper says, "Would you like something to drink?"

I dig my hands into my pockets. "No, I'm good, thanks."

Tense silence fills the room.

"I'm sorry I upset you," I say.

She narrows her eyes. "You accused me of stealing Juliette's design. I've had better days."

I rub the back of my neck. "I know it wasn't you. It was—"

"Bianca. I know," she cuts in.

"I'm assuming Tamara told you." Everyone in the office must be gossiping.

Harper throws her hands up. "How could you believe it was me?"

I drop my head to stare at my feet for a beat. Looking back at Harper, I say, "I knew it wasn't you."

Harper lifts an eyebrow and pulls a dubious expression. "It sure sounded like you believed I'd done it. You threw me out of your office!"

Asking her to leave the boardroom wasn't exactly throwing her out, but I can understand why she'd see it that way. "It was the only way I could get to the truth. I know you never saw the headpiece."

Harper frowns. "So?"

"Only a handful of people saw it. Portia, her stylist, Juliette, Bianca, and me. Bianca had it boxed for Portia's stylist a couple of weeks ago. I got suspicious of her when she pointed the finger at you."

"But you threw me out," she says grudgingly.

I blow out a breath. I hate that I've hurt her like this. "I wanted you out of the room because I needed Bianca to think I believed her. I hoped she'd slip up, and she did. As soon as she brought up the headpiece, I had her. The proof was also on her phone. She'd sent messages and pictures to Matteo."

Harper covers her mouth. "Why would she do that?"

Exhaustion from the day catches up with me, and I slump down on the sofa. With a heavy shrug, I say, "Jealousy? That's what my brothers think. I knew she had feelings for me. I ignored them, hoping eventually she'd get over it and move on when she realized I didn't reciprocate them. When she noticed my interest in you—that we shared something—she acted out in a way she knew would hurt me—the company. Except, it's not the company I care about…it's you." Harper is still standing, so I reach for her hand and pull her down to take a seat next to me. Still holding her hand, I bring it to my lips and kiss her knuckles. "I'll never let anyone hurt you like that again. I'm sorry for my part. I should have dealt with it better."

"Was there even a moment where you believed I could have done that?" She studies my face for the answer. I'm ashamed to admit, that for a second, the thought crossed my mind. At my hesitation, Harper pulls her hand free. "You did!" She jumps up from the sofa and hugs her arms around her waist.

I rise from the seat and stand in front of her. I want to gather her in my arms, but with the pissed expression on her face, she'd probably pull away. So, I slide my hands into my pockets to stop myself from touching her. "Shock then rage at seeing our design on someone else overwhelmed me. I was confused. I was ready to blame anyone. It's no excuse. As soon as the thought entered my mind, I dismissed it immediately."

Biting her bottom lip, she doesn't look convinced. I step closer, risk touching her. I cup her face in my hands. Relief washes over me when she doesn't pull away.

I rub my thumbs along her jaw and say, "I'm sorry. God, I'm sorry." I kiss her cheek. "If I could go back and do things differently, I would."

Harper's face softens. "It was a shitty thing to do."

I rest my forehead on Harper's. "I know. I was a dick. Please, forgive me." My chest squeezes tight.

With lips curling into a smile, she says, "I forgive you. I understand the stress of the moment couldn't have been easy."

Pent-up tension expels from my lungs, and I smash my lips on Harper's mouth. Her hands land on my waist as she kisses me back with equal fervor. Pulling away, I stare into her eyes. "I love you." The words slip from my mouth. I didn't mean to say them so soon. I'd only recently worked out my feelings. Thought I needed more time to process them. But with the love of my life in my arms, this moment feels right. Why should I wait to tell her how I feel? When she gazes back at me with shocked, glassy eyes, her mouth slightly open, I say again, "I love you."

A tear slides down her left cheek. Fuck, is that a good or bad sign?

Harper's bottom lip trembles. "You love me? After everything I've done—"

"Shh." I place a feather-light kiss on her lips. "I've told you before, it's in the past. I want to focus on our future. If we're up-front and honest with each other from now on, we can get through anything."

She still hasn't told me she loves me back. Have I read her feelings wrong? She averts her eyes and focuses on something over my shoulder. A cold shiver travels down my spine. Shit! I'm an idiot. She doesn't feel the same way.

I take a step back, letting my arms fall to my sides. "You don't want this." I wave a hand between us.

Harper's eyes grow round. "No...I mean, yes. Yes, I want this." She grabs hold of my hands and clasps them to her chest. "I'm just finding it hard to believe you love me."

I kiss the top of her nose. "Believe it. It's true. To be honest, I've never stopped."

She gives me a watery smile. "I love you too, Finn. I've never stopped." She wraps her arms around my neck, kissing the relieved breath from my lungs.

This is where I'm meant to be. There's nothing now that can tear us apart.

Chapter Thirty-Four

HARPER

I LAY NAKED AND spent on my bed, wrapped in Finn's arms. Our heavy breathing echoes through the room. I should be overjoyed at hearing Finn tell me he loves me. I never believed I'd hear those words again. The words wrap around my damaged heart, mending it. While part of me is elated, guilt worms through like a dark cloud. Blanketing the moment. *If we're up-front and honest with each other from now on, we can get through anything.* But I haven't been completely honest with him. Guilt claws my chest. Can I tell him? After he's told me he loves me, how can I keep this from him?

Finn props onto an elbow and brushes my hair from my face. "Why so serious? I've just given you the best fucking orgasm you'll ever have. You should be grinning from ear to ear. What's on your mind?"

With a chuckle, and wanting to avoid the question, I say, "The best orgasm ever? That's all you've got?"

He pokes me in the ribs, and I squeal. "It was outstanding, and you know it. I'll be giving you a lifetime of them."

"Mmmm, I can't wait." I sigh as his hand covers my breast.

Finn pulls away. "But you're going to have to wait. I want to know what you were thinking about earlier. You looked too serious for someone who'd just been fucked."

I try to sit up, but Finn pulls me down onto my back and hovers above me.

"Honesty. Remember?" His gaze burrows into me, asking for the truth. The truth clogs in my throat, making my heart speed up at a dangerous level.

"I'm not coming back to Alessi's," I say.

I'm such a coward for not telling him what I was really thinking. Why is it so hard to tell him about his father? But what good would it do if I told him? He has a great relationship with his father. Believed his parents loved each other. Why would I want to ruin that for him? Hopefully, not telling him won't one day bite me in the ass.

"What?" Finn jerks back.

"I'm not coming back to work."

Finn pushes away from me and sits up on the bed. I get up too and gather the sheet to wrap around my body.

"You can't quit," he says.

"I've already told Tamara. She wasn't happy about it, but she understands."

Finn runs his fingers through his already tousled hair. "Make *me* understand."

"Everyone in the office knows we're in a relationship. I saw the way they looked and whispered about me. At first, I thought

I didn't care too much, but after what happened at the Gala, I don't want to have any speculation thrown my way again."

"The Gala was a one-time incident, and I don't care what other people think. If I move back to London, you're coming with me. You can work from the London office."

I shake my head. "It's the same thing. If I come with you to work in Alessi London, everyone will know you got me the job. I want to keep our personal and working relationship separate. Look what happened today. I don't want to feel that way again."

"That won't happen again."

"I know it won't, because I won't work for you. I have to do this."

Finn blows out a long, frustrated breath. "What will you do for work?"

"Alyssa is going to talk to her manager about getting me a job at The Temple."

Finn's eyebrows slam together. "The Temple? You're not working as a stripper!"

Crossing my arms over my chest, I frown. "Alyssa is not a stripper—not that there's anything wrong with that if she were. If that's what I want to do, you can't stop me."

Finn crosses his arms over his chest, mirroring me. "I fucking can, and I will."

"You don't own me."

"I own you as much as you own me," his voice grows deep. "If I say you're not stripping, you're not stripping.

God, controlling men drive me nuts! "She's going to ask about me getting a bar position."

His shoulders sag with relief. He pinches the bridge of his nose. "You could have led with that."

"You didn't let me explain. You jumped in, acting like a caveman. What were you going to do? Club me on the head and toss me over your shoulder to stop me?"

He rubs his chin and grins. "If I have to."

I roll my eyes. "For future reference, I will *not* be told what to do. I'm not living like that again. Understood?"

The smile on Finn's face drops. "Understood. Although, if you get the bar job, I'll be there at every shift."

My jaw falls open. "Why would you do that?"

"Because The Temple has a bad reputation?"

"How do you know?" I cock an eyebrow.

"I've *heard* it has a bad reputation. *I've* never been there."

Fiddling with the edge of the sheet, I say, "I don't even know if I'll get the job. So, calm down."

I got the job.

Finn made good on his promise.

At every shift, Finn sits at the bar. He keeps his back turned toward the stage, and not once have I caught him turning his head over his shoulder to watch the entertainment on stage. It's so cute. He nurses one whiskey all night and watches me as I work. Being new and learning the ropes, at first I found it a little awkward. Now, I enjoy his company. Especially if a man gets overly friendly with me, thinking I'm part of the less-clothed entertainment. All Finn has to do is give them a back-the-fuck-off glare and they quickly step away, never to bother me again.

Although it's a different story when a woman approaches Finn. They don't ignore *my* back-the-fuck-off glare. Even though the girls need payment for private lap dances, I can bet my next paycheck they'd offer one to him for free. As soon as he walks through the club's doors, the women fluff out their hair, lift their skirts, and make a beeline for him to see who gets to him first. They are shamefully flirty, not caring when he tells them he has a girlfriend…me!

Tonight, Finn shows up with Hayden and Lucas. I'm not sure how they feel about Finn and I being back together. If they're wary of me, I guess I can't blame them. Though they smile and greet me with politeness, I'm sure they'll cut me down if I ever hurt Finn again.

The three men slide onto barstools. They have some serious good-looking genes going on. All tall, dark, and handsome. The women are going to flock around them like flies. Great!

"What can I get you to drink?" I ask. They give me a whiskey order. Thank God they want nothing too fancy. Whiskey straight up I can manage without turning to Google.

Passing them each their drink, I move onto the next customer. I'd love to stay and chat with Finn and his brothers, but it's a busy night and I have work to do.

Like I predicted, with three handsome men in the club, it doesn't take long for the women to notice them. Fresh blood. One by one, they pump up their boobs in their tiny tops and sway their hips as they approach. Princess P—the P standing for Pussy—is in the front line, zeroing in on Finn.

Before Princess P can make her move on him, I slide a tray with drinks along the counter in front of her. "Table six is waiting for their order."

Princess P cocks an eyebrow. "Get someone else to do it. I'm busy." Her cat-like claws scratches over Finn's shoulder. Finn shakes her off. Her hand drops to her side and she pouts with disappointment.

Bitch. Get it through your thick head. He doesn't want you! is what I want to say. Instead, I say, "They asked for you." I just made that up to get rid of her.

Rolling her eyes, Princess P huffs. "Fine." She picks up the tray. Leaning toward Finn, she purrs, "I'll be back soon." Sashaying away, her hips rock from side to side. The pink faux leather skirt she's wearing barely covers her ass. Unlike Hayden and Lucas, Finn doesn't glance her way.

"Damn, she's hot," Lucas exclaims. "She's into you too." He gives Finn's shoulder a light punch. "Lucky Dog."

I clear my throat behind him. Swiveling toward me on his chair, his eyes pop. "I mean, not that Finn will do anything... He's obviously not into her... He will always—"

"I think Harper gets the message," Finn interrupts, his lips quirking into a grin over the rim of his glass. I can't help but smile back at him even though Lucas' comment annoyed me.

Hayden and Lucas turn to watch the performance happening on stage, looking like they're enjoying it. Why wouldn't they? Angel, who is an amazing pole dancer, spins around the pole to the song *Pony* in nothing but a cowboy hat, purple nipple tassels, and a G-string.

Alyssa slides behind the bar. A blonde wig conceals her dark hair. A black trench coat covers her dance costume. "Hey, who did Finn bring with him? They're *hot*! Although, one looks a little too flirty for my taste." Lady Cherry has sided up to Lucas, and he's lapping up her attention. "I bet it only takes her ten seconds to convince him to get a lap dance."

As soon as Alyssa says the words, Lucas grabs onto Cherry's hand, and she leads him to the private area. We snicker behind our hands.

"The man with Lady Cherry is Finn's younger brother, Lucas." I point a finger at Hayden sitting with Finn. "That's Finn's older brother, Hayden."

"Wow, three hotties from one family. Nice."

I see Alyssa eyeballing Hayden. He's a little older than she is, but who am I to judge? I check the time on my watch. "You better get backstage. You're up next."

"Shit." Alyssa quickly pours a glass of water, guzzles it down, and dashes around the bar to the door that leads backstage. "Wish me luck!" she calls over her shoulder.

"Good luck!" I yell back. She doesn't need it. I've finally gotten to see her dance in person, and she's amazing. Watching her gives me goosebumps. Broadway doesn't know what they're missing.

Making my way along the counter of the bar, I say to Finn, "Alyssa's up next. She told me earlier she's changed her routine. I can't wait to see it."

When Angel finishes her set the lights dim, plunging the stage into darkness. Silence fills the room. The regulars know what's coming. A golden spotlight hits the stage. Alyssa, in her trench coat, stands under the beam of light. With a hand resting on a chair, wearing six-inch heels, she is ready to rock the room.

Chapter Thirty-Five

―――◆―――

FINN

Watching Alyssa dance is like watching something choreographed for an upscale performance. Something you'd never find at a cheap strip club. It's sexy, yet not slutty. She doesn't take her clothes off or gyrate all over the stage for tips. She keeps it classy, and all eyes are glued on her. Including Hayden's.

"Who is that?" Hayden asks in awe.

"It's Harper's roommate, Alyssa."

"She's amazing," Hayden says with wide eyes.

I have a feeling Hayden isn't just talking about Alyssa's dancing skills. He hasn't blinked since the spotlight covered her with golden light. I hide my smile. Hayden never gets distracted by a woman—choosing to focus only on his daughter and career. The last woman I saw him with was Lily's mother. I may spend most of my time living in London, but if there were women in his life, Lucas would have told me. Unless Hayden is dating in secret, which I doubt. It took a lot of effort to get him here tonight even though Lily is at a sleepover.

The music ends and the stage goes dark. Alyssa's performance is over. I know from coming here the last three nights, she'll have another two dances later.

Harper props her forearms on the counter and leans toward me. "Isn't she amazing?"

"Who's amazing?" Lucas, with a huge grin, takes a seat next to me. I don't have to guess how his lap dance went. His unzipped fly is proof it went well.

"You missed my friend Alyssa dance on stage," Harper informs him.

"Did she get her gear off?" Lucas asks.

I turn back to Harper, and I catch her eyeroll. "No. She's a performer, not a stripper."

"Then I had a better time with Lady Cherry," he says to Harper. To me, he whispers with a wink, "Her *cherry* was delicious."

I shake my head. When will Lucas grow up? All he wants to do is go out and fuck women until his dick falls off. Wait...wasn't that what I was doing before Harper came back into my life? How quickly things can change when you're happy and with the person you love. Glancing over at her smiling and chatting with a customer, all I want to do is drag her home and make love to her over and over again. Make her a permanent part of my life.

"I think I want to marry Harper," I say to Hayden and Lucas.

"What?" my brothers say at the same time.

Making sure Harper is still serving customers and out of earshot, I say again, "I think I want to marry Harper—no, I *know* I want to marry her."

Hayden's eyes narrow. "I thought you said there was something not quite right. Like maybe she was holding something back."

It had crossed my mind. Lately, I've been so wrapped up in her, I haven't visited that thought again. Well, except for the nanosecond I thought she was working with Matteo. Surely if she's hiding something, I'd feel it, right? I flick another glance at her wiping down the counter. Like she feels my gaze on her, she lifts her head and smiles at me. The smile smashes into my chest. God, I love her.

"I think she's told me everything," I say.

"You think?" Lucas raises an eyebrow.

I spin the glass in my hand. "What more can there be?"

Hayden scratches the side of his neck and shrugs. "Who knows? But if you are thinking something is off, trust your gut."

Trust my gut. My gut is telling me I want Harper permanently in my life.

"Why do you want to get married anyway?" Lucas waves a hand in the direction of the stage and the women chatting up customers. "When you can have a variety of women who will suck your dick until your eyeballs pop."

Choking on a laugh, I shake my head. I don't want a variety of women.

I only want Harper.

Chapter Thirty-Six

HARPER

The shrill sound of my phone on the nightstand wakes me from a deep sleep. I groan at the interruption, cursing myself for not putting it on silent before I went to bed. Working late nights at The Temple has me sleeping in longer in the mornings than I normally would. I place a pillow over my head and try to ignore the annoying sound. Finn has already left for work, and I'm hoping for a couple more hours of sleep.

When the ringing stops, I sigh with relief and nuzzle my face in the pillow. A few seconds later, it rings again. Pushing my hair from my face, I crack my eyes open and glare at the offending device. I better answer it. It could be important. Picking the phone up, I see Finn's name on the display.

"Finn," I answer. "Is everything okay?"

"No, everything is not okay."

I spring into a sitting position and fling my legs off the bed, ready to go wherever I'm needed. The fog of sleepiness evaporating. "What's wrong?"

I search the closet for jeans and a t-shirt. I don't have the beautiful clothes from Alessi's anymore. I gave them back after I quit. Finn insisted I keep them, but it didn't feel right.

"You're not at work," his deep voice grumbles.

I pause with my clothes in my hands. "I don't work there anymore. I haven't in days."

"What can I do to change your mind? Sexual favors didn't do the trick."

I giggle and sit on the bed. "You can keep trying with sexual favors if you like. Maybe I need a little more convincing. I really liked the way you did that thing with your tongue—"

"Get your ass in the office now!" he growls. "I'll be happy to do it again and again and again."

I clench my thighs together. Just the sound of his voice makes me hot. "I'm not coming into the office to have sex with you."

"As much as I'd love for you to do that, there is another reason I need you here."

"Oh, why?"

"I'll tell you when you get here. Just so you know, we'll get to the tongue thing tonight. Love you." With that, he disconnects the call.

I flop onto my back. Covering my rapidly beating heart with my hands, I sigh with happiness. I'll never tire of hearing Finn tell me he loves me. Once he opened up and let those words out, he hasn't stopped telling me. He's giving me his all. And I'm giving him...secrets.

The smile on my face drops as guilt once again plagues me, smothering the feelings of elation. I'm not giving him *my* all. Not when I have a secret hanging over my head like a dark cloud. I can't keep it to myself anymore. Not if I want an open and honest relationship with Finn. I need to tell him soon and hope it doesn't shatter his heart. I pray he'll forgive me for keeping it from him.

At Alessi's, I duck into Tamara's office before meeting up with Finn. She's sitting at her desk, typing something on the computer. When she sees me, she smiles and gestures for me to take a seat. "Has Finn convinced you to come back?"

"No, although he called me here. Has something happened? Does this have anything to do with Bianca and Matteo?" Surely not, Finn would have sounded pissed on the phone if it had anything to do with them.

Tamara clasps her hands together and places them on the desk. "Everything's good. Especially now that Bianca's gone, the office is a much happier place. Like it usually is when she's working in London. Thank God the wicked witch is dead."

"I'm glad things are back to normal." I peer out the door to the hallway that leads to my desk. Apart from dealing with Bianca, I loved working at Alessi's. Being surrounded by such beauty had unearthed my love for fashion again.

"You can always come back." Tamara must have picked up on my longing. "With Bianca gone we could use the help. I'm looking for another PA for Finn. The job's yours if you want it."

"As tempting as that sounds, you know it's a bad idea. I want to enroll in a fashion design course again."

"That's wonderful. If design is what you want to do, I'm sure Finn can help—"

"No. I want to do this on my own and not get any special assistance because I'm Finn Alessi's girlfriend."

"Good for you." Tamara smiles encouragingly.

Starting again after all these years is scary. Yet excitement also drums through my body. Can I do it? I'll never know unless I try. Where I enroll will depend on where I'm living. Will it be New York or London? Either will be amazing. I'll have to research schools in London just in case.

Finn pops his head inside the door. "I heard you were here. Do you want more time with Tamara, or are you done?" His gaze flicks between the both of us.

"I'm done." I rise. "If you have time, do you want to have lunch?" I ask Tamara.

"I'd love to. Come back when you've finished with Finn," she says.

Finn holds out a hand for me to take. I hesitate for a moment. What will people say? Then it hits me. I don't work at Alessi's anymore. Finn isn't my boss. If I want to hold his hand, there's nothing stopping me. I lace our fingers together and follow him to his office. My old co-workers greet me with friendly waves and hellos.

Once in the office, Finn closes the door behind us. Sliding his arms around my waist, he tugs me to him and kisses me. "I miss you," he mumbles against my lips.

I giggle. "I saw you a few hours ago."

"Still too long." He tunnels his fingers through my hair and deepens the kiss, his tongue sweeping into my mouth. "I can't get enough of you." He groans against my mouth with frustration. "But this is going to have to wait until tonight." Reluctantly, he pulls away.

We sit on the sofa looking over the city. "So, why am I here?"

"I'm attending a charity event tonight. With everything going on, I forgot about it. I'd love for you to come with me. Do you think you can get a night off work or get someone to cover your shift? I know it's last minute."

"You're in luck, I have the next two nights off."

"Excellent. Juliette can fit you with a gown."

"You want to go to a charity event after what happened at the Met Gala? The media will only hound you with questions about the duplicate gown." Why would he want to be put through that?

"If I cancel, it will look like I'm guilty and in hiding. With you wearing one of Juliette's creations, the media will see Matteo's designs can't hold a candle against Alessi. They'll see who really stole the dress."

"I'll be happy to go with you." If I can support Finn in any way, I'll do it. "Do you have anything in mind you want me to wear?"

"I'll leave that up to you and Juliette."

We kiss goodbye, and I make my way to Juliette's room, eager to see what's waiting for me. This will be like playing dress-up with the most exquisite dresses. In her office, I see three gowns displayed on mannequins. All of them stunning. The one that catches my eye is the ice-blue, looks-like-a-cloud gown I tried on for Juliette for the photoshoot. I finger the soft fabric.

Juliette struts into the room, waving the folding fan in front of her face. She flicks it closed and tosses it onto the table. "I see you've chosen the gown you want to wear. Great choice. It looked amazing on you. Not that the others wouldn't."

"I felt amazing in it."

We take the dress off the mannequin, and I duck behind the privacy screen to change.

Stepping out, the skirt swishes around my legs. "How do I look?"

Juliette claps her hands. "*Magnifique*! As beautiful as I remember. I can't imagine anyone else wearing this gown now." Juliette's gaze travels over me from head to toe, examining the dress. She twirls her finger in the air, indicating for me to spin. "Perfect!"

Once I'm back in my jeans and t-shirt, I find Juliette studying a sketch on an easel.

She turns to me and says, "Darling, why on earth did you leave Alessi's?"

"I had to move on." It wasn't an easy choice, but one I needed to make.

One manicured eyebrow rose. "To a strip club?"

"I'm sure Finn told you I'm not stripping. I'm working behind the bar."

"What about going back to design school? If you did, I'm sure Finn would hire you as an intern." Juliette moves from the easel and to a dress on a mannequin. She adjusts the thin straps and fluffs out the skirt.

"I'm thinking about enrolling in school again. I'd love to finish it this time and see where it takes me. But it won't be here at Alessi's. I need to make my own way. I can't have my boyfriend plan out my future."

"There's nothing wrong with a little help. Most of the time, to get into this industry it's 'who you know'."

"Yes, but I'll always be wondering if I'm actually good enough or if it's only because of Finn."

Juliette nods. "I understand. When you decide what you want to do, let me know. I'll be happy to put in a good word for you." I open my mouth to protest, but Juliette holds up her hand, stopping me. "I'm not handing you a job. People need references when applying for positions. I'll be happy to provide one."

After Derek's death, I never would have pictured things turning out like this. I have amazing people in my life. People who genuinely care for me. Finn *loves* me. It all seems too good to be true. I'm afraid this euphoric bubble I'm living in will pop. I don't want that to happen. Best to stay away from sharp edges.

The rest of the afternoon is a hive of activity. Not only do I get to wear one of Juliette's creations, Finn also sent a style team to my apartment. I've been pampered with a manicure, pedicure, facial, and every other beauty treatment possible. The hairdresser created a work of art with my hair. Old school Hollywood waves cascade over my right shoulder, exposing the deep plunge at my back. My makeup is simple and elegant with neutral colors except for the pop of red lips. When the team leaves, I anxiously look in the mirror. I'm amazed at the transformation.

A few minutes later, a knock sounds at the door. I take a deep breath and open it. Finn's gaze roams over me from my head to toes, a look of admiration on his face. "You look amazing!"

"You like?" I swish my skirt from side to side.

Finn's eyes lock with mine. "Very much. You're beautiful with or without the gown." My heart does a backflip.

Finn's wearing a black tuxedo, white shirt, and black bow tie. He slicked his hair back into a neat style. Gold cufflinks glint at his wrists. "You look beautiful too."

He cocks an eyebrow. "Beautiful?"

Rolling my eyes, I say, "Yes. Men can be beautiful too." With a laugh, I adjust his tie. "You also look sexy as hell, and if I wasn't so dressed up, I'd do you right here."

His eyes blaze down at me with heat. "Fuck the dress, fuck the event. I want to stay here and *fuck* you!"

With a giggle, I step out of his reach in case he touches me. I can't risk ruining all the hard work his team did on me. "As much as I love the sound of that, we have to go to the event. It will look good for Alessi Fashion."

Finn blows out a frustrated breath. He knows I'm right. "Fine, but as soon as possible, we're leaving so I can strip that dress from your body."

I shiver with desire. "I'm looking forward to it."

"Before we leave, I have something for you." Reaching a hand inside his jacket, he pulls out a small, black, velvet box and hands it to me. "This is for you."

My gaze flicks from the box to Finn's face. He rolls his lips. Does he look nervous? This can't be...no, surely not an engagement ring? The oxygen squeezes from my lungs. He wouldn't propose before leaving to go to an event, would he? If he is, what will I say? With his father's secret burning a hole in my gut, I can't accept. Not when I haven't been totally honest with him. Oh...but to be married to Finn. It would make me the happiest woman in the world. I have to tell the truth before we get deeper into this relationship. It's only fair to Finn.

"It's not an engagement ring. If that's what you're wondering." He chuckles like he can read my mind. "I'll find a better time and place to do that."

A better time and place? Does that mean... Oh God...he wants to propose! My legs shake.

Lifting the lid on the box, I see a diamond necklace set in a delicate and intricate gold setting sitting on the black velvet. I gasp. "It's beautiful."

"It's the diamond from the engagement ring I bought you years ago. I had the gold melted down and set the diamond into a pendant and chain. It was always meant to be yours, so I wanted you to have it." When I don't say anything, just stare at the box, he scrubs his fingers through his neatly styled hair, tousling it. "Shit. It's weird, isn't it? I should have gotten you a new one not this—"

I cup his cheek with my free hand, kissing his lips again. "It's not weird. It's perfect. I love it. Can you put it on me please?" I'm not sure if Juliette would approve of the addition. I don't care, I want to wear it. I'm so happy he no longer needs it to remind him of the past. Is this his way of erasing it and looking to the future?

"Are you sure?" he asks with uncertainty.

"Yes." I pluck it from the box and hand it to him. The huge diamond glitters under the light. I turn my back to him and lift my hair out of the way. Finn clips the necklace on, kissing the top of my shoulder when it's in place. I turn around and smile. "Ready to go?"

Now is not the time to tell him about his father. It can wait until after the charity event. No point upsetting him after such a touching moment shared between us. When we get home though, I'll lay everything out on the table.

As I follow him from the apartment, I pray he'll forgive me.

Chapter Thirty-Seven

FINN

IN THE BACK OF the limo, Harper snuggles as close to me as her dress allows. The diamond around her neck sparkles as it catches the streetlights whizzing past. The other diamond I'm holding onto is burning a hole in my pocket. I'm waiting for the right moment to propose to Harper. Before the event wasn't the time. Not when she had looked at the box with the necklace like what was inside was going to bite. It made me question whether proposing is the right thing to do. Is she scared of a commitment? Why? With the way our relationship is going...yes, we've had a few bumps along the way, but everything is looking great now. Harper is my woman. Maybe I'm overthinking this.

Harper stares out the window, fidgeting with her fingers sitting in her lap. Her leg is bouncing under the layers of fabric. Placing a hand on her leg, I say, "Hey, is everything okay?"

Turning to look at me, she gives me a stiff smile that doesn't reach her eyes. "I'm fine."

Something's not right. "No, you're not." I link our fingers together. "Talk to me."

She drops her head and glances at our hands. "I'm nervous. That's all."

"Why?"

"I'm in this glamorous dress, with one of the owners of Alessi Fashion. I'm sure there'll be a red carpet. What if I mess up? I might trip and fall. If I'm asked a question, I might say something stupid and embarrass you."

Placing a finger under her chin, I tilt her face up to look at me. "You won't mess up or embarrass me." I kiss her palm. "Relax. Just be yourself. Everyone will love you. If, at any point, you feel uncomfortable, let me know and we'll leave. Okay?"

"Okay." She still looks tense.

"I know a way that can help you relax." I dust a finger over Harper's collarbone and dip it behind the neckline of the bodice.

Harper's eyes widen. "We can't. You'll ruin my hair and makeup. Do you know how much work went into this?"

Dropping to my knees in front of her, I rest my hands on her legs. "What I have planned won't put a hair out of place." I toss the skirt of the dress to her waist and slide my hands up her smooth thighs.

"Finn, we can't. What about the driver?" Her legs fall open, making her protest sound weak and unconvincing.

"He can't hear or see anything with the privacy screen up." I pick up her left leg and kiss her calf. My tongue slowly glides to her thigh, and I hover over her pale blue lace covered pussy. Her head falls back on the seat, and she tilts her pelvis up toward me, giving me permission. "Relax and enjoy the ride."

Arriving at the charity event, Harper steps from the limousine and smiles like the cat that ate the cream, looking extremely relaxed. My planned worked. Anything to make my woman happy, I'll do it.

When we step onto the red carpet, journalists call my name and cameras flash in front of our faces. Harper's hand grips mine. I whisper in her ear, "Are you okay? Do you want to leave?"

She smiles reassuringly but doesn't ease off on her grip. "I'm fine."

Soon Met Gala questions are fired our way.

"Did you steal Matteo Blanchett's design?" one reporter asks.

"No. Someone stole it from Juliette Monet. This is another of Ms. Monet's creations," I say, gesturing to Harper's dress. "As you can see by this stunning dress, Ms. Monet has too much talent to steal from anyone."

Cameras flash blinding bright at Harper to capture the gown. She smiles at them. Not looking at all as uncomfortable as I know she's feeling inside. That's my girl!

"Who did it?" another reporter yells.

"I don't know. We're looking into it." I never reported Bianca's involvement and won't release it to the media. It would be too messy. I'd rather forget about her and the shitstorm she created.

Once I have enough of answering questions, I usher Harper inside.

"Are you okay?" I rub a hand down Harper's back.

"Yes. It wasn't so bad. Do you think they believe you didn't steal the design?"

I shrug. "They'll believe what they want. There's nothing I can do about it. When Juliette's collection comes out, they'll know who needs to steal designs. Matteo's designs won't come close." I tap a finger on her nose. "We've made an appearance. We can slip out the back and go home if you like."

"Maybe we should do a lap of the room first and show off this gorgeous Juliette Monet creation."

That's a good idea. With my peers in the room—if they have any doubt, it's a good idea to remind them how good Alessi Fashion is. I hook Harper's arm in the crook of my elbow and enter the ballroom. Soft gold walls shimmer in the light of crystal chandeliers. Pillars of floral decorations are meticulously placed around the room, filling the air with their sweet scent. We mingle with the other guests, and it doesn't take long to learn who they believe the thief is. They all know Blanchett Fashion House is declining and he's clutching on for dear life.

When Harper and I are in a quiet area of the room, I let out a long breath I didn't realize I was holding. Even though I had faith in our designs and reputation, it's a relief to have the industry on our side.

Harper squeezes my hand and smiles brightly at me. "Alessi Fashion is, and will always be, on top. They know it wasn't you. I'm so proud of you." She gives me a quick kiss on the lips.

As long as Harper is by my side cheering me on, I can get through anything. God, I love her. I want to get her home and ask her to marry me as soon as possible. Make her mine forever. I can't wait much longer.

Something over my shoulder grabs Harper's attention. Her face screws up with anger. "They have a lot of nerve showing up here! How can they show their faces after what they've done?"

I turn to see Matteo walking into the ballroom with Bianca on his arm. "Because Matteo thinks the industry believes him. That's how conceited he is."

We watch them as they make their way around the room. One by one, people are lifting their noses up and turning their backs. It's obvious they've shunned Matteo.

"It looks like it's confirmed who everyone believes," I say. "He'll be lucky to work in fashion again. I kind of feel sorry for him."

Harper's eyes widen. "You do?"

"No. He deserves everything he gets."

Harper giggles. "You're bad."

"I want to get you home and show you how *bad* I can be, but I see my dad and brothers coming over, so it's going to have to wait a little longer."

She sighs with disappointment.

I chuckle. "Patience, my love."

I wave to my family. When they approach, I shake their hands and they all say hello to Harper.

My father even gives Harper a kiss on the cheek. I'm so grateful he's trying. "Good to see you, Harper. You look beautiful."

Harper stiffens at my side, and the color drains from her face. It couldn't be easy for her being around my father after hearing the things he said about her in my office. Hopefully, he's sincerely trying to attempt to get along.

"Nice to see you too." Her smile is frozen on her face.

"Thankfully, this Met Gala disaster can be put to rest," my father says to me.

"I still think we should get the police involved and have Bianca and Matteo charged. We have proof," Hayden says.

"Why you didn't release that information, I don't understand. You risked the industry not believing us. That was a ballsy move." Lucas raises his glass of scotch in the air.

Holding my arm out to Harper, I say, "Look at this gown. Who would ever believe we'd copy anyone else?"

"It's stunning." My father gives the dress an appreciative look.

Harper shuffles her feet, probably uncomfortable with the attention on her. I place my hand on the small of her back to soothe her.

"Matteo and Bianca could have cost us millions," Hayden says with agitation. "They need to be punished."

My father taps him on the back. "Always thinking about money."

Hayden shuffles slightly away from our father. The movement so minor you'd hardly notice. I notice because for years Hayden has had a problem with him. Why?

"I think we should let it go," Dad says. "Do we really want the media circus involved? They've already hung themselves. They'll pay the price."

"I agree with Dad. Let's drop it. If they cause any more problems, then we'll do something," I say.

My father claps his hands. "Now that's settled, there's someone I see that I'd like to speak to. Enjoy your evening, boys." He nods his head to Harper. "Harper." With that, he heads off into the crowd.

Harper turns to me, looking a little flustered. This could still be a sensitive subject considering she believed we blamed her. "I'm going to the bar to get a drink."

"I'll get it. What would you like?"

She shakes her head. "That's okay. Stay and talk with your brothers. I'll be right back." She spins on her heels and rushes away before I can object.

I don't want to talk to my brothers. I want to make sure Harper is okay. Before I can go to her, I get stopped by a colleague and lose sight of her.

Chapter Thirty-Eight

HARPER

At the bar, I sip—or more like guzzle—my glass of champagne. Seeing Marco makes my blood run cold. I saw through his fake smile and friendly kiss on the cheek he gave me. It took all my might not to wipe it off my face. Swallowing the rest of the drink, I put the glass on the counter. If Finn is ready to leave, I'll ask him to take me home. Then I'll tell him what I know about his father. Hopefully he'll forgive me for keeping the secret for so long.

Before making my way to him, I need to make a stop at the ladies' room. As I walk down the long, narrow corridor, I spot Marco and Bianca in what looks like a heated discussion. Marco has his arms crossed over his chest. Bianca's hands are waving in front of his face with agitation. So they don't see me, which is good, because they're the last two people I want to bump into. I duck into an open doorway that appears to be a sitting room. I listen as their voices grow louder and travel through the corridor.

"I'm an outcast, and it's all your fault," Bianca hisses resentfully.

"Don't be so dramatic."

What did she mean *it's all your fault*. I pop my head out slightly, not wanting to be seen, but hoping to get a better understanding as to what is happening.

Bianca is jabbing a finger at Marco's chest, her face twisting with rage. "Have you seen the way everyone is looking at me? Or should I say *not* looking at me? They believe Matteo stole the design, and because I worked for Alessi's and have arrived on Matteo's arm, they've put two and two together."

Marco rolls his eyes. "So I was wrong. They'll get over it."

"Get over it! Get over it! They will not *get over it*. Because of you, I'll never work in the fashion industry again," Bianca's voice rises with anger.

Marco pinches the bridge of his nose. "You're being ridiculous. In a couple of months it will be forgotten."

"This is your fault," she says again. "You told me Finn would believe Harper stole the designs and boot her out of his life."

I gasp with shock, cover my mouth, and duck my head back into the sitting room. Marco arranged for the design to be stolen? Just so he could get me away from Finn? This man is insane! How can he do this to his son? He stood in front of his sons and acted like he knew nothing about it. No wonder he didn't want Bianca charged. Because he knew she'd drag him down with her. The sooner Finn knows the truth about him, the better.

"Enough," I hear Marco growl. "I paid you enough to last for years. You've lost nothing. I can lose my sons if they find out about this. If you dare breathe a word to anyone, I will make your life a living hell. Not only will you never step foot in the fashion industry again, you'll never find work in any reputable establishment. Is that clear?"

I don't hear Bianca's answer. I can't hear anything over the pounding of my heart. After watching her race past the sitting room, I assume she agreed. A red haze covers my eyes, my chest heaves, and with clenched fists, I step out of the room and into the corridor.

Marco's eyes widen with surprise at seeing me, and he quickly masks his menacing expression with a fake smile. "Harper, I didn't see you coming this way. Are you having a good time?"

"Cut the crap, Marco," I say through gritted teeth.

He raises an eyebrow. "Excuse me?"

Pointing a thumb over my shoulder, I say, "I heard you talking to Bianca. How could you do that to your sons? They've worked so hard. Built the company up ten times better since they've managed it. For what? So you can tear it down just to get me out of Finn's life?"

Marco slides his hands into the pockets of his trousers, the stance appearing casual to anyone walking by. But I can feel the animosity rolling off him in waves. "You don't deserve to be in his life. You nearly killed him."

I toss my head back and scoff. "You don't want me around because of what I know. Not because of Finn's feelings. I've kept your dirty, little secret long enough. It's time your sons find out about how their father cheated on their mother while she lay dying. I'm sure they'll also love to know about your little scheme with Bianca."

Giving me a sly smirk, he says, "With what proof? Do you think they're going to believe any of this? They know how much I loved their mother and our company. Go ahead. Tell them. See what happens to you."

It's my time to give him a sly smirk. "I might not have proof for the stolen design, but I have proof about your affair. I have the woman's name, address, and where she works. Oh, and lots and lots of photos of the two of you intimately together, courtesy of Derek. Who knew by giving me his blackmail file on you, he'd done something decent in his life? I'm not sure why he did it, but he had someone pack it in my suitcase after his death."

Marco's face grows pale. He swallows hard. "I don't believe you."

I shrug. "I don't care if you believe me. Let's find out if Finn does." I need to talk to Finn now! This can't go on a moment longer.

I turn away to go find Finn, but Marco clamps a hand around my bicep and swings me around. He clutches his hands on my shoulders in a tight grip. I wince with pain. Marco stands nose to nose in front of me. "If you tell them anything, I will destroy you."

Flinging his hands off me, I step out of his reach. "I've had enough of dealing with men like you. You threaten and bully people to get your way. Well, not anymore. It's time for the truth to come out. I'm not covering for you anymore. I thought I was doing Finn a favor. I didn't want your behavior to hurt him. What a mistake."

I hurry away on shaky legs before he can stop me again. He yells my name. I don't stop. *Where's Finn?* I frantically scan the room, pushing through the crowd, not caring about the annoyed expressions thrown my way. I finally spot him talking with a group of men.

Reaching him, I clasp his hand. "Finn, I need to talk to you."

He steps away from the group. Concern is etched on his face. "What's wrong? Has something happened?"

Before I can answer, behind me people gasp and squeal with fright. Turning, I see Marco clutching the back of a chair, then he collapses onto the floor.

"Dad!" Finn cries. Stepping around me, he races to his father. Hayden and Lucas aren't far behind. "Someone call 911," Finn yells, dropping to his knees.

For a moment I stare at Marco, wondering if this is all an act to stop me from talking to Finn. Would he go this far? He runs the risk of losing his family. Then I snap out of it. This could be serious. He has a lot to lose. The stress could have done some damage. Digging into my purse, I pull out my phone and call for an ambulance.

Finn and his brothers don't leave Marco's side while waiting for the paramedics. When they arrive, they settle him and get him ready to take to the hospital. Finn turns to me. "I'm going with him."

"I'll come with you." I need to be by his side to support him.

"No, I don't know how long we'll be. The limo is waiting for you. Take it home. I'll call you as soon as I can." With a quick kiss on my lips, he follows the paramedics from the ballroom.

My trembling fingers touch my mouth, hoping for Finn's sake his father will be okay. I can't tell Finn the truth now. After this, will I ever be able to?

I arrive home and change out of the gown and into sweats. Pacing the small living room, I keep glancing at the time, waiting for Finn's call. Is Marco really sick, or is it just a ruse to stop me from talking to Finn? God, I hope he isn't so conniving to go that far. Had the stress of the moment brought on what appeared to be a heart attack? Guilt washes over me. Maybe I could have dealt with it better. When I learned about his involvement in the design scandal, I was so angry, I couldn't hold back a moment longer.

Dropping onto the sofa, I check my phone. Still no text from Finn. I wish Alyssa were home. She'd help me take my mind off things. Should I message Finn? No, he's probably busy with Marco. He told me he'd call me when he could. Tucking my legs up onto the sofa, I lay my head down and wait. The events of the day catch up with me, and my heavy eyelids flutter closed.

Knock. Knock.

I wake with a start. *What was that?* I stretch and search groggily around the room with confusion.

Knock. Knock.

Someone is at the door. Finn! Jumping to my feet, I run and open the door. With his hair tousled, rumpled clothes, and dark smudges under his eyes, he looks exhausted.

"How's Marco? Is he okay?" I ask as he steps into the apartment.

He nods. "Looks like severe heartburn. He's staying overnight to be monitored and run more tests."

I blow out a relieved breath. I throw my arms around his neck. "Thank God."

When his arms stay stiff by his sides, I pull back to stare at him. He takes two steps away from me. Cold eyes look back at me. A chill runs down my spine. Did Marco say something to Finn? Did he confess the truth and now Finn is angry with me for keeping it from him?

"Finn, what's wrong?"

With an edge to his voice, he says, "While I was at the hospital, I got a text. You might be interested in seeing it." Pulling out his phone from his jacket pocket, he swipes the screen and hands it to me.

Frowning with confusion, I look at the screen. Blood rushes to my ears and pounds at my temples. "Where did you get this?"

Finn glowers. "Does it matter!"

"Yes, it matters." I wave the phone in the air. "Whoever sent this is trying to cause trouble between us." I put my money on Bianca. I thought she rushed away. Maybe she stuck around to do this. Desperate enough to want to rip Finn and I apart and also get her revenge on Marco.

With a snort of contemptuous laughter, he nods at the phone. "It looks like you're the one who's caused trouble between us. Well, you and my father."

Fear thrums through my veins. "This is not what it looks like." I look back at the photo someone sent Finn of Marco and I. Taken from a distance, it shows Marco's hands on my shoulders, our noses almost touching. It looks like Marco and I are in a lover's embrace with him about to kiss me. Not how Marco's eyes were striking me with venom. "Someone wants to hurt us. It was Bianca, wasn't it?" I ask, my voice shaking.

Ignoring my question, he says, "Was I the stepping-stone to get to my father? The patriarch of the family? Are his pockets deeper than mine? Was the 'friction' between you both purely for my sake? A distraction as to what was really going on?" He scrubs his hands over his face. His voice cracks, "I fucking fell for it."

My world is crumbling around me. *Please, no. I can't lose him again.* "Finn, I can explain." I step closer, needing to be near him.

Finn holds up his hand, stopping me from touching him. "There's nothing to explain. I'm such a fool for trusting you again. I had this feeling in my gut…" He splays his hand over his stomach. "…telling me something was off. Like you were keeping something from me. I ignored it. Believed your story. But that's the last time I'll ever believe anything you say."

A sob catches in my throat, and tears roll down my hot cheeks. "It's not a story. I've wanted to talk to you—tell you something about Marco—something I wasn't sure you wanted to hear. But I'm not involved with Marco. Please, let me explain what this photo is really about."

He hangs his head. "No more lies, please." He turns to leave.

I rush after him, grabbing his arm to stop him. He glances at my hand like something crapped on him and shakes it away. With a sinking heart, I take a step back. "Did you show Marco the photo? He'll tell you it's not what it looks like."

"He told me you've been coming onto him since the minute your *husband* died. Begging to be together. He said that photo was a moment of weakness on his part."

An icy wave washes over me, ripping the breath from my lungs. "No," I say, my voice cracking. *How could Marco do this to his son?* "He's lying. He's been lying to you for years. Finn, I love you—"

"Don't say those words to me again!" His expression is more distant than I've ever seen it before.

My body shakes. *This can't be happening.* There's nothing more I can say or do, so I watch Finn storm out of the apartment and slam the door behind him. My legs give out, and I slide onto the floor, hugging my knees to my chest. I rock as sobs wrack through my body.

How can Marco do this? How can Finn believe I'd *do* this? The evidence is damning. I wish I had told Finn about Marco sooner, then we wouldn't be in this mess. Now he hates me so much, he won't listen to my side of the story.

I've lost him. Again. It was torture the first time. It took years to pull myself out of a dark hole. How am I supposed to do it again?

Chapter Thirty-Nine

FINN

I arrive at Alessi's the next day and barrel into Juliette's office. The designer has two colored pencils in her hair and one between her lips. Not taking her gaze off the sketch she's working on, she mumbles, "Hello, darling. If you're marching in here about to demand to know what's happening with the designs, I have good news, they'll be finished next week."

Pulling out a chair from behind the desk, I straddle it and lean my forearms on the backrest. "You'll have to send them to London. I'm leaving." With everything that's happened, I can't get out of town fast enough.

Juliette plucks the pencil from her lips. "You're not due back for another couple of weeks." Tossing the pencil on the desk, she takes a seat next to me. "What's happened?"

What's happened? The woman I love is a lying, scheming fucking cheat. My father is just as bad. If he weren't already in the hospital, I'd put him there. "I'm needed at the London branch."

"What about Harper, will she be joining you?"

"We broke up."

Her eyes widen. "Why?"

Because she had her sights set on my father. *My father!* Nausea rolls in my gut. "Everything about her is a lie. The reason she left me nine years ago, why she's working at Alessi's, and her lov..." I choke on the word *love*. That was the biggest lie of them all. The one that killed me the most. For the second time in my life, Harper has ripped my heart out. "Her feelings for me."

Juliette picks up her fan and waves it in front of her face. "You need to explain from the beginning."

I give her a recap of last night's events. Her face is expressionless as she listens. I hand over my phone to show her the incriminating photo. Her eyes narrow at the screen.

"Did you ask her for her side of the story?"

With a frown, I say, "Why would I? The photo says it all. My father even admitted it."

She taps her fan on the screen. "So, you've looked at this photo and have assumed she's up to no good with Marco? To me, this looks like a tense situation. Harper does not look at all comfortable."

Jumping up from the chair, I pace the room. "He *told* me what happened. Told me she's been trying to seduce him."

Juliette pushes from the desk and rises. "I've known Marco for years...you're a big boy now, so I'll tell you a little secret. He's no saint. After your mother passed away, I watched him pursue many women. Sometimes a little too eagerly. And when these women reject him, he has not behaved in a gentlemanly manner toward them. That photo could be something entirely different from what you're thinking. Have you considered that maybe it's Marco who's not telling the truth?"

I abruptly stop my pacing. "Are you saying my father has been inappropriate with women? With Harper? That's fucking ridiculous."

Dropping her hands on her hips, Juliette gives me a sad expression. "Not inappropriate, but pursued a woman too strongly when feelings weren't reciprocated."

My father isn't like that. He plays golf and hangs out with his buddies. I've never seen him with another woman, much less pursuing one. But how would I know for sure? I live in London for most of the year. How would I know what he does when I'm not around? No, surely Hayden or Lucas would have said something if it were true.

"My father's not like that," I say. "Harper wants to get her claws into his money."

Juliette sits on the edge of the desk. "What I see when I look at that photo isn't Harper looking at Marco with any kind of affection. Again, I'd say she looks uncomfortable. Whenever she looked at you, her face lit up with love. If you believe there's nothing more to the story than Marco's rendition, then you're a fool. I haven't known Harper long, but I know for certain there's not a malicious bone in her body. Listen to her side before you judge."

I can't stay and listen to Juliette defend Harper. "I gotta go."

"Just think about what I said before you make any hasty decisions," she calls after me as I leave her office.

On my way out, my phone beeps with a message.

Harper.

I don't want to open it, yet my finger swipes the screen.

I need to talk to you. Please let me explain.

Tilting my head to the ceiling, I blow out a breath. Juliette's words run through my mind. *If you believe there's nothing more to the story than Marco's rendition, then you're a fool.* Do I listen to Juliette and let Harper tell her side of the story? Why would my father lie? No...*she's* the liar. I don't need to hear Harper's side of the story.

Ignoring her message, I slip the phone into my jacket pocket. She buried herself in this mess. I'm not fool enough to fall for her lies again.

It's over. For good.

Chapter Forty

HARPER

I mix up a gin and tonic, add ice, and slide the tumbler to the customer sitting at the bar. I wouldn't mind a shot or two myself to numb my mind from the nightmare I'm living. Alyssa suggested I not come in on my night off, but mixing drinks is distracting me from thinking of Finn every second of the day. I wipe the counter in vigorous circular motions. He's answered none of my text messages. Obviously, he's made his mind up. In his eyes, I'm guilty, and he has cut me out of his life.

"Hey, if you keep scrubbing like that, you're going to wear a hole in the counter." Alyssa sidles up next to me. "Do you need a break? You've been working non-stop for hours. I can cover for you before my performance if you'd like."

I find another sticky spot on the counter to clean. Work is the only thing keeping me going. If I stop, I'm scared I'll fall into a blubbering mess and never be able to get back up. "I don't want a break. Thanks for offering though."

"Are you sure? Earlier I saw you put cut lemons into the tiny umbrella drawer."

"I did?" I pull the drawer open. Sure enough, slices of lemons are sitting on top of colorful umbrellas, soaking through the thin paper. "Shit." I pull the lemons out. The umbrellas are unsalvageable, and I toss them into the trash.

"Let me know if you change your mind." Alyssa gives my shoulder a gentle squeeze.

I nod.

To my left, someone approaches the bar. I turn and try to pull up a smile for the customer, but it freezes on my face. Finn is standing at the end of the counter. For a second, my heart fills with joy. God, I've missed him. One day without him feels like a year. I want to throw my arms around him and never let go. Has he come to listen to what I have to say? The glare he aims at me stops me in my tracks. No, I don't think so. So why is he here?

"I need a drink," he says and clicks his fingers at me. With his disheveled clothes, messy hair, and slurred speech, I can tell he's drunk.

"Do you want me to deal with him?" Alyssa asks.

I shake my head. My heart races as I approach him. "Why are you here?"

He taps a finger on the counter. "I'm here to drink. Why else?" Sliding onto a stool, he glances at the stage where Angel's dancing. "Maybe watch a show. She's talented." He makes circling motions with his head, following the stripper's twirling tassels.

Rolling my lips, I take a deep breath. He's never watched a stripper before. I know he's doing this to hurt me.

Turning back to me, he looks at me with bloodshot eyes and snarls, "Where's my drink?"

If I didn't know how hurt he was, I'd get security to kick him out of the club for being such a dick. Instead, I fill a glass and pass it to him. "Here, drink this."

Finn sticks his nose in the tumbler and sniffs. Screwing up his face, he scoffs, "It's water," and pushes it away. With the force it tips over, spilling water on the counter and onto the floor. I jump away before I get splashed. If Finn keeps behaving this way, my manager will throw him out.

"I'll clean it up." Alyssa rushes to me. "Go sort Finn out."

"Thank you," I say to Alyssa. To Finn, I point in the direction of the room behind the bar. "Come with me.

"Ooh, am I-I getting a private lap dance?" He gives me a cruel sneer. "I'll pass. Been there, done that. Maybe there's someone else I can try? Where's Princess P?" He's deliberately being cruel and trying to hurt me. It's working. Tears sting the backs of my eyes. My heart aches for the love I've lost.

Clasping onto his bicep, I drag him to the breakroom. Thankfully, it's empty. "Why are you here?" I ask again.

"Can't a man go to a strip club whenever he wants?" He digs his hands on his hips.

"There are plenty of clubs in New York City. Why this one?"

"For the talent." He loses his footing, stumbles, and quickly rights himself. Shaking off my attempt to steady him, he points a finger at my face. "You've been texting me, wanting to talk." He spreads his arms wide. "Here I am. T-talk."

How am I supposed to talk to him when he's so drunk? But he won't answer any of my messages, so what other option do I have? This might be the only time I can do it. "The photo someone sent you isn't what it looks like."

He rolls his eyes. "You've already said that. Tell me something new."

God, he's an ass when he's drunk. "I tried. You wouldn't listen."

"How rude of me." He waves a wonky hand in the air for me to continue.

"The night of the charity event, I overheard a conversation between Marco and Bianca. Bianca was angry at him because she got blamed for the Met Gala dress fiasco when it was Marco who put her up to it."

Rubbing his brow, Finn frowns. "Wait…wait…wait. Dad *made* her do it?"

"Yes. I heard him admit he was involved. He threatened Bianca to keep quiet about it or she'd never work in the fashion industry again."

Finn tosses his head back and laughs. "Why would my father, the man who helped create the most prestigious fashion label in the world, sabotage his own company?"

"He wanted to get rid of me and asked Bianca for help."

Scrubbing a hand over his face, Finn says, "I'm so drunk and confused right now. If you think he'd fuck up his company just because you left me years ago, you're wrong. He might not like that we're together, but he wouldn't destroy our reputation."

I pick at my fingernails. "That's not why."

Finn runs his fingers through his hair, messing it up more. "Then why?"

"It's because of something he did to your mother while she lay dying in the hospital. I only found out about it when I threatened to leave Derek. Along with threatening your company, he told me if I left him, he'd tell you, Hayden, and Lucas what your father had done. You and your brothers worshipped him and had already lost your mother. I didn't want to hurt you even more."

Finn grows still, suddenly looking sober. "What did he do?"

Drawing a deep breath, I say, "Marco was having an affair. The night the hospital called the family to say their goodbyes, he never made it. He'd gotten the call—or so Derek said—and stayed with his mistress. Derek had pictures taken from cameras in the hotel room Marco was staying at with timestamps."

Finn's face grows dark and dangerous. "You're lying."

"It's the truth. I wanted to tell you when we got back together, was going to after the charity event, but Marco collapsed and...well, you got the photo. Before he collapsed, I confronted him. Told him I wanted to tell you. He got mad and threatened me. That's what that photo is about."

"You're lying!" he says again with a clenched jaw. He paces the small room.

Why won't Finn believe me? The answer comes quickly. He doesn't trust me. Never did. I give it one more try. "Why would I lie?"

Finn crosses his arms over his chest. "Where did Derek say my father was on the night of my mother's death?"

I twist my hands together. "At his casino in Atlantic City. Apparently, unbeknownst to his guests, he put cameras in the rooms his big spenders stayed in. They were the people he wanted to blackmail one day."

Jabbing a finger at me, he spits, "Lie! My father was rushing back from London to get to her. He worshiped the ground she walked on. Showered her with love. This is bullshit. You've dug yourself into a deep hole, and you're trying to climb out of it. I've seen your true colors. I won't fall for your games again."

My heart sinks to my stomach. There's nothing more I can say to make him see the truth. Except...there's something I can show him. No one wants to see photos of their parents during their most private times—especially with another woman. But it's all I have left to convince Finn I'm not lying.

"I have proof," I say. "Derek gave me the photos."

"I wouldn't trust anything coming from Derek...or you."

Shards of glass cut through my heart. No matter what I say, Finn will never believe me. I've lost him forever.

We stand staring at each other. I have no words left. There's nothing more I can say. He looks at me with a blank expression. Love isn't shining from his eyes anymore.

Tears clog my throat. Turning my back, I whisper, "Just go." I can't take a moment more of him looking at me like I'm shit under his shoe.

The sound of the door closing tells me he's left. I sink into the nearest chair, prop my elbows onto my knees, and drop my face in my hands. Silent tears rattle my chest. It feels like I'm being ripped apart. My body aches from head to toe.

After a few minutes, I get to my feet, push my hair back from my face, and swipe the tears from my cheeks. I can't hide in the breakroom all night. My heart is broken, and I can barely breathe, but I have work to do. It's that or fall apart.

When I go back to the bar, I don't expect Finn to still be here. But I find him sitting at the end of the counter, his shoulders slumped, staring into the glass of amber liquid in his hands. He doesn't look up and acknowledge me, nor does he watch the performance on stage. I hate how dejected he looks. I hate that I'm the cause. If only I'd spoken up sooner, maybe none of this would be happening.

While I work the rest of my shift, Finn stays like he's done every other shift. Except this time, he doesn't see me home.

Chapter Forty-One

FINN

At my desk, I cradle my throbbing head in my hands. It's like a hammer is pounding against my skull. The lights pierce my eyes, my mouth is dry with a bitter taste, and my stomach is churning, threatening to spill. Yet after all the alcohol I consumed, I still remember every fucked-up detail at The Temple. I've come into the office to finalize things before I leave for London, but I can't focus on anything except Harper. How gorgeous she looked. What she said. The broken expression on her face when I left her at the doorway of the club after her shift.

The door swings open and Hayden and Lucas saunter in, taking seats opposite me.

"You look like shit," Lucas points out.

I pull a face. "Thanks."

"Big night?" Hayden wrinkles his nose at my messy hair and rumpled clothes I'd worn yesterday. I'd slept in these clothes and hadn't bothered changing.

"You could say that."

"I thought you'd come to the hospital to see Dad. They released him early this morning. All the tests came back clear," Hayden informs me.

With my head messed up with Harper, I hadn't given my father being in the hospital a second thought. Fuck, what kind of son am I? "Had a lot to do. I'm glad he's fine."

Hayden and Lucas exchange a curious look. "Everything okay?" Lucas asks. They'd been getting coffee in the hospital cafeteria when I received the message with the photo. I haven't seen them since. They don't know what happened.

"I broke things off with Harper."

"Why?" Hayden asks at the same time Lucas says, "You're joking?"

I wish I was joking. Instead, I'm living a fucking nightmare. One I'd promised myself I'd never star in again.

I push off from the chair, walk to the window, and stare sightlessly to the street below. I tell them about receiving a photo of Harper and our father in an intimate embrace. How when I approached him about it, he admitted that she'd been pursuing him, and he succumbed to a moment of weakness. "Of course she denied it. Even tried telling me one hell of a story about Dad." I tell them about the affair while our mother lay dying in the hospital. God, did Harper really think I'd fall for that?

"Holy shit! Is it true?" Lucas says.

I spin around. "Of course not! Dad would never cheat on Mom. Especially when she got diagnosed with brain cancer. He loved her." How can Lucas even question it?

"Why the hell would she make something like that up?" Lucas asked. Can he not see that it's bullshit?

"To get out of the hole she'd dug for herself," I reply.

"She'd make up lies about Dad cheating on Mom to cover up the affair she's having with him?" Lucas pulls a disbelieving face. "He's...*old*."

I link my fingers at the back of my head. "Didn't stop her before. Derek wasn't much younger than Dad." Last night's whiskey churns in my gut at the thought of them together. I notice Hayden sitting quietly, not saying a word. "You have nothing to say?"

Hayden hooks an ankle over his knee. "I have lots to say. I'm not sure you'll want to hear it."

I drop my hands. "Tell me."

Hayden's foot hits the floor, he cups his hands and lets them fall between his knees as he leans forward. "I believe Harper."

If Hayden hit me over the head with a sledgehammer, I'd be less surprised. "You believe Dad was cheating on Mom?"

"Yes." How can Hayden sit there so calmly? Like we're discussing nothing more important than the weather.

"You knew?" Lucas yells and stands beside me.

Hayden blows out a rough breath. "I've known for years. Dad was screwing around with many different women. About ten years ago, without either of us knowing, we were staying at the same hotel in Paris. I stepped into an elevator and found him sucking face with a twenty-something-year-old blonde." Scrubbing his hands over his eyes like he wanted to remove the image, he lifts his head. He screws up his face with disgust. "He made me promise not to tell Mom. Said it wouldn't happen again. At first, I believed him. But as time went on, I watched him closely and saw through the lies he told Mom. He was telling Mom he was away on business, but I know he was fucking other women. It made me sick. I couldn't understand how he could do such a thing. Mom adored him. When I couldn't take it anymore, and wanted to tell her, she got sick. How could I tell her about Dad's affairs while she was fighting for her life? Would that have killed her sooner? I couldn't take the risk. I wanted her last moments to be happy ones. So when Dad didn't make it to the hospital, I knew where he was. When he finally arrived after she'd passed, he couldn't look me in the eye. Fuck, I wanted to punch him in the face."

The room becomes so quiet I can hear the pounding of my heart. Icy tentacles trail up and down my spine. My breathing is erratic. I clench my fists. Everything I believed about my family is a fucking lie.

Lucas speaks up first. "Why the hell didn't you tell us?"

Hayden rubs his palms on his thighs. "What good would that have done? You both think his shit don't stink. You believed you had parents who loved each other—maybe Dad loved Mom in a sick, twisted way. I didn't want to ruin it for you."

"That wasn't your decision to make. We had a right to know what was happening under our noses." I clench onto the top of a chair.

Hayden drops his head down. "I was trying to save you from the hurt. It fucking killed me to know about it. What good would it have done if we all knew? We all would have hated the bastard for what he did."

I ground my teeth together and say through tight lips, "I wouldn't have accused Harper of lying!" My shoulders sag. Oh God. What have I done? I put my trust in the wrong person. A sudden urgency grips me. I swipe my keys and phone off the desk. "I have to go."

"Where?" Lucas asks with a worried expression.

"I need to say a few things to Dad. Then I need to get to Harper and beg for her forgiveness." Christ! How could I have been so blind?

Lucas clasps onto my arm, stopping me from leaving. "I have a few things to ask him too. I'll go with you." His worried expression deepens. "You look like you're going to murder him."

I jerk my arm free. "With the way I'm feeling, I might. I need time alone with him."

Hayden rises. Placing a hand on my shoulder, he says, "Maybe you should calm down before you talk to him."

Why are they so concerned about what I'll do to him? After what he did, he deserves everything coming to him. To placate Hayden, I nod. "I'll go for a drive first."

Twenty minutes later, I pull into my father's driveway. I lied and came straight to his house. The drive hadn't calmed me down. I'm still vibrating with anger.

Letting myself into the family home, I yell, "Dad, where are you?" My voice echoes through the spacious marble foyer. When I don't hear a response, I yell again, "Dad!" I storm through the bottom level of the house looking for him.

"What's going on?" My father is standing at the top of the staircase, his eyes wide.

Dressed in tailored, gray pants and a crisp, white shirt, he doesn't look like a man who'd spent time in the hospital with a suspected heart condition. Had that been an act? Did he collapse to stop Harper from telling me what he'd done? My muscles quiver.

"Finn, are you okay?" He plods down the stairs.

When he gets to the bottom step, I point a finger at his face. "You *lied* to me! You've been lying to me...*us* for years!"

"I don't know what you're talking about. Let's go into the kitchen. I'll make coffee, and you can tell me what this is about." His hand shakes as he gestures for me to follow him into the kitchen. Yeah, he knows I'm onto him.

I don't move. "You had affairs when Mom was alive. You left her to die in a hospital while you were fucking your mistress!" He jerks back like I slapped him. "On her last breath, she asked for you. On. Her. Last. Breath!" I say through gritted teeth.

"You know I was stuck in London—"

Clenching my fists at my sides, I lean into his face. "Stop *lying*! I know the fucking truth."

"If Harper is telling you this nonsense, she's trying to come between us." My father is visibly shaking.

"Harper tried to tell me. I didn't believe her. My father would never be such an asshole. So, I cut her out of my life. Imagine my surprise when Hayden confirmed her story. Not only that, he informed Lucas and I about the multiple affairs you had under Mom's nose."

His shoulders slump forward. "I loved your mother."

"You had a sick way of showing it. You couldn't keep your dick in your pants."

Swaying on his feet, he rests his hand on the nearest wall to steady himself. Never did my father look so old. In his late sixties, he was still fit and handsome. Now, in the blink of an eye, age has caught up with him.

"Forgive me," he pleads, tears swimming in his eyes. "I never wanted to hurt anyone."

"Don't feed me that bullshit. You only care about yourself. You're a liar and a cheat. You even tried to ruin our company. A company me, Hayden, and Lucas have worked our asses off to get it where it is today. We could have lost everything! For what? So you could keep your dirty, little secret. You disgust me."

"I'll make things right."

I step away as he reaches for me. "Don't touch me. In fact, never speak to me again. There's nothing you can do or say to make this right."

"Finn... Please..."

"Thank God Mom isn't alive to see what a pathetic excuse of a man you are." With that, I blow from the house. I can't stand to look at him a moment longer.

In my car, I clench the steering wheel. Taking deep breaths, I wait until the trembling inside me subsides. Once I'm semi under control, I pull out of the driveway, and I make my way to Harper's apartment. I need to fix things. I fucked up big time. Not believing her was a huge mistake. *Please let her forgive me*, I say over and over again. Praying that God or whoever the hell can hear me, helps me get her back.

I get to her apartment in record time. Pulling up in front of her building, I bound from the car. Before I make it to her door, I bump into Alyssa on her way out. When she sees me, she gives me an I-want-to-kick-your-ass look. Disgusts screws up her face. I don't blame her.

"Harper's not home," she says before I can ask.

"Are you saying that so I don't go in there? I just want to talk."

Alyssa narrows her eyes. "Oh, now you want to talk. You've ignored all her attempts to talk to you." She digs her hands on her hips. "Oh, except for last night when you turned up at The Temple drunk as fuck. Do you even remember a word she said to you?"

"Yeah, I do." And I acted like a complete ass.

"And you still didn't believe her?" She screws her nose up. "You don't deserve her."

"My brother told me the truth. I was wrong."

"Oh, your *brother* told you the truth. So, everything is fine now? You expect by turning up here, Harper is going to fall into your arms like nothing happened? Like you didn't destroy her heart and soul?"

"Where can I find her? Please, I need to fix this."

Without answering, Alyssa throws me a scathing look. Spinning on the heels of her biker boots, she swings the duffle bag over her shoulder, just missing my face, and storms up the sidewalk.

I sink to the bottom step and pull my phone from my pocket. I dial Harper's number and wait for her to answer. After a few rings, it goes to voicemail. If she won't answer my call, maybe she'll respond to a text. I can't explain what I've learned over a message, so I tell her I need to talk to her urgently. I sit staring at my phone, waiting and hoping for a reply. After fifteen minutes, I assume she's ignoring me. I try calling again. No answer.

Blowing out a frustrated breath, I rise and go back to my car. Where can she be? The Temple doesn't open until six PM. I glance at the time on the dashboard. That's not for another four hours. Surely she'll have to come back home to get ready for work. I get back out of my car; sitting there feels too comfortable for what I've done. So, I walk to the front of the apartment and sit on the cold, concrete step and wait.

Chapter Forty-Two

HARPER

I SPEND THE AFTERNOON sitting on a hard bench in Central Park, hoping the cold day will numb the pain of losing Finn. My heart is broken—shattered. I don't think it will ever feel whole again.

Another text from Finn hits my phone. He wants to talk to me. What more can he say? I already know he can't trust me anymore. Hates me. Thinks I'm having an affair with his father. I turn off the phone. I can't listen to any more of his harsh words. Not when I'm feeling so fragile—ready to crumble at any moment.

As the afternoon drags on, the temperature drops, and I force myself to move so I don't freeze to death. I slowly make my way home. Finn is sitting on the bottom step of my apartment. His head is hanging low, and his hands dangle between his knees. My steps falter, and my stomach drops. What is he doing here? I watch him. I can't move.

Like Finn feels me staring at him, his head snaps up. When he sees me, he propels from the step. "Harper! I've been calling you for hours."

"I know." I dig my keys out of my bag. I'm proud of myself for being able to form words from my tight throat.

"Why haven't you answered my calls?"

"I have nothing left to say." I push past him and enter the building. He follows close behind.

"I have something to say. I need to talk to you." His eyes plead with me. What had made his gaze turn from anger and disgust to…I'm not sure what this is—maybe sadness and desperation?

Crossing my arms over my chest, I say, "When I wanted to talk, you didn't want to listen. You had to be drunk before you'd hear me out. Even then, you didn't really care what I had to say. So, no Finn, I can't bear to hear more insults."

I try slipping the key into the lock of my door, but my hand is shaking so much I keep missing. Finn's big, strong hand covers mine and steadies me. The warmth of his body surrounds me. I squeeze my eyes shut and draw in a deep breath. Fighting the temptation to lean back.

"A lot has happened since we last spoke. Please," he says the word with such desperation.

My bottom lip trembles. I unlock the door and gesture for him to come inside. I set my bag on the sofa and I sit down.

Finn takes the chair opposite me and rubs his palms up and down his thighs. "I know you told the truth about my father."

I shoot up straight in my seat.

"Hayden told me about the multiple affairs he had while my mother was alive. He was even suspicious where he was the night Mom died and knew he was with a mistress. So, I confronted my father. Of course, he tried to deny it. Then the truth came out. I'm so sorry for not trusting you. I acted like an asshole. Please forgive me."

I stare down at my lap again, taking a moment to let what he said sink in. Now he believes me, but not because of what I told him. Disappointment washes over me. He should have trusted me in the first place.

When minutes tick by, he leans forward and holds onto my hands. "Say something."

Snatching my hands free, I say, "You had to hear it from Hayden before you believed *me*!"

He hangs his head. "I know. I'm sorry.

"You accused me of having an affair with your father. That's what hurts the most. After everything we've been through, you didn't think my love for you was real."

"I know. I'm so fucking sorry. It all happened so suddenly, and my mind was a mess."

I point a finger at him. "It's because you never trusted me. You've been holding onto that, and at the first challenge in our relationship, you put that mistrust between us." A single tear slides down my cheek. I swipe it away. "You broke my heart."

Reaching for my hands again, he pulls back at the last second, probably realizing I'll shake him off again. "I was wrong. What can I do to make it up to you? I'll do anything. Please don't walk away from us."

My chest heaves. "*You* walked away from us."

Finn scrubs his hands over his face. "Harper, I'm sorry."

"If there's no trust, what do we have?"

"I trust you."

"You didn't."

"It was a mistake."

"And what happens if life throws us some unfortunate hurdle? Will I be faced with accusations again?" Before he can answer with what he thinks I want to hear, I stand and open the door. "You promised me you'd let no one hurt me again. You've hurt me. Now, I don't trust you."

One month later, I'm sitting in a pizza restaurant, staring at my pepperoni pizza, wishing I was home in my sweats watching TV. Alyssa and Tamara suggested a girls' night. Said it was what I needed to pull me out of my funk. Said I needed to have some fun. Sticking needles under my fingernails sounds more appealing than mingling with the world. How long will it take for me to want to have *fun* again? Another month...six months...a year?

The fog of emptiness clings to me every moment of every day. Will I ever find my way out? Tamara's sister says it will take time. Says I need to push myself little by little. So, here I am—having girls' night. I agreed only to dinner. I refuse to go clubbing. That is too big of a step.

During the day, I spend my time with Juliette. She asked me if I'd like to sit with her and watch her work. If it wasn't for such an amazing opportunity to study her, I would never step foot back at Alessi Fashion. With Finn in London, I have no chance of running into him at the office, and I've kept my distance from Hayden and Lucas. It's hard going into the office and not thinking about Finn. Memories of him are everywhere. I made Tamara and Juliette promise to tell me if he was ever back in New York City so I can stay away.

With Juliette's encouragement and guidance, I've enrolled for the winter semester for fashion school. She also set me up with an internship with Sempre Fashion when my course starts. Finally, my career is heading in the right direction. My dreams are coming true. Well, except for one—Finn.

Tamara clicks her fingers in front of my face. "Earth to Harper!"

I have a habit of zoning out lately. I snap back to attention. "Sorry, what were you saying?" Placing my napkin on the table, I leave my meal untouched.

Tamara and Alyssa exchange worried glances. Tamara says, "We finally get you out of the apartment and you are miles away. We hate seeing you like this. What can we do to help?"

"I'm fine," I lie with a fake smile on my face. Will it convince them? Again, Tamara and Alyssa exchange worried glances. Maybe not. "Will you stop that!"

"What?" Alyssa and Tamara say at the same time.

"Looking at me like I'm going to crack or something."

Alyssa pushes her empty plate aside. "Well, are you?"

I run my finger along the crease in the tablecloth. "No. I'm not. I'm good. Really, stop worrying." I'm far from good, but I can't let them know or they'll be hovering over me more than they already are. I love them for caring, but sometimes it can be too much.

"If it helps, I've heard Finn's a nightmare to work with in London. I'd say he's still hurting too," Tamara says, obviously not believing me when I said I'm fine.

At the sound of his name, my heart shudders. Is he missing me as much as I miss him? Have I made a mistake letting him walk away?

"Is there any chance you two can work things out?" Tamara asks. I had told Tamara and Alyssa the full story. They were shocked and disgusted to learn about Marco Alessi's deceit and threats.

Giving up on pretending to eat, I push my plate aside. "He never trusted me. Took one look at a photo and assumed the worst. I can't keep worrying that whatever I do or say, he'll be wondering if I'm telling the truth."

Tamara pats her mouth with her napkin and places it on the table. "For years, Finn believed you left him for another man. One older with money coming out of his ears. A powerful man. Then, out of nowhere, you burst back into his life, confusing the hell out of him. Before he even knew the truth about your marriage, he was softening toward you. With all that, he gave you back his heart. If he held on to mistrust...well, his gut was right. You had kept something from him."

My back stiffens. "I was trying to protect him."

"I know. I'm sure he realizes that now too."

My shoulders sag. "He only believed me because Hayden confirmed it. Otherwise, he'd still hate me." That hurt.

"A lot happened. He must have been so confused. Yes, he should have believed you—*trusted* you. He made a mistake. In time, I'm sure he would have seen the truth."

Would he have? I'm not so sure. Maybe if I had been the one to tell him from the start, things might have turned out differently. I've gone over and over it in my mind dozens of times.

Playing the 'what if' game is driving me nuts. What if I wasn't so harsh on him? What if I'd accepted his apology and put the trust issue behind us? I could play that game all day every day, but it still won't change the outcome. Finn is in London. He didn't stay and fight.

Because I didn't let him.

Chapter Forty-Three

FINN

On my desk, my phone beeps with a message. I glance at it. It's another text from my father. He's been texting or calling every week since I confronted him about his affairs, the night my mother died, and how he threw Harper into his mess. I'd hoped once he moved into his *château* in France, he'd stop calling. No such luck.

I have nothing more to say to him. Because of him, I've lost Harper. No, I can't blame him entirely. I screwed up. I accused her of having an affair. I didn't believe her when she told me the truth. Now I'm paying the price. Life isn't the same without her. I don't want to go out and see people. London looks grayer than normal. Not even throwing myself into work has helped me forget her. All I see when I close my eyes at night is her beautiful, smiling face. Hear her soft laughter.

Once I thought London was the only place I wanted to be. The only place that made me happy. How wrong was I? My place—my *heart*—is with Harper. *She* makes me happy. If only I had acted differently. *Believed* her. We'd still be together.

Picking up my phone, I delete my father's message without even reading it. Then I select Harper's name. It's been a month since I last spoke to her. Saw her. Touched her. So many times, I've wanted to call her to hear her voice. I rub a hand over my chest. A constant ache lived under my ribs. I'm so mad at myself for fucking up the only good thing in my life. I want a connection with her again—need it. I type a message and hit send before I can stop myself.

Me: I miss you.

Will she answer? Probably not. Maybe she'll delete it without reading it.

The three dots appear on the screen telling me she's typing. I hold my breath. Then the dots disappear. I exhale with disappointment. The dots reappear. Again, I hold my breath.

Harper: I miss you too.

A huge, relieved grin spreads across my face. It's not a declaration of love, but she didn't tell me to fuck off and leave her alone. I clutch my phone in my hand. My only connection to Harper—I want to keep it close.

For the next week, at the same time each day, I send Harper the exact message.

Me: I miss you.

And every time, the three dots appear, disappear, and reappear before she replies. Like she is hesitating on whether she should hit send.

On the seventh day, when I send the text, I get a different response.

Me: I miss you.

Harper: What are we doing?

My finger hovers above the screen before typing.

Me: I'm not sure. All I know is that I miss you.

Dots…Dots…Dots…

Harper: I miss you too.

What *are* we doing? How long will we send each other messages? If it means keeping Harper in my life in some small way, I'll do it for as long as she'll let me. My place is with Harper. *She makes me happy. She is home.* Words I often think ricochet through my mind. *Home.* Conjuring up memories of a little slice of paradise where we lay on the spongy grass by the lake, soaking up the sun, planning our futures together. When young love was simple with no complications. A place that always made Harper happy.

Hitting the intercom on the desk, I call for my assistant to come into my office.

Marie scuttles in the room, notepad ready. A look of fear on her face. God, my foul mood has scared the staff. I'll have to do something nice to apologize—maybe give her a few days off to make up for being such a jerk.

"Marie, can you please look up the name Judith Richardson?" And I give her all the information I know about her, which isn't much.

Marie bobs her head. "Yes, sir. I'll get right on it." She spins on her heels and leaves.

If *I* can't make Harper happy, I'll move heaven and earth to get her back one thing that did.

Chapter Forty-Four

HARPER

Sitting in Juliette's office, I stare at my phone. Every day at the same time, I wait anxiously for Finn's text. It's the best and hardest part of my day. How am I supposed to get over him and move on? Every time I reply to one, I promise myself it will be the last. Then I'd receive one more and I can't help writing back.

Like clockwork, my phone beeps with a message.

Finn: I miss you.

Me: I miss you too.

God, I miss him so much. Not having him in my life is crushing. It's worse than anything I've ever been through. My parents' betrayal and marrying Derek don't compare to the emptiness I feel without Finn.

Juliette sails into the room in a flourish of yellow organza fabric looking too bright and cheerful for my mood. "Morning, darling. I have special plans for you today." Whipping a fan out of her pocket, she waves it in front of her face.

"What is it?" I ask with interest. Hopefully it will take my mind off Finn. Though I doubt it.

With a flick of her wrist, she closes the fan. "You, my darling, are going to check a property for me that we've scouted for an upcoming photoshoot."

I frown. "What photoshoot? I didn't think there were any scheduled for a few months. I heard you going over the photoshoot schedule with your assistant."

"This is something exclusive that I've been keeping under wraps."

"And you want me to check out the site? You're coming with me, right?" This is a huge responsibility for someone who doesn't work here anymore.

She holds her arms out wide. "I can't. I have too much to do here."

What? She's not coming? "How am I to know if the location is suitable? I've done nothing like this before." Although I'm happy Juliette trusts me with such a task, I'm not sure if I'm the right person for the job.

Juliette moves to a mannequin, turning her back to me, and adjusts the garment. Over her shoulder, she says, "I've seen photographs. It looks like the perfect location. All I need you to do is to confirm the property looks as good as the photos."

Okay, that doesn't sound so hard. I can do that. "When would you like me to go?"

"Now," she says, lifting the hem of the dress and examining the stitching.

"Now? But I haven't seen the photos."

"I'll text them to you while you're on your way."

I rise from the chair. "Where am I going?"

Juliette picks up a pencil from the desk and stands behind an easel. Only the top of her bright red hair is visible. "Mirror Lake."

"As in Lake Placid?"

"Yes, darling. It's such a beautiful location. Have you ever been there?"

On a shuddery breath, I say, "Yes, I have."

Mirror Lake! My heart drops to my feet. The last time I was there was with Finn. We spent the weekend swimming in the lake, laughing, making love, and planning the rest of our lives together. The cabin, the lake, the solitude was wonderful. We dreamed of buying it from my father one day. Soon after that magical day, my life turned to hell.

"I can't go." Even being in the town would be too much. My heart is too raw and bruised to relive some of the happiest days with Finn.

"Why not?" Juliette says from behind the easel.

"Umm...because..." I can't think of an excuse quick enough.

"I have no one else to send. Everyone is busy working. It will really help me out. Of course, we'll compensate you for your time."

My shoulders slump on a ragged breath. How can I refuse a request from Juliette Monet, especially when she's been so generous with her time? "Okay, send me the photos, and I'll get back to you as soon as I can." The sooner I get the job done, the sooner I can get the hell out of Mirror Lake.

Juliette pops her head around the easel and smiles. "Excellent! Now hurry along, darling. I have a car waiting for you. The driver knows the address."

During the long drive, I try to distract myself by playing Candy Crush on my phone. Anything to stop myself from thinking about the lake and especially Finn. I soon realize I'm fighting a losing battle and give up my game. I rest my head on the headrest and close my eyes. I've come to the conclusion that no matter where I am, who I'm with, or what I'm doing, I'm never going to get Finn out of my head—my heart. I feel like I'm drowning without him.

After nearly five hours we enter the town. I pull out my phone, checking for a message from Juliette. She still hasn't sent me the photos. *How am I supposed to know if the location is acceptable if I can't compare it?* I send her a text to remind her to send them. I stare at the phone waiting for a response—nothing. I blow out a frustrated breath and toss it on the seat next to me.

After a few minutes, my phone beeps with a text. I press a palm to my heart. Finally! I look at the screen. The message isn't from Juliette. It's from Finn. My breath catches in my lungs. Two messages in one day? Why? My heart races as I swipe the screen. What a coincidence he's contacting me while I'm in Mirror Lake.

Finn: I miss you.

Me: I miss you too.

Moisture gathers in my eyes as I stare at his message. Being back in Mirror Lake with Finn's message on my phone makes my body shake.

Finally, the car slows down and comes to a stop. I have to put my thoughts aside or I'll never be able to do the job Juliette has sent me here to do. I try calling her, and my call goes to voicemail. I leave a message for her to get in touch with me right away.

"We've arrived, Ms. Madden," the driver says, glancing at me through the review mirror.

"Thank you." I tuck the phone into my bag.

The driver comes to my door and opens it. I step out into the fresh, crisp air I know so well. I take in my surroundings, and I freeze. Preoccupied with Finn's message, I hadn't noticed the location I was at.

The cabin!

A surge of nostalgia pierces through my chest. How? Why? Of all the properties, why did Juliette pick this one? Urgency to leave races through me. If I stay a moment longer, memories of a past filled with hope and dreams—a past I can never get back—will suffocate me.

Spinning around, I knock on the limo driver's side window. The glass slides down. "You need to take me back to New York City."

The driver shakes his head. "I'm sorry, Ms. Madden. I've got another job to get to and won't be heading back into the city. Another driver will arrive for you shortly."

I grip the bottom of the window frame. "Please, I need to leave now! Take me with you to your next job, and I'll find my way back from there."

"I'm sorry. I can't." He shrugs with regret. The window slides up, darkening the interior of the car.

With the palm of my hand, I slap the glass. "Wait...please!"

But the car reverses and drives away, leaving me with my mouth hanging open in shock. *What is happening?* Out of all the properties on Mirror Lake, how have I ended up at my parents' old cabin?

Taking a deep, shuddery breath, I slowly turn around. The cabin looks the same. The house was made to look rustic with its timber walls and finishes to blend in with the surrounding nature. Hanging planter baskets with purple geraniums and bird boxes hang from the rafters. Huge windows overlook the blue lake. The clouds above mirrored in its reflection. The creaky, wooden pier stretches over the water, and birdsong fills the peaceful air.

With hesitant steps, I walk toward the cabin, my fingertips brushing over the wildflowers growing in the tall grass. Emotions are overwhelming me. The love I feel for Finn is so strong here. He is in everything I look at, smell, and touch.

As I get closer, I'm startled by movement on the porch. Someone steps out from the shadows and into the afternoon sun. That someone is Finn. At the sight of him, a pang of longing rips through my heart. I want to run to him and throw myself into his arms. Instead, I hold myself back. I'm not sure why he's here. Is he looking at the property for Juliette too? Why didn't she tell me? Questions buzz through my mind. All I can do is stare at Finn.

He approaches, keeping some distance between us. His eyes travel over me like he's drinking me in. I know I'm doing the same to him. His hair is a little longer. Dark smudges blemish the skin under his eyes, like he hasn't slept in days. The sleeves of the creased navy shirt he's wearing are rolled up his forearms. For a few moments, no one speaks. Our eyes lock onto each other. Our chests rising and falling with heavy breaths.

After a moment, Finn says, "I miss you."

Chapter Forty-Five

FINN

As I watch the limo arrive, my nerves stomp inside my body, my legs shake, and my palms sweat. Have I done the right thing bringing Harper here? What if she doesn't want to see me? She's answering my text messages, but what if that was all she wanted?

The limo door opens, and I hold my breath as she steps out. Every day I tell her I miss her. It kills me to communicate with only three simple words. What I really want to say to her is how much I love her. Need her. Tell her everything that's in my heart. Then pull her into my arms and kiss her until neither one of us can breathe.

As much as I desperately want to do that, I've come here for one reason: to give her back the cabin she loves. Something no one can take away from her again. It had taken heavy negotiations to buy it—Judith is nearly as ruthless as her brother Derek. It was worth every penny. It's only a small gesture considering everything Harper had to sacrifice and give up. If I could, I'd give back everything Harper has lost.

When she steps toward the cabin and sees me, for a second, I wonder if she'll be angry at what I've done. Doubt clouds my thoughts. Maybe she doesn't want all this again. Maybe the memories will be too much for her. Fuck. It's too late. It's done. I can't turn back now.

"I miss you," I say, my voice rough with emotion at seeing her again.

Harper's chin wobbles as she averts her gaze and fixes on something over my shoulder. When she looks back at me, she takes a deep breath, like she's trying to compose herself—trying to stop herself from crying. Fuck, I've made her sad. That's not what I wanted to do. I want to see her smile again. Hopefully giving her this cabin will do it.

"Why are you here?" Not the same words she texts back. That doesn't matter. Hearing her voice is like sunshine has burst through my body. Never have I heard anything so beautiful. "Why am *I* here? What's going on?" Confusion is etched on her face.

"I needed to see you. I asked Juliette to send you here."

Her eyes widen. "You know I've been seeing Juliette?"

I nod with a small smile. "I'm so happy you're getting back into fashion again." We're talking to each other like strangers. My heart squeezes at the distance between us.

"Why am I here?" she asks again.

I scuff the toe of my shoe into the spongy grass. "I fucked up. Big time. I had a second chance with you. I let the past and my insecurities get in the way. Instead of letting all the bullshit cloud my mind, I should have held onto your love...trusted it. Not toss it aside like it meant nothing. I'm sorry for what I've put you through." I open my arms wide. "I know how much you loved this place. How happy you were here. So, if I can give you back a tiny piece of happiness, I hope this will do it. I bought it for you."

Harper bites her bottom lip. She glances from the house to the lake and then back at me. "You bought it for me?"

I nod. "Yes. I can't imagine this place without you in it. It belongs to you." What if she wants nothing from me? I was so hell-bent on getting it back for her I never stopped to wonder if she wanted it. "That's if you want it. Sell it. Burn it. It's yours. Derek never should have kept it from you."

Twisting her fingers together in front of her, she says, "I don't know what to say."

"You don't have to say anything. I hope whatever you decide to do with it makes you happy." I take a few steps to walk away then stop and turn back toward her. There's something I need to say before I leave. "Harper, living my life without you won't be easy. Because my heart is yours. It's been yours from the moment we met. I probably never told you enough...I love you." Emotion clogs my throat. "Always will."

Turning back around, I force my feet to take one step in front of the other. Walking away from Harper is the hardest thing I've ever done in my life.

Chapter Forty-Six

HARPER

I stand rooted to the ground. *Finn bought my family's cabin for me!* Not because he was using it as a tool to win me back, but because he loves me and wants me to be happy. From the moment he stepped off the porch, I saw the love for me in his eyes. The same longing to touch me like I had for him. I felt the emotion vibrate off him and into my heart. He wants me to be happy. But I'm not happy. I haven't been since we broke up.

Covering my face with my hands, my shoulders shake with silent tears. I drop my hands, spin around, and I call out, "Wait!" Finn stops, dips his head before turning back around. "I miss you too." My words are only a whisper. With Finn's eyes widening, I know he's heard me. My heart is pounding so hard. I take two steps closer to Finn. "I'm sorry."

Finn frowns. "Why?"

"If I had been completely honest about everything from the start...about Marco—"

"My father is the one to blame. Not you." Finn's jaw clenches. "You have nothing to be sorry about. I don't want to talk about him anymore. Tell me again what you said."

I'm happy to say it again. "I miss you too."

Finn swallows hard. "You do?"

I nod as tears stream down my face. "I do. My heart is yours. It's been yours from the moment we met. I probably never told you enough…I love you," I repeat his words.

With two long strides, Finn stands in front of me. Chest to chest. Nose to nose.

His hand cups my face. "You love me?"

"I love you." I want to tell him so every day of my life.

"I promise to spend the rest of my life making you happy."

"You can start by kissing me." Being in his arms feels as natural as breathing. Never do I want to be gasping for breath again.

Groaning low in his throat, he covers my lips with his. Our mouths melding together, tongues entwining, sucking the air from my lungs. Finally breaking apart, Finn's gaze travels over my face. He links his fingers through mine and brings my hands to his mouth, kissing each fingertip. "You've made me the happiest man in the world."

I can't believe this is my life now. Never could I imagine it working out this way. "Thank you for buying the cabin for me. This place will always be special. Although, I can only accept it on one condition."

Finn cocks an eyebrow. "What's the condition?"

"This cabin isn't just mine. It's ours. I want to make new and better memories here...with you."

His lips quirk into a smile. "Deal. I want you to know, Harper, that you are my home. Whether it's here, New York City, or fucking Timbuktu, my place is with you. You're stuck with me."

My heart flutters. "Forever?"

Finn places a gentle kiss on my lips. "For as long as you want me."

Cupping his face, I say, "I will always want you."

Finn rests his forehead on mine. "Then forever it is."

Epilogue

HARPER

One year later

Standing by the lake, I wrap the blanket tight around my shoulders. I love this time of the morning at the cabin. It's so peaceful and quiet. I wish I could spend more than weekends here, but with work and finishing my degree, I have to spend most of my time in New York City. Watching the mist swirl over the water until the first rays of the warm sun evaporates it, I draw in the tranquility. The only sounds are coming from birds waking up in nearby trees and frogs croaking among the weeds lining the shore. Breathing in the cool air, I smile. Never did I imagine I'd ever feel such peace again. Spending time at the cabin I love with the man I adore; I have to pinch myself.

Rubbing a loving hand over my still-flat belly, I hear my husband's footsteps on the timber jetty. When he reaches me, he slides his arms around my waist, pulling me back to his front. He rests his chin on my shoulder and turns his head to kiss my cheek.

"Good morning," he says, his voice husky from sleep.

"Good morning." I turn around to face him, placing my hands on his hips.

Life the past year with Finn has been wonderful. We've been making up for lost time with plenty of love and laughter. Two months ago, we got married in a simple ceremony by the lake with our closest friends and family. It was magical and everything I could have wished for. With the news I'm about to tell Finn, our lives are going to become even better.

"Are you ready to head back to the city soon?" Finn asks. "Tonight, I'm taking you out to celebrate you passing your exams."

I blow out a breath. "I'm so relieved I passed."

Finn brushes a lock of hair from my face. "I knew you would. I'm so proud of you."

"Just five thousand more exams to go!" I laugh. How am I going to finish school with a newborn? Oh well, we'll figure it out.

"You'll smash them all," he beams with confidence.

"I'm so grateful for your support, especially when I wanted to quit." So many times, I thought my creativity sucked and I couldn't keep going. Finn always helped me through.

"Does this mean you'll come back to Alessi's and design for us?" Finn quirks an eyebrow.

He knows my reasons for not working at Alessi's. I want to make it on my own without the help of my husband's company. That hasn't changed. Although, he likes to jokingly ask from time to time.

"After I finish my degree, you won't be able to afford me." I give him a teasing grin.

"That is true." He chuckles. "Where would you like to go for dinner?" he asks.

"I think we should cancel dinner and stay in tonight."

Finn frowns with concern. "Is everything okay?"

"Yes, everything is fine. I'd prefer to celebrate at home."

Finn gives me a knee-melting, sexy smile and snuggles into me. "I like the sound of that." He places a kiss on the curve of my neck.

Before I get distracted by his magical mouth and forget to tell him my news, I push back. "Finn, I need to tell you something."

I suspected that I might be pregnant when I threw up yesterday. Before heading to the cabin, I raced to the drugstore to buy a pregnancy test. I waited until this morning to take the test just in case something I ate might have made me sick. I decided not to tell Finn anything because I didn't want to get his hopes up for nothing. We weren't planning a family yet—I have school to finish—but I know he'll be ecstatic. When nausea rolled in my stomach again as soon as I woke up this morning, while Finn still slept, I took the test.

"What is it?"

Now that I have his full attention, the words get stuck in my throat. How do you blurt out something so important? Should I have done something special like given him a baby onesie with "World's Greatest Dad" printed on the front like

I've seen people do online? Was telling him on a jetty dressed in pajamas and wrapped in a blanket the best way to do it?

Suddenly, my nerves evaporate like the morning mist on the lake. Here is the perfect place. The perfect time. Where we promised each other we'd make beautiful memories.

Finn cups my face. "Is everything okay?"

Smiling at the man I love, my heart swells with joy. "Everything is perfect. Finn, I'm pregnant."

Finn's eyes grow wide. His mouth drops open. "You're pregnant?"

I nod. Happy tears clog my throat.

"We're having a baby?" His voice drops to a whisper.

"Yes."

Finn places his hands on my waist, picks me up, and spins me around, smiling at me with tears in his eyes. When he sets me back on my feet, he gives me a long, slow kiss. Pulling away, he gazes at me with so much love and affection, my heart skips a beat.

Placing a hand on my belly, he says, "You, me, and peanut...forever."

Tears pour down my face. "Forever."

Acknowledgements

Firstly, I want to thank my loving family Tom, Jaime, Ryan and Leah. They continually show me love and support and are my number one fans. A huge thank you to TL Swan and the Cygnet Inkers. The ladies in the group are amazing. To my wonderful beta readers, Jillian, Michelle, Kirstie and Becky thank you for taking the time to read Unforgettable. Your feedback and praise over the book was amazing.

Finally to my amazing readers. I can't tell you enough how much I appreciate you reading my books. Thank you from the bottom of my heart! xx

About Sonia Stanizzo

Sonia Stanizzo is a contemporary romance author living in the beautiful south coast of New South Wales, Australia with her husband and three children. When she's not dreaming up stories about couples and their road to finding love, sometimes bumpy but always a lot of fun, she can be found taking pole dancing lessons, reading and writing.

Thank you so much for reading Unforgettable. I hope you enjoyed meeting Finn and Harper and loved them as much as I loved writing them.

Say Hello!

Want to follow me on social media? Follow me here:
Facebook: facebook.com/soniastanizzowriter
Instagram: instagram.com/soniastanizzowriter
Tiktock: ticktok.com/@soniastanizzowriter
Sonia's Website: www.soniastanizzo.com
Sonia's email: soniastanizzo@gmail.com
Join my newsletter for free books, new releases and giveaways: www.soniastanizzo.com

More Titles By Sonia Stanizzo

Trouble in Love Series

The Trouble with Mr. Pretty

Chasing Trouble

Trouble in Disguise

Acting on Love Series

Risk Taker

Rule Breaker

Matchmaker